THE MURDER OF MADISON GARCIA

THE MURDER OF MADISON GARCIA

A FORD FAMILY MYSTERY

MARCY McCREARY

CamCat
Books

CamCat Publishing, LLC
Brentwood, Tennessee 37027
camcatpublishing.com

© 2023 by Marcy McCreary

Hardcover ISBN 9780744308303
Paperback ISBN 9780744308402
Large-Print Paperback ISBN 9780744308419
eBook ISBN 9780744308426
Audiobook ISBN 9780744308433

Library of Congress Control Number: 2022945185

Book and cover design by Maryann Appel

5   3   1   2   4

FOR LEW

1

SUNDAY | JUNE 30, 2019

I SLID underneath the bubbles. My knees poked out above the surface. One. Two. Three. Four. Five. When I came up for air I heard "Radiate"—my phone's ringtone. I lifted my body, turning toward the sound, and my boobs collided with the edge of the tub. Damn, that hurt. I inched my fingers across the floor but the phone was unreachable, resting on the far edge of the bathmat. I gave up and submerged my body back into the warmish water. *If it's important they'll leave a voice mail.*

With the tips of my fingers sufficiently wrinkled, I reached for the towel that lay crumpled on the toilet lid. With the towel secured around my midsection, I picked up my phone. A missed call from my daughter Natalie. I hit "Recents" to call her back and noticed an incoming call from the night before. A red phone number, indicating a person who was not in my contact list. Boston, Massachusetts, was displayed below the number. Probably one of those spam calls—a request for my social security number or a plea from a political fundraiser. There seemed to be a lot of that lately with the presidential campaign heating up. The

American people had taken sides—lefties, centrists, right-wingers—and it wasn't pretty. *It never used to be this way.* Or maybe it was, but social media and cable news were exaggerating and exacerbating the divisiveness. Made me think of that Stealers Wheel lyric: "Clowns to the left of me / Jokers to the right / Here I am stuck in the middle with you."

After applying a fair amount of goop to tame and defrizz my curls, I slipped into my black yoga pants and gray drawstring hoodie. I settled on my bed, opened my laptop, and googled "reverse lookup." Curiosity is a strong motivator to get to the bottom of things—and as a detective, it was hard to pass up the chance to solve this little mystery. I entered the phone number into the rectangular box at the top of the screen. The results page displayed the name Madison Garcia, a resident of Brooklyn, New York, not Boston, Massachusetts. I opened my Facebook page and typed "Madison Garcia" in the search box. There was one Madison Garcia living in Brooklyn. But the page was private. And her profile picture was a black cat. When I clicked on the name, I was greeted with a handful of pictures she must have designated shareable and therefore accessible to the public. There were people—mostly millennials—in the photographs, but no one I recognized. All personal info was hidden.

"Susan, you up there?"

"Yeah!" I shouted, closing the lid. "I'll be right down!" I plucked a tissue from the box on the bedside table and blew my nose, then headed downstairs with the laptop tucked under my armpit and the box of tissues in my grip.

"Feeling any better?" Ray asked.

"Fucking summer cold. Just popped a DayQuil." I shook the tissue box. "And I got these bad boys."

"You look like shit." A beat later he added, "And I mean that in the nicest way."

"Good save," I said before I blew my nose with more force than necessary. "What's your plan today?"

"I'm heading into the station soon. Chief assigned me to work on those bungalow robberies. Seems we have a serial cat burglar in the area." Ray put on his serious face and wagged his finger. "You are to stay put. I'll pick up dinner tonight."

"Yes sir," I said, military salute included.

My phone rang and we both glanced at it. I swiped to answer. "Chief?" I bobbed my head a few times as Ray shot me dirty looks. "Got it. On my way."

"Susan, is this your idea of staying put?"

"Dead body over at Sackett Lake." I blew my nose again in my semi-used tissue. "Besides . . . it's just a little summer cold." I coughed up some phlegm and headed back upstairs to change into real clothes.

A POLICE vehicle and an ambulance were parked along the road leading down to the lake. I spotted Officer Sally McIver and her partner, Ron Wallace, at the edge of the parking area. Two paramedics stood beside a black Lexus, the only car in the small lakefront parking lot.

Sally waved as I got out of my car. Ron held up a roll of police tape and shook it like a tambourine. I looked out toward the lake and took in the scene. From this distance, the dead woman in the car simply looked like she was daydreaming, staring out at the placid water without a care in the world. Her platinum-blonde hair was the only visible trait from this vantage point. I retrieved my packet of protective outerwear from the trunk, then joined them.

"What can you tell me?" I asked Sally.

"You sound like shit," she replied.

"Top of the morning to you too."

"That guy over there tapped on the driver's side window," she said, pointing to the gray-haired gentleman with a German shepherd by his side. "Thought she might be sleeping or something. When she didn't respond he opened the door. Saw the blood. Then he called 9-1-1. Ron and I got here about five minutes ago."

One of the paramedics approached us. "Multiple stab wounds to her torso. I noticed a bathing suit in the back seat. Perhaps here for a swim and was robbed?" He shrugged, then sighed, clearly not thrilled with how his day was starting out. "All yours." He turned and headed back to his partner.

There wasn't much we could do until Gloria and Mark showed up. Gloria Weinberg was our forensic photographer. Back in the Borscht Belt days, when the Catskills resort hotels were in full swing, she took pictures of the guests who would then purchase their portraits encased in mini keychain viewers.

Now she photographed crime scenes . . . and the occasional wedding. And once, the crime scene of a murder victim whose wedding she had photographed. Mark Sheffield was our crime-scene death investigator. He had joined the Sullivan County ME's office last fall—wanted to get away from the grim murder scenes of the city. Wait until he got a load of this blood-soaked tableau.

I turned to Ron. "Let's get a perimeter going. From this area here all the way around to the water," I said, sweeping my arm across the landscape to indicate the area I wanted cordoned off. I wiped my nose on my sleeve. "Sally, run the plates. I'm going to have a little chat with the man who found her."

I approached the gray-haired man and introduced myself.

"Benjamin Worsky," he said in response.

"Okay, Mr. Worsky. Just a few standard questions and you can be on your way."

"It's no trouble. None at all. In all my years, never thought I'd come across a . . . a dead body. Poor woman."

"When did you happen upon the car?"

"I left my house at seven o'clock on the dot. I'm a man of habit. Seven on the dot every morning to walk Elsa." He petted the top of

Elsa's head. "It takes me ten minutes to walk from my house to this spot, so I would say I spotted the car around seven ten. But I didn't think anything of it and continued my walk past the car. But when I came back this way—and I'm thinking that would be around seven thirty, because I walked another ten minutes and then turned around—the car was still here."

"Why did you approach the car?"

"I'm not really sure. Perhaps a sense that something was wrong." He looked down at Elsa who looked up at him. "Elsa was a bit agitated. Maybe it was that. So I peered in and the driver didn't look well." He frowned and raised his hand to his heart. "I tapped on the window just to ask her if she was okay and when she didn't answer, I opened the car door. That's when I saw the blood and called 9-1-1."

"Did you touch anything?"

"Just the car door handle."

"Did you see anyone else around, either when you came through or off further on your walk?"

"No. But you might want to visit with a woman who lives up the road a bit. She walks along the lake every morning at six o'clock. She might be able to tell you if the car was here at that time."

"Yeah, that would be great. Her name?"

"Eleanor Campbell."

"I know her. The woman with the birds, right?" I chuckled softly, recalling Eleanor Campbell's birds driving Dad crazy when we were working the Trudy Solomon cold case last year. She was a character you didn't easily forget.

"Yeah, budgies, I believe," Mr. Worsky replied.

"Okay, great. If you can just give your address to that officer over there," I said, pointing at Sally, "then you're free to go."

"I don't mean to step out of line here, but you sound awful." Mr. Worsky tugged at his whiskers. "You should really be in bed."

I suppressed an eye roll. Or maybe I didn't.

✳

A BLUE Honda Accord pulled into the parking lot. The blaring rock music ended abruptly when the ignition cut out. Mark's lanky legs emerged first. When he fully stood, he maxed out at six feet, six inches. His nickname was Pencil, and he seemed to have no qualms about that. He had a penchant for wearing khaki pants and tan shirts and his hair was the color of graphite.

He was such a good sport about his nickname that at last year's Halloween party he wore a tan T-shirt with "No. 2" emblazoned on the front. He opened the trunk of his car, pulled out a pair of overalls, and suited up.

"Good morning, ladies! What brings you out on this fine, fine day?" Mark winked. He looked over at the black Lexus. "Ah. Has the scene been photographed yet?"

"No. Still waiting on Gloria," I said checking my watch. "Thought she would've been here by now. She lives just a little ways up the road." As if on cue, Gloria's Chevy pickup rumbled up the road. "The gang's all here."

I coughed into the crux of my elbow.

"You sound like shit," Mark said. "Bad cold?"

"Yeah, I'm on the back end of it." He nodded and lifted an eyebrow in that way people do when they don't believe you. So I added, "No longer contagious."

We watched as Gloria pulled off the tarp and lifted her gear from the rear bed.

"Sorry for the delay, guys. I was over at Horizon Meadows." Gloria laid her camera bag on the ground and slipped into her protective wear. "My sister was in a bad state this morning. Fucking Alzheimer's. They're moving her to Level Six care." She knelt and removed two cameras. She hung one of the cameras around her neck and held the other. "There but for the Grace of God go I."

We all nodded.

"I'll start with a few global photos," Gloria said, snapping the shutter to capture the entirety of the crime scene from a distance.

I donned my PPE, then trailed behind Mark and Gloria as they walked toward the victim. As we neared the body, she threw a question over her shoulder, "Is this how you found everything?"

"Minor scene contamination," I replied. "A passerby opened the driver-side door and the paramedics checked for life. But we haven't touched a thing."

"You sound like shit," Gloria said.

"That seems to be the consensus today."

The humidity was setting in, further irritating my sinuses and making it harder to breathe. My hands were also a sweaty mess. More so than usual.

On days like this it was hard to tell whether my palmar hyperhidrosis (both an annoyance and source of embarrassment, especially when it came to handshakes) was the cause of my sweaty palms or whether the clammy air was simply making my hands wet. I dragged my palms along the front of my pants to sop up the moisture. Then I slipped on my bright blue latex gloves.

We stood bunched together at the open driver's-side door while Gloria laid her duffel bag on the pavement and unpacked her yellow number markers and photo scales.

"Do we have an ID on the woman?" Mark asked.

"Still working on that," Sally replied, as she zipped up her white Tyvek jumpsuit.

Mark crouched down next to the body. "What a fucking bloodbath."

"Looks like someone stabbed her and walked, drove"—I looked out at the lake—"or swam away." I peered over his shoulder to get a closer look. "Mid- to late twenties. Maybe early thirties?" I sniffled, trying to suction back the escaping mucus. "I suck at guessing ages."

"I'm getting a late twenties vibe," Mark said.

"No signs of a struggle. Perhaps she knew her attacker. A date gone sideways?" I inferred.

"I don't see a purse," Sally said, cupping her hand like a visor over her eyes and gazing into the passenger's-side window. "There's a duffel and a bathing suit on the backseat."

"Try the door," Mark said.

Sally opened the passenger's side door. "Not locked."

"How about the rear door?" I asked.

Sally opened the rear door. "Not locked."

Gloria moved around the rear of the car to take midrange and closeup photographs of the items on the backseat.

Sally's phone pinged. She glanced at it, then said, "Car is registered to a Samantha Fields, a doctor who lives in Brooklyn. Should be easy enough to find someone who can provide a positive identification." She drummed her fingers on her cheek. "Unlocked doors. No handbag. No phone. I'm thinking robbery."

"Or someone trying to make our job harder by making us think it's a robbery," I suggested.

Mark leaned over the body to get a closer look at the stab wounds. "Three wounds . . . here, here, and here," he said pointing to each incision. "What's this?" he muttered, mainly to himself. "Well, lookie here." Mark reached down into the footwell and pulled out an iPhone. He held the phone up to the woman's face and the device sprang to life. "Here you go," he said handing me the phone.

I hit the green-and-white phone icon on the lower left corner of the phone. "Holy shit. This is *not* Dr. Samantha Fields."

ELDRIDGE SUMMONED me into his office as soon as I got back to the station.

"Everyone's going to be breathing down my neck on this. The press. The sheriff. Whaddya got so far?" he asked.

I set the scene, then said, "I believe the victim is Madison Garcia. I received a call last night at nine forty from her number and that outgoing call is on her phone's "Recents" list."

"What did she say?"

"I was asleep when the call came in and she didn't leave a message. Sally tracked down the owner of the Lexus, a Dr. Samantha Fields, who said she had loaned her car to a Madison Garcia for the weekend. There's also a husband, Rafael Garcia, who we have yet to connect with. Left him a message about an hour ago."

"Rafael Garcia? Hmm. Why do I know that name?" Eldridge strode to the door of his office. "Hey Roger. Get in here."

Roger placed both hands on his desk and pushed downward as he stood. Phlebitis in his legs made it hard for him to stand from a seated position. He was just a few months away from retirement and had no intention of hanging up his badge early just because his legs felt like two pieces of lumber. "Yes, sir."

"Does the name Rafael Garcia sound familiar to you?"

Roger scratched at his chin and nodded. "Sure does. Isabela and Luis's kid. A bit rough around the edges, if I recall. Bad-boy type. Heard he's in finance, or maybe it's banking. Same difference, I suppose. Anyway, done good for himself. Married a local girl, Madison Garmin. Joke was she married him because she only had to change the last three letters of her last name. Get it? Garmin to Garcia."

"The *i* stays the same right?" Eldridge said.

Roger's eyes narrowed. "Oh yeah! You're right, Chief. Just the *m* and the *n*." He turned to me, as if to fill me in. "Her parents died when she was in high school. From carbon monoxide poisoning. Her mother left the car running in the garage after returning from grocery shopping."

"Madison Garmin? That name sounds familiar." I pulled a Kleenex from the tissue box on Eldridge's desk and gently blew my nose.

"Your dad is good buddies with her grandfather . . . Irving. In fact, Madison ended up living with her grandparents after her parents died. Your dad can probably tell you more than I can." Roger puckered his lips and sighed. "Y'know Susan, you really should be home in bed. You're going to infect us all."

My irritation grew but I held my tongue. He was right, of course. I shouldn't be out and about breathing on people. But I was on the back end of this thing, and I was pretty sure that meant I was no longer contagious. But just try and explain that to anyone while you're wheezing and sneezing. "Is this Madison?" I asked, showing him a polaroid of our murder victim that Gloria took at the scene.

"Haven't seen her in a while, but pretty sure that's her. Shit, man, so young," Roger mumbled. "Am I excused?"

Eldridge nodded, then turned toward me. "So your dad knows the family?"

"Yeah," I answered tentatively, sensing where this was going.

Eldridge laid his palms on the desk and leaned forward. "I'm thinking of assigning this to someone else. Perhaps Marty. I don't need your family intertwined with yet another case like last year's Trudy Solomon—"

"That's exactly why I should be on this case," I snapped. I took a deep breath, knowing I needed to back off a bit. "My dad knows the family—they like him, trust him. That could work to my advantage."

"Or it could cloud everyone's judgment."

I met and held Eldridge's stare. "Look, I'll recuse myself if lines get blurred or crossed, but at least let me take a first stab at this."

Eldridge grunted and leaned back. About five seconds ticked by until he said, "What's your next move?"

"Sally is canvassing the area, asking nearby residents if they saw anyone lurking around the area last night or this morning. The witness we interviewed at the scene—a guy named Benjamin Worsky—told me there's a woman who walks the area every morning. Just so happens to be a woman who helped us with the Trudy Solomon case last year. Remember Eleanor Campbell?"

"Yeah, the woman with the uncanny memory and the two birds named after a sitcom. Laverne and Shirley?"

"Yup. That's her. Heading over there now." My phone rang. "Detective Susan Ford." I glanced up and mouthed to Eldridge, "It's him . . . Rafael Garcia."

ELEANOR CAMPBELL'S house was situated at the edge of Firemans Camp Road, the road leading down to Sackett Lake. I was surprised to find Eleanor in the throes of packing, being that just eight months ago she informed my dad and me that she would never move from this house. ("I plan to die here with my budgies," she had said.) Stacks of boxes lined the hallway and most of the furniture was gone. I peered into the living room. The green velvet sofa with the faded armrests was still there. As were the birds, Laverne and Shirley.

"Change of heart?" I asked, motioning toward the boxes.

"My nephew insisted after I took a nasty spill a few months ago. It took a lot of finagling but the folks at Lochmore Manor said I can keep my budgies . . . as long as they don't disturb anyone." She led me into her kitchen. "You alone this time?"

"I am."

"I so enjoyed your father's company. He's at Horizon Meadows, right?"

"Yes. You still have a great memory."

"I wanted to move there, but they wouldn't budge when it came to my budgies. They said it's a slippery slope. If they allow my budgies, then they open the floodgates to pet snakes and exotic monkeys. What a load of crap." Eleanor handed me a cup of coffee. "So, are you here because of the murder?"

"You know about that?"

"Word travels fast in these parts, Detective Ford. Benny rang me this morning, said you might be paying a visit. Hence the fresh pot of coffee." She held up her cup.

"Mr. Worsky—Benny—told me that you take early-morning walks down by the lake. Did you see a black Lexus in the parking lot?"

"I do and I did." She turned her head abruptly at the sound of the birds chirping in the other room. "Mind if we go to the living room?"

I followed Eleanor and wove my way around the boxes to the green sofa. I carefully lowered myself on the edge of the worn seat cushion, remembering the last time I sat on it and nearly sank to the floor.

"Hello Laverne. Hello Shirley," I said in the direction of the cage.

"*Hello! Hello!*" Shirley screeched. Laverne paced sideways on her swing.

"So you took a walk this morning?"

"Sure did. I walk almost every morning. Beautiful birds down by the lake. Lovely blue herons. I get up at six o'clock and I'm out the door by six twenty. It takes me fifteen minutes to walk down to the lake, and then I walk along the shoreline a bit. My daily exercise."

"Which means you saw the car in the parking lot at around six thirty-five this morning?" I asked, hoping to speed along the interview.

"Correct. You're very good at math, Detective Ford," Eleanor said with a quick smile.

"I was an art history major, but I can do simple math if I have to." I took a sip of coffee. "Did you see anyone in the car?"

"I did. I saw a young woman with long blonde hair. I assumed she was sleeping and didn't want to disturb her. I now wish I'd taken a closer look."

"Did you see anyone else, either near the car or along your walk?"

"No. But I did see something strange last night. Well, not strange. But different."

"Go on. Anything you saw might be helpful."

"Sometimes I have trouble sleeping, especially on humid nights. So I went out on my porch at around ten thirty. I remember because the news had just ended. Figured I'd get some fresh air before turning in, rock on my rocker. That's when I saw headlights coming up the road and turn onto Firemans Camp Road."

"Was it the black Lexus?"

"That I can't be sure of. It was dark. But it was a dark car."

"Did that strike you as odd? A car turning onto that road."

"Not really. Back in the day it was a necking spot. Do they still say necking? Anyway, it was a place where teenagers went to kiss and swim. 'Midnight Swim' it was called. At least that's what my nephew told me when I used to see cars head down there at night. But I don't think it's a thing anymore. That was like ten, fifteen years ago. So no, I didn't think twice about it." She sighed. "I wish I did though . . . could have saved someone's life if I called the police."

"You did nothing wrong, Eleanor. You had every reason to believe it was just a bunch of teenagers out for a swim."

Eleanor forced a smile. "You're right, of course. But still."

"By any chance, did you see the driver?"

"Not really. Even though they passed right in front of my house, it was too dark to see them clearly."

"Them? So there were several people in the car?"

"Just two."

"Are you sure of that?"

"The whatchamacallit light was on in the car…"

"The dome light?"

"No. The light under the rearview mirror."

"The map light."

"Look at that, never too old to learn something new." She tapped the side of her head. "So, yes, that map light was on. Thing is, couldn't tell you if they were male or female, but there were definitely two of them."

DAD WAS as predictable as a solar eclipse. You knew exactly where he would be and when. At noon on a Sunday he would be on his second cup of coffee in the lunch cafe at Horizon Meadows, reading the sports section of the *New York Daily News*, poring over the stats of recent baseball games. You can set your watch by it.

"Hey Dad," I said taking the empty seat beside him.

He glanced up and then back at the paper. A barely audible ha-rumph escaped his lips. He was still nursing his anger toward me. But it was nothing compared to the animus directed at my mother upon learning how she deceived him those many years ago. Two weeks ago, Mom did what she promised me she would do when she hit her six months sobriety mark—reveal to Dad a secret she'd harbored for forty years . . . that she knew all along what had happened to Trudy Solomon, a local woman who went missing in 1978, a case Dad was assigned to and couldn't crack. And even worse, she'd helped Trudy "disappear." Sure, Mom had her reasons for doing what she did, but Dad was having none of it. And honestly, I didn't blame him one iota. I had hoped the tension between them would be at a simmer by now, but that was naive, considering how much that case affected his life. My bigger worry was whether my mother would turn back to the bottle for solace. Recovering alcoholics don't need a reason to start drinking again. But if she wanted an excuse, this was it. Clearly my father understood this, but he couldn't see past his own anger.

Not yet.

"So you get wind of the Madison Garcia murder?" I asked.

Dad tipped down the edge of the newspaper. "Yeah. Irving called me. He and Audrey are a wreck, as you might imagine. First their daughter, now their granddaughter. That there is some serious grief to deal with. Any leads?"

"Remember Eleanor Campbell, the woman with the birds?"

"Yeah." Dad chuckled, probably recalling how Eleanor flirted with him last year when we interviewed her about Trudy Solomon. "She a suspect?" he said with a smirk.

"A witness, smart aleck."

"She saw what happened?"

"Not exactly." I explained to Dad what she saw and then described the crime scene.

"Shit."

I thought he would say more, but he just solemnly shook his head. "Dad? You okay?"

"Yeah, go on."

"I thought you might be able to fill me in on what happened to her parents. Just looking to get the big picture on her life."

Dad folded the newspaper in half and stuffed it into his backpack. He ran his fingers along the edge of the table as if he was playing piano. He abruptly stopped, then sighed. "Sad story. I remember it like it was yesterday. Huge snowstorm that day, and Robin—Madison's mother—drove up to the ShopRite to get some provisions. Maybe she was distracted or flustered or something, but when she got home, she left the car running in the garage. The fumes got to them."

I had scanned the incident report. The door from the garage to the house was halfway open, giving the fumes a pathway into the house. Madison's father, Todd, was in the spare bedroom on the first floor. Madison told the police he had the flu and had been staying in that room, quarantining himself.

The assumption was that after Robin put the groceries away, she went into the den to watch TV. That's where she was found: in the den, TV on.

"And Madison found them?"

"No. Her boyfriend did. Rafael Garcia—who, as you know, became her husband."

"So where was Madison?"

"Madison was at a girlfriend's house at the time. At some point that afternoon, she texted Rafael and asked if he wanted to join her at the friend's house. She also asked him to stop by her house on the way and pick up 'the stuff.' Which we later found out was pot she had stashed in a box under her bed. He said he rang the doorbell and when no one answered he peered into the windows and saw Robin. He banged on the glass, and when she didn't respond, he walked around to the garage. He said he heard the car running and put two and two together, broke a window, crawled in, then called 9-1-1."

I had heard dribs and drabs of this story through the years, but never the details. Dad and Irving were—still are—good friends. Robin met Todd at Boston University in 1987—both majored in hospitality management. Robin got pregnant her senior year at BU but graduated with honors. Todd secured a management position at a boutique hotel in Boston and Robin worked part-time at a catering company. According to Dad, Irving and Audrey campaigned like crazy to get Robin and Todd to return so they could be more involved in Madison's life. They finally relented in 1996 when Madison was five years old.

The area was in steep decline by then. Hotels were shuttering their doors, one after the other. It also meant property was cheap and easy to come by. Todd bought several acres of land adjacent to Sackett Lake. In the 1960s, a hotel on that parcel had burned to the ground; from the ashes rose an exclusive spa, attracting a far different clientele than the older hotels, bungalow colonies, and sleepaway camps that once dotted the lakefront. Shangri-La, Todd named it. 'Escape to Paradise,' its tagline.

And escape people did. People with money. That place was super expensive, super exclusive, and super secretive.

"She called me last night."

"Who? Madison?"

I nodded. "Maybe she was in some kind of trouble. But she didn't leave a message. So perhaps it was something she thought could wait until she got ahold of me. That tells me she wasn't afraid for her life. Well, at least last night, when she called me."

My phone rang and I swiped to answer. "Yeah."

"Rafael's on his way," Eldridge said. "He'll be here in two hours."

"Roger that. I'll head back shortly." I slid my phone into my back pocket.

"Have you spoken to Jacob Bowman?" Dad asked.

"Who?" I turned my head slightly and expelled a delicate sneeze.

"You really shouldn't be out and about with that bad cold."

I waved my right hand, swatting away his reprimand. "Who is Jacob Bowman?"

"Old business partner of Todd's. And the one guy I know who would benefit from Madison's death."

I LED Rafael into a room in the precinct that looked more like a cramped den than an interrogation room—two beige loveseats faced each other, a light oak coffee table in between. A lamp with a low-watt bulb graced one of the two teak end tables, casting a shadow across the far corner of the room. The decades-old carpet was a dull brown with a mosaic pattern that hid the myriad of coffee stains spilled over the years. A plug-in air freshener did little to mask the amalgam of body odor that seemed to never dissipate. This room was meant to feel less confrontational, an attempt to re-create an informal chat in someone's home. It fooled no one.

"I get it. The husband is always the prime suspect," Rafael offered up. His downturned eyes, surrounded by thick, long eyelashes women would die for, gave him an inherent melancholy quality. Maybe he was happy on the inside, but his eyes innately played the part of a deeply saddened husband.

"Until we rule them out," I countered.

"Of course. That's why I'm here. Rule me out and get on with finding out who did this," he said in a let's-get-down-to-business kind of way.

"We'll need your fingerprints and a DNA sample."

Rafael nodded. "I got no problem with that. Expected as much."

"We spoke to Madison's grandparents and they had no idea she was even up here. Do you know why she was in the area?"

"She had a meeting with Jacob Bowman."

Okay, that got my attention. Two mentions of this guy in one day.

Rafael continued, "If I were you, I would look closely at him. He was her father's silent partner." He air-quoted silent. "That guy couldn't be silent if you stuck a sock in his mouth and covered it with duct tape."

"In what way was he a partner? And why do you think I should be looking closely at him?"

"Todd and Jacob held shares in each other's businesses. Todd was the majority owner of Shangri-La with 55 percent of the shares. Jacob was and still is the majority owner of New Beginnings, that posh recovery center in Liberty, with 55 percent of those shares. They had a mutual agreement that their shares would be bequeathed to each other if they were to die." He leaned forward and slightly tilted his head, as though letting me in on a secret. "Except, Todd left his Shangri-La and New Beginnings shares to Madison. Seems Todd had changed his will without conferring with Jacob . . . or Madison. It was a surprise to her as well." He snickered, as though slightly amused by this business backstabbing. "But on the plus side, Todd didn't completely fuck over his business partner—it was stipulated that if—" He pressed his lips together, then cleared his throat. "If Madison passed away before Jacob, Jacob would inherit Madison's New Beginnings shares."

"And the Shangri-La shares? Who would get those upon Madison's death?"

Rafael swallowed hard and his eyes watered when I said the word "death," but he quickly regained his composure. "As her husband, those shares would end up with me." He must have seen my eyebrows shoot up, and added, "If you're thinking that's a motive for murder, Detective, think again. I had no interest in that business. None."

Plausible, I thought. The guy was seemingly successful. But greed is a powerful motivator to do awful things.

I made a mental note to revisit his interest in obtaining those shares when I had a better handle on the state of their marriage and Madison's involvement in the two businesses. "Any idea why Todd bequeathed his shares to Madison?"

"I think he wanted Madison to earn income from these businesses. Maybe he thought she would be interested in running Shangri-La one day." Rafael clenched his fists. "But Jacob was impatient and constantly badgering Madison to sell her shares to him. And if I find out he did this . . ."

"Wait, are you about to confess to a future crime?"

Rafael jabbed his finger in the air. "The point is, if I don't think you guys are getting the job done, I'll go and hire a private detective to sort this out. You sure you're up for this? You sound mighty sick to me."

"It's just a summer cold." I shifted slightly, then leaned over the coffee table. "You've been mighty cooperative and I appreciate that, but threatening to involve a third party won't get this case solved any faster. And in fact, it might muck things up. I will keep you informed as much as I can." I leaned back. "Tell me, what is it you do? For a living?"

"I'm a hedge fund manager. At Paulson Capital."

I nodded as I made a note of that. I hadn't a clue as to what a hedge fund was, let alone what managing one would entail. But I kept my ignorance to myself. In matters like this, the Internet came in handy. Plug in "hedge fund manager" and, voilà, the answer would be at my fingertips—perhaps a website titled "Everything You Wanted to Know about Hedge Fund Management but Were Afraid to Ask."

"Did you glean anything from her journal?"

"Journal?"

"Yeah, she kept it in her handbag. Red leather, with her initials embossed on the cover. Always had it with her to ensure no one read it." He tapped his chin. "I offered to get her a real diary, with one of those little locks, but she was afraid she would lose the little key." He flashed a closemouthed smile at the thought of that.

"The only personal items we found in the car were her phone and overnight duffel. But we've got officers searching the area and a dive team scouring the lake for the murder weapon and perhaps other evidence. Can you describe her handbag?"

"It was one of those brown-checkered Louis Vuitton bags. Yea big," he said holding his hands out apart twenty inches or so. "She spent nearly three thousand dollars on the thing. She said it was unique in that it had a red lining and red strap, but they all look the same to—"

I sneezed, a bit unexpectedly, and raised my arm just a hair too slowly to catch the outgoing spray.

Rafael leaped from his loveseat. "Jeez. We done here?"

"No." I stood, resuming eye-to-eye contact. "When was the last time you spoke to Madison?"

He expelled a breath of air, then paced a couple of steps to his right, then back to his left. "The last time we spoke was Saturday afternoon," he said, pulling out his phone and scrolling through the call history screen. "The time stamp says four o'clock. She told me she'd borrowed Samantha's car and planned to meet with Bowman Sunday morning."

"And she didn't call you after that? To tell you she arrived in the area? To say good night?"

"No. She said she would call me Sunday morning." He sat back down.

I retook my seat. "Where were you Saturday night into Sunday morning? It's not like you couldn't have driven up here, done this, and then drove back to the city."

"I was home. Alone. I was in the shower when you called and I didn't notice your message until I was heading out the door to meet my sister for breakfast."

"Okay. I'd like to get in touch with your sister. Camilla, right? Just to substantiate your whereabouts."

"Sure, she came up here with me. As you can well imagine, Camilla is a bit distraught. I dropped her off at Shangri-La. Perhaps this can wait until tomorrow?"

MADISON

Monday, January 14, 2019

M*y first journal entry. Yay for me. I read somewhere that journaling can help resolve personal issues. Not sure how jotting down my thoughts and activities will resolve the mess that I'm in (or about to get in), but okay, sure, I'm game.*

The bottom line is this: I need to come clean. I just need a little more time, but I know it's soon or never. I think it was Erma Bombeck who said guilt is the gift that keeps on giving. Amen, sister. But this is a "gift" I need to return. And that's where you come in, dear journal—help me weigh the pros and cons. Do I tell the truth? Or let sleeping dogs lie?

So, where to start? Maybe I'll leave the heavy stuff for another day when I get the hang of this. I'll be positive and happy for now. And I'll talk about my favorite topic for a bit—me! I turn 28 next month. A strange age. Too old for music festivals, too young for garden parties. Too old for reckless partying, too young for country club soirees. An age when it feels most people have set a path for themselves and are steadfastly sticking to whatever they set out to do. I didn't set out to be a copywriter. I fell into the role. Got a bunch of internships at ad agencies while in college and was assigned copy tasks. The writing came easy. Naturally, even. Need a catchy headline, I'm your gal. Need convincing ad copy, my pen was at the ready. Need a snappy line for that Insta post, I'm the queen of captioning! My bosses would say, "Oh Madison, you are so good at this." I didn't get to choose my profession. It chose me. Was there a different path to follow, one that would have led me in a more fulfilling direction? At least I can take solace in the fact that I can't hurt anyone in my field of work (well, unless I make a false claim about a product that turns out to be harmful, or my pen flies from my hand and pokes someone in the eye).

Is my marriage like my career? Did I choose Rafael . . . or did he choose me? The answer is as plain and simple as vanilla ice cream. I set my sights on him. He had this bad-boy reputation. Man, he was just so sexy. And I knew my parents would be dead set against us dating. Three for three. Ticked off all the "teenage rebellion" boxes. Didn't matter that he was dating someone else at the time. I wanted him, and I usually got what I wanted.

So, yes, at first Rafael was a conquest. But let me make this perfectly clear, dear journal: I love Rafael. I might not know what I want to do with my life, but if I wanted to, I could just ride his coattails into a predictable and cushy future. And what would be so bad about that? Plenty of women choose this path.

Well, that's it for today, I will be satisfied with these few paragraphs and a pat on my back for starting this thing.

2

MONDAY | JULY 1, 2019

MY FIRST order of business was Jacob Bowman. The talkative silent partner. According to both Dad and Rafael, the person with motive. Greed. Or perhaps revenge, stemming from a long-simmering anger for not getting what he believed was rightfully his upon Todd Garmin's death—100 percent ownership in the two properties. He agreed to meet me in his office at Shangri-La.

Shangri-La was located on the north side of Sackett Lake. The narrow road that led to the entrance was easy to miss. The small wood sign nailed to a tree bark was well camouflaged. If you squinted, you could make out the shallow engraving: SHANGRI-LA. Designed to keep the curious riffraff out, I presumed.

I turned left at the sign and proceeded down a semi-paved, rock-strewn single-lane road.

My unforgiving Prius let me know every time I hit a hole or rock. A few turnoffs along the way presented an opportunity for one car to pass another, if encountered.

Jacob had directed me to park in Lot C, the lot furthest from the spa entrance. I ignored his directive and parked in Lot A. What was he going to do about it? Call the police?

As I emerged from the car, I spotted a burly man hurrying toward me. Skip-walking. Waving his hands as though shooing away a fly. When he got within shouting distance, I could hear him yell, "You can't park there, ma'am." I took out my badge and held it out in front of me until he got near enough to see what I was holding.

His breathing was labored from that short jog over to my car and he was sweating profusely. He placed his hands on his thighs and bent over, trying to catch his breath. He glanced at my badge. Then tilted his head up at me. "Detective Susan Ford?"

"That's me."

"Oh, I thought I told you to park in Lot C."

"Yeah, well, I wasn't in the mood to walk from there. So, why don't we just go inside, where it's, hopefully, cooler. I presume you have air-conditioning."

He nodded, still gasping for breath.

"Are you okay?"

"Just mildly winded. I'm a tad out of shape and this sticky weather gets to me." He gestured up at the sky as though the stickiness was there to be seen.

As we slowly walked up to the lamasery-style main building, I took in the scene around me. I had been here once before when one guest accused another guest of stealing her jewelry and threatened to kill her. Turned out she never even brought it with her. Her son found the jewelry in her safe at home. Case solved.

The wooded area of the parking lot gave way to rows of flower beds, each row a different color and height, meticulously maintained. The landscaping had that English country-estate vibe.

"Pretty, huh?" Jacob said. "Todd took the reference to Shangri-La literally. He hired a Buddhist architect who designed the main building, guest dwellings, dining area, meditation rooms, and spa facilities. A Buddhist landscape architect designed the grounds based on the notion of Shambhala."

"Shambhala?"

"It's a core concept of Tibetan Buddhism—the realm of harmony between man and nature connected to the wheel of time."

"Wheel of time?"

"The wheel of time is a concept found in several religious philosophies, not just Buddhism. The belief that time is cyclical, consisting of repeating ages."

"What comes around goes around?"

"That's karma. Different."

"So, what's the origin of Shangri-La?" I asked as we headed down a long corridor. I felt I should have known this, but I was drawing a blank. The only reference I could conjure up was Stevie Nicks's album, *Trouble in Shangri-La*, which felt very apropos right now.

"British author James Hilton wrote about a mystical, utopian paradise in the Tibetan mountains called Shangri-La in his nineteen thirty-three novel, *Lost Horizon*. A place isolated from the world where the people age slowly and live for hundreds of years. We don't promise you eternal life, but we do offer peace, relaxation, and an opportunity to escape the rat race for a while."

"Well, this place is in the mountains."

"The *ri* in *Shangri* actually means 'mountain.'" He pushed open an ornately engraved wooden door. "Well, here we are."

We weren't in Shangri-La anymore. The office was in disarray with cabinets flung open and papers and folders piled on the floor. The furniture looked like it had been picked up at a yard sale; the veneer on the desk had peeled away, exposing cheap wood underneath. There was an oniony smell, perhaps from a sandwich or salad disposed of in the small wastebasket next to the desk.

Or perhaps lingering BO.

"Sorry for the mess." Jacob removed a stack of folders from an old armchair. "Wasn't expecting company."

I inspected the seat, sure that fleas were lurking in the folds of the torn fabric. "That's okay, I'll stand."

"Suit yourself," Jacob said as he sat on the wooden swivel chair behind the desk. He leaned back and clasped his hands behind his bald head. "So, you want to talk about Madison. I imagine you probably heard about my beef with her. But that's all water under the bridge. We had come to terms."

I was going to ask him if he'd thought about getting a lawyer. But I wasn't formally interrogating him. We were just having a friendly chat. And since this guy liked to talk, I gave him all the leeway in the world, or as Dad would say, enough rope to hang himself with—but that metaphor was always a bit too gory for my taste. "Go on."

"Sure, we've had our . . . um . . . differences through the years, but she finally came to her senses. And by that I mean she realized that being part owner in a couple of businesses she had nothing to do with wasn't worth her time or effort and it was just practical and financially smart for her to sell her interests to me." He unclasped his hands, placed his palms on the desk, and leaned forward. "But now, I have no idea what's going to happen. For all I know, Rafael can make a big stink. This thing could end up in probate and I'm no better off now than before her murder. So, I'm really the last person you should be contemplating for this. We were supposed to meet yesterday and discuss the details." He leaned back in his chair and folded his hands in his lap, seemingly satisfied with his explanation of why he should not be considered a suspect.

"From where I'm sitting, you stand to benefit greatly from her death. Todd's wishes were quite clear . . . Rafael would have a hard time disputing your right to the New Beginnings shares."

"That might be. But I stand to lose the majority shares to Shangri-La, a business I poured my sweat into, in both the down years and the up years. Now I have to deal with Rafael, which trust me, is not to my benefit." He swiveled his chair back and forth a couple of times. "I didn't do this, and happy to undergo a polygraph test if that's what it takes."

"Is it possible that someone did not want Madison to sell her shares of Shangri-La to you?"

"That's what I was thinking. Her husband, maybe? Who knows? That's your job, Detective. I'm just here to say, if you think it's me, you're barking up the wrong tree."

I stepped closer to his desk. "Do you have any proof that she was planning to sell her shares to you? Perhaps text or email messages."

"Yeah. We exchanged a few emails on the matter. I'll get those over to you."

"When was the last time you heard from Madison?"

"That would be Friday afternoon. I remember because I was in a meeting with Ryan Joyner."

"And that would be who?"

"After Todd and Robin passed away, I hired Ryan as general manager. He runs the day-to-day operations here; I manage the books. My baby is New Beginnings—that's where I spend most of my time . . . and energy. But I have a warm spot in my heart for Shangri-La, so I stay involved as much as possible."

"And what did Madison say when she called?"

"She asked if we could meet at nine o'clock instead of ten. Yesterday. Sunday. That she needed to take care of something else while she was up here. I said sure and that was the end of the phone call."

"And when she didn't show up?"

"I figured she blew me off. Wouldn't have been the first time."

"Where were you the night of June twenty-ninth and early morning of June thirtieth?"

He gnawed at his thumbnail. "Here." He swiveled his chair and motioned around the room with his chubby hand. Every fingernail was bitten to the quick. "Working late, getting ready for the July Fourth holiday."

"Can anyone back that up?"

"I'm sure there were staff and guests who saw me here. I'll try and remember who and get a list to you."

"Any security cameras in the parking lot? To see who's coming and going?"

"No," he snapped, followed by a close-lipped smile intended to soften the outburst. "We value our guests' privacy."

In my experience, lack of cameras at a place of business sometimes had more to do with protecting the privacy of the owners than protecting the privacy of customers. But I kept that thought to myself. I eyed the door. "Would you mind if I took a look around the property?" I asked, eager to leave this rank-smelling office.

He rose and I followed him out the door into the main lobby. Abstract paintings in ornate frames hung on the beige-painted walls. Clusters of sofas, love seats, and armchairs were generously spaced apart. A group of guests occupied one of the clusters, chatting and laughing.

"Renovating?" I asked, pointing out the window to a small building under construction, shielded by blue tarps.

"I just got a gaming license for ETGs. Electronic table games—roulette, baccarat, blackjack. Adds a little Monte Carlo flavor to the place." He stopped before he got to the front entrance. "Y'know, this might have nothing to do with Madison. My guests are spooked right now. We could have a serial killer on the loose, for all we know. Have you considered that, Detective?"

I was going to spew statistics but wasn't in the mood. Sure, sometimes murder is random—victim in the wrong place at the wrong time—but unfortunately, and more often, murder is perpetrated by someone you know . . . and trust. "Right now we're considering everything."

Jacob escorted me across the lawn behind the main building to an L-shaped bungalow where Camilla was staying. A quarter board affixed to the porch railing read "Serene Scene."

"Every bungalow has a unique name, depending on where it's situated on the property," Jacob explained.

I glanced around. Yup, definitely serene.

"Further down this path we see a lot of blue herons, so that bungalow over there is named—"

"Blue Heron?"

"Exactly. You catch on fast, Detective. And speaking of birds, the reporters trying to contact me are like vultures. I told my staff to speak to no one."

"That's wise."

He swept his hand across his midsection, motioning me up the three stairs to the wraparound porch. "This is where Camilla stays when she visits." He joined me on the porch. "Only the best for Camilla." He sneered.

Jacob planted himself in front of Camilla's door.

"Well, okay, I can take it from here," I said.

Jacob rocked from foot to foot, then backed away. "Um, oh, okay," he stuttered, acknowledging his dismissal, obviously disappointed.

I waited until he was halfway across the lawn, then knocked on the door.

"Coming!" The door swung open. "Hello!" She tilted her head sideways. "Detective Susan Ford, I presume?"

The resemblance to her twin brother was uncanny. Same drooping eyelids, same caterpillar-like lashes, same charcoal pupils. Her cheekbones were high and prominent, no contouring needed. Her lips full and pouty, no lipstick needed.

Barefoot, she was clad in Daisy Dukes and a white crop top exposing her midriff. I'm five five, and she was a good five inches taller than me.

"That's me!" I answered, trying to mimic her chipper intonation.

"Come in, come in. Tea?" she asked with a hint of a British accent that I didn't detect when she first addressed me.

When I stepped inside, she silently pointed to my shoes. I got the hint. I slipped them off and lined them up with the other pairs of shoes neatly arranged by the door.

The bungalow was sparsely furnished in an Asian motif consisting of a bamboo coffee table atop an oriental rug, a futon-style couch flanked by hip-high wicker baskets containing fake cattails. Lantern lighting above. Scrolls with Chinese calligraphy hung over the futon couch. A four-paneled room divider, screen-painted with reeds and long-necked birds, blocked off a corner of the open space. Behind the divider, I spied a pile of small suitcases.

I followed her through the living area into the kitchen. Her perfume drifted behind her—the scent was hard to put a finger on, somewhere between spicy and cloying.

"It's been a rough couple of days," she lamented with a deep sigh. "This is the kind of thing that happens to *other* people." She poured the tea into two hand-thrown ceramic mugs. "Here you go."

I hear that a lot. *This happens to other people.* But aren't we all other people to someone? Or perhaps she was referring to class and status. *This only happens to the little people.* Which, unfortunately, is true. Those on the lower socioeconomic rung are statistically more exposed to such jeopardy.

An article I recently read by some hotshot sociologist spelled out the correlation between poverty and violent crime: Sometimes it's a fight for survival. A person living on the margins, feeling alienated, might weigh the chance of being caught committing a crime versus a perceived benefit worth the risk. If that's the case here, what was to be gained by killing Madison?

Was it a random robbery? Or did someone have something to gain from her death?

I cradled the mug in my hands, letting it cool slightly before taking a sip. "Thank you for seeing me this morning. Just a few questions, formalities really, just to get pointed in the right direction."

"I saw you come up the walkway with Jacob. Not sure what he told you, but I wouldn't trust that guy one lick. He's probably thrilled Madison is dead." The air conditioner kicked on and she jumped slightly.

"Why do you say that?"

"Well, now Jacob will get his wish, full control of New Beginnings," she said, slipping in and out of the British affectation.

"Do you have any reason to believe that Jacob would do something this extreme to get his wish?"

Camilla shrugged. "He's a wanker. A real nob. Madison told me about him being a relentless bully and all-around pain in the ass about selling her shares of Shangri-La to him. He insists they are rightfully his. That he wants the freedom to make financial and aesthetic decisions without her interference.

"But the funny thing is, I don't think she ever gave him advice or stood in the way of any decision he has ever made. I think on some level she just hung on to them to piss him off." A single tear made its way down Camilla's right cheek and she swatted it away with the heel of her hand.

I reached into my bag and offered her a tissue, which she declined. "Rafael told me that you had plans to meet him for breakfast Sunday morning. Can you confirm that?"

"Yes, yes." She ran her fingers through her long mane of ebony hair. "We had planned to meet for breakfast on Clark Street . . . in Brooklyn Heights. I have a flat in the neighborhood. Rafael called me about Madison just as I was walking out the door. So instead of meeting him for breakfast, I packed a bag, grabbed something at Starbucks, and drove up here with him." She sighed. "I usually work on Sundays, preparing for the week ahead, but I didn't think he should be alone during this trying time," she said, just shy of swooning.

"What is it you do for a living?" I asked, not because I thought it was pertinent to this investigation but because I was curious, or wondered if it might shed some light on why she spoke with a strange British accent and used words like *flat* and *wanker* instead of *apartment* and *jerk*.

"I'm an influencer."

"An influencer? Like on YouTube?"

"Well, Instagram and TikTok. Health and beauty products, make-up, and fashion mostly. It started as a lark a few years ago, but when I amassed hundreds of thousands of followers, the brands came knocking. Now I've got millions of fans." She deployed air quotes around *fans*. "When I was at King's College, I did some modeling to pay for expenses, and this seemed like a perfect extension to that."

"King's College in London?" Perhaps that explained the on-again, off-again Queen's English. Or maybe her strange affectation was associated with her TikTok persona and she had a hard time turning it off in real life. Either way, it was a bit kooky.

"Yes. Lovely really. But I prefer this side of the pond."

"Do you know why Madison borrowed a friend's car to come up here?"

"Did she? Is that how she got up here?" Camilla said with no accent. "I really had no idea that she had even left the city," she continued, the British accent now in full swing.

"I'd like to get a list of Madison's friends. Is that something you can help me with?"

"Sure. You should start with Madison's business partner, Annabelle Pratt."

"What kind of business?"

"Madison is . . . oh, dear . . ." She took a deep breath. "She *was* a copywriter. Annabelle was . . . is a graphic designer. They called themselves Mad Bell. Digital and print advertising, social content, that kind of thing." Camilla cocked her head sideways and tapped her chin.

"They had a bit of a falling-out a few months ago—March, or maybe it was April. Anyhoo, a parting of the ways."

"Why the split?"

"I have no idea. But it was not amicable. Something happened between the two of them." A text message lit up her phone. She glanced down at it, then placed it face down on the counter. "Work related, but this is more important. I can send you a list of Madison's friends, if you like. It's not like she had a ton."

I sat silently, waiting for an explanation. Most people liked to fill the void with their own voice. I found they were more likely to tell me more if I let their last statement hang in the air a bit.

"She wasn't particularly social," Camilla said, filling the silence, as expected. "Always had an excuse for not wanting to come out and play. If you ask me, she was more interested in smoking a joint alone than . . ." Camilla gasped. "Oh dear, how gauche of me to be speaking of Madison like this. But I guess we all have our little vices. Pot was hers. Mine is not knowing when to shut up." She smiled and the dimples tucked under her cheekbones deepened, making her already high cheekbones soar to greater heights.

Camilla's phone rang. She tilted it toward her. "Gotta take this. It's Rafael."

She opened the slider and stepped out onto the porch. She bopped down the three steps and walked along a gravel path that led to a circular stone patio; the large stones shimmered in the sunlight, a mix of copper, gray, and silver hues. At the center of the patio was a stone-constructed fire pit with four white Adirondack chairs forming a circle around it. Just beyond the patio a hammock hung between two maple trees. *Serene.*

Camilla turned to me, smiled and held up her index finger. She turned away and continued her conversation with Rafael. The DayQuil was wearing off, as was my patience. My left sinus cavity was beginning to throb and Ray was going to pitch a fit if I came home sicker than I left.

"Told you so" was definitely in my future. Camilla spun around and started back toward the house.

"Sorry about that. Rafael is trying to make arrangements for the funeral. He's over at Madison's grandparents' house. They are pretty distraught that they can't bury her within twenty-four hours of her passing. It's a Jewish thing, y'know."

"I'm aware of the custom, but they know we need to complete the autopsy, which is this afternoon." We stood in silence for a few moments. "Okay, then. Well, I'll be on my way. Oh, and don't forget to email me that list of her friends."

Camilla looked out toward the hammock. She cupped her right hand above her eyes, shielding the sun. Staring out ahead, she asked, "Do you have any leads? Do you think this was planned or random? Should we be worried that there's a mad killer running around here?" Before I could answer, she lowered her hand and turned to me. "Oh, and Detective, if you want something for that cold, one of my clients sells an herbal remedy that'll knock that shit right out of you."

I HELD my breath as Mark rolled down the sheet exposing Madison's upper body. I exhaled slowly. Here was an instance when I was glad to have a stuffed nose. Even after nearly twenty-five years on the force, this was something I'd never get used to. Some people do. Or maybe they pretend to.

"I didn't peg you for the squeamish type, Ford."

"Just get on with it," I muttered.

"Madison Garcia, nee Garmin. Female, age twenty-eight, Caucasian. Height, sixty-three inches. Approximate weight, one hundred and fifteen pounds. Blonde hair, brown eyes. Two tattoos. A butterfly, seven point six two centimeters wide on her right shoulder blade and"—he picked up her right arm and turned it over—"a quill pen and inkwell on her inside right forearm." Mark picked up a laser pointer and aimed it at her torso. A beam of red light illuminated the space between Mark's hand and Madison's midsection. "Three stab wounds. One to the heart, one to the left lung, one to the liver." The light moved from one incision point to the next. "All sideways entry. Death caused by exsanguination leading to hypoxia."

"Which stab was the fatal one?"

"Any one of them could have killed her. I would say the assailant knew what he was doing."

"Or she."

"Or she. Of course."

"The assailant's aim was quite impressive. The stab to the left lung could have been the first wound and would have silenced her as her lungs filled with blood. In this second stab wound, the knife penetrated the two chambers of the right side of the heart causing damage to the ventricular wall and bleeding around the heart and lungs. And down here, the assailant aimed between the fourth and fifth ribs and went for the liver."

"Overkill?"

"Not necessarily. Efficiency may be the reason—hit all the key spots. Ensure her death."

"Defensive wounds?" I asked.

Mark lifted her right hand. "No. So, she never saw it coming."

I stepped away from the body.

"So if they were both sitting in the car next to each other, the person in the passenger's seat—someone she presumably knows and trusts—swings his . . . or her arm around and stabs Madison in the left lung, heart, and liver in quick succession?"

"That's what it looks like." Mark picked up a scalpel and held it in his right hand like he was gripping a bicycle handlebar. "Probably holding the knife as so." He reached across his body and made three jabbing motions. "The knife goes in straight and makes a slight slit to the right, meaning he—or she—is naturally tugging it toward himself before pulling it back out and going for the next target."

"Can you tell what kind of knife was used?"

"Small knife, the blade eight to nine centimeters long. Smooth, not serrated. I can't be 100 percent sure, but the size and shape of the wound leads me to believe a plain reverse tanto was used."

"A plain reverse tanto?"

"It's a combat-slash-hunting knife with a triangle tip that sharply angles down to the blade. Pretty popular these days. Lots of manufacturers, and lots of places to buy them. I know because I have one."

I raised an eyebrow.

"Happy to show you mine, Detective," he said, with a sly wink. "Hasn't been used in a while."

"How much blood would have gotten on the assailant?"

"These wounds don't project that much blood spatter. But I can't imagine the assailant didn't get blood on his hands and arms. Now, if the assailant went for the axillary artery of the armpit, well, that's your typical horror movie scenario." He pulled up the sheet to cover Madison.

I closed my eyes and conjured up the crime scene. "There was blood on the passenger's-side inside door latch. But whoever did this seemed mighty prepared, so I'm thinking gloves, right?"

"Right. There was no fingerprint in the blood found on that latch. But we did lift lots of different fingerprints from inside the car. So you might get lucky there."

"What puzzles me is that there was no sign of a struggle. No defensive wounds." I glanced at the sheeted corpse, then back at Mark. "As you know, Madison tried to call me earlier that night. I'm not sure why, but perhaps she sensed she was in trouble.

"But, if that was the case, you would think she'd get suspicious if someone sitting next to her was donning a pair of gloves in the dead of summer."

"Well, if I wanted to, I could surreptitiously slip on a pair of gloves. So perhaps Madison didn't notice as she was driving along."

"Any drugs in her system? I heard she was into weed."

"I ran a standard tox panel and nothing. No stimulants. No depressants. No analgesics. No cannabis. No dissociative anesthetics. No hallucinogens. No inhalants. Clean as a whistle."

"Hmm. Estimated time of death?"

"Based on body temp, rigor mortis, and lividity when we found her, I'd say between nine p.m. and three a.m. It was a hot and humid night, so that may throw off the calculation."

"Based on Eleanor Campbell's statement, she saw a car drive toward the lake around ten thirty. So, that narrows it down a wee bit more."

"What time did Madison call you?"

"Nine forty." I shuddered to think how differently this might have played out had I picked up the phone.

MADISON

Tuesday, February 12, 2019

Okay, shoot me . . . I haven't exactly been on top of this journal-writing thing. But here I go. I'm going to do it. See, I'm doing it. Yeah, I'm stoned. A habit I plan to quit this year (my New Year's resolution). But I like it. Why does everyone think it's such a big fucking deal? It's just weed.

Rafael says my pot smoking makes me spacey. I am a forgetful person, maybe weed has something to do with it. He wants to buy me a real diary—the kind with a little lock and key. Told him I would lose the key and have to cut open the latch, so what's the point? It'll become just another broken thing in my life.

No, this is better. Just have to safeguard it. Keep it with me at all times.

I got a whole lot of shit going on right now. That's why I got this journal in the first place. Put down my innermost thoughts. Work through thorny dilemmas.

Get past my stuckness. Is that even a word? Well, now it is.

Maybe I should start by airing grievances. Like that Seinfeld *episode. Every entry can be a celebration of Festivus! Rafael LOVES* Seinfeld. *Some evenings, while I'm cooking, he's on his computer with his headphones on, and I catch glimpses of him watching that show and laughing out loud. Claims it's the funniest thing ever conceived for television. I watched three episodes (including that Festivus episode) and thought it was stupid. If I'm going to watch vintage television programs, I'll fire up* Friends.

Yes, grievances. My most heavy beef is with Jacob Bowman. Yuck. How in the world did Dad get involved with that shlub? What an asshole. An asshole of the highest degree. The king of assholes! I wonder if he thinks I'm an asshole. I certainly treat him with disdain. He acts like he's doing me a favor by running the businesses without my involvement. He was running them into the ground until a few years ago. I'll admit he's turned the business around lately, but so what? He's still an asshole.

Honestly, I want out. I need to cut ties with those places. Give me my money so I can walk away from it all.

Ugh, what am I saying? I can't just walk away. There are things you cannot walk away from. I have to pay the price. Have to come clean. Will anyone stick by my side if I do, or will everyone cast me aside?

There are days when I feel that I can't move forward until I deal with what happened. Yet on other days, I manage to convince myself that reopening this old wound will only bring more pain and suffering. Perhaps I'm waiting for a sign. Some clear signal that it's time to loosen this noose of guilt that squeezes tighter with every passing day.

To some people guilt feels overwhelming. They are desperately trying to stay afloat in a body of water where their feet can't touch the bottom and the waves are crashing over their heads. They bob and bob and bob, treading water, and yell, "Help, help, I'm sinking." But it's not like that for me. Not at all. I'm drowning in the shallow end. I could stand—if I wanted to—and save myself.

3

TUESDAY | JULY 2, 2019

I LET myself into my mother's house and made a beeline for the kitchen. Mom was upstairs in the shower, running late as usual. The kitchen was in a bit of disarray. She had taken out a home equity loan last month—a present to herself for six months of sobriety—to update her 1970s era kitchen. I glanced around at the mustard-colored appliances, the faux-brick linoleum floor, the dark knotty-pine cabinets, the Formica countertops. She also planned to hire a contractor to strip the faded and smoke-stained wallpaper plastered throughout the house and replace it with a fresh coat of paint. ("Seems tried-and-true wallpaper isn't in anymore," Mom moaned, clearly disappointed that the world had moved away from this decorating trend.)

I removed a black ceramic mug from the cabinet and placed it under the Keurig spout. A tray on the counter held an assortment of coffee flavors. I inserted a French Roast pod into the contraption, then leaned against the counter as the machine did its thing. Mom appeared in the kitchen doorway as I neared the end of my coffee. She leaned on her cane—one of those classic-styled, scorched chestnut Derby walking canes. Her knee surgery being only a partial success, she needed the assistance once in a while.

She eyed my coffee. "Do we have time for a cup of coffee?" She opened the cabinet door and grabbed a mug before I had time to protest.

I glanced up at the wall where the clock would be, but in its place was a round void, unsullied by the kitchen grease that covered the rest of the wallpaper. I peered down at my watch. "Ten minutes tops, then we need to be on our way."

Mom plucked a Hazelnut pod from the rack and inserted it in the gaping mouth of the machine. "I did get up early, by the way. I just got sidetracked playing Words with Friends. It's very addictive."

"Better that than a morning highball."

She snorted. "Ain't that the truth." She walked over to a drawer and pulled out a pack of Marlboros and a Bic lighter, then glanced in my direction. "Don't worry, Susan. I'll take it outside."

I followed her out onto the small back deck. She placed her mug on the porch railing, then thumbed the wheel of the lighter and inhaled her first drag. "One cigarette, and I'll be ready to go." She exhaled, then said, "Besides, it's a shiva. Irving and Audrey will be stuck in their house for the next few days with tons of people coming and going. If we're a few minutes late, who's going to notice?" She took four more drags then snubbed the tip of the cigarette on the side of the railing before depositing it into a metal can near the sliding door.

IRVING AND Audrey Feinberg's house was an architectural beauty, one of those Swiss chalet-style homes. The A-frame structure, constructed from rough-hewn timber, featured a steeply pitched gable roof with wide eaves shading a broad porch. Enormous picture windows soared from the base of the house to just below the eaves, symmetrically flanking the front door. The house was situated in the woods a mile or so from the Woodstock Music Festival site, not far from where Ray and I lived. There were four cars parked in the clearing to the right of their house. I pulled in next to a silver Volvo.

"You aren't planning to interrogate anyone here, are you?" Mom asked as she unlatched her seatbelt. "This is a shiva, y'know. Would seem a bit disrespectful and all that."

"What makes you think I'm going to grill anyone?"

"You underestimate my knowledge of you."

I had to smile. I wasn't planning on interrogating anyone, but I did time our arrival to coincide with Madison's business partner, Annabelle. Rafael had mentioned the night before that she would be here in the morning to pay her respects.

"Let's not forget the lasagna," Mom said when I opened the car door. "With this heat, that'll reek to high heavens if we leave it in the car."

Madison's grandparents were Reform Jews, not very religious. Dad told me he had attended Passover dinners and Yom Kippur break fasts with Irving and Audrey, but they had pretty much fallen away from the temple after their daughter, Robin, and son-in-law, Todd, had died. Even so, they were quite insistent that we release Madison's body as soon as possible to adhere to Jewish burial traditions. The shiva usually followed the burial, but I guess they decided to bend the rules a bit, considering the circumstances.

The door was slightly ajar, so we walked right in. Just as I was about to close it behind me, an elderly gentleman with a piece of black cloth pinned to his lapel stepped into the foyer and said, "Please leave it open."

Mom elbowed me and whispered, "Guests aren't supposed to knock or ring the doorbell during shiva. So the door is left open."

"And you know this how?"

Mom lifted her finger to her lips. "I'll tell you later."

The man led us into the spacious exposed-post-and-beam living room. A towering stone fireplace took up nearly an entire wall. Flameless of course, considering the excessive heat and humidity outside. Recesses to its left and right held several cords of firewood. A toffee-hued leather couch, matching love seat, and two wingback chairs surrounded a misshapen piece of reclaimed wood, polished to perfection. The wide pine floors were partially covered by plush earth-toned rugs. Above us hung an antler-inspired chandelier. Audrey Feinberg was seated on one of the wingback chairs; a man I recognized but couldn't quite place sat beside her on a wooden crate.

We walked over to Audrey. The bottom rims of her eyes were pink. Her foundation was smeared, presumably caused by several swipes at her cheeks to clear falling tears. I placed the lasagna on the side table and crouched beside her. My mother lingered at my side. "Sorry for your loss," I said softly.

"Our deepest condolences," Mom added, bending over slightly.

Audrey tilted her head ever so slightly. "Thank you. And thank you for stopping by." Her voice was subdued, and I got the sense she had been prescribed a sedative to get through this day. "Your dad was here most of the afternoon yesterday," she said flatly, then shifted her attention to Mom. "He'll be back later today."

I looked around the room for her husband, Irving, but he wasn't present. Neither was Annabelle.

"We'll just put this in the refrigerator," I said, retrieving the lasagna pan.

Audrey blinked slowly and a flutter of a smile came and went. "Thank you, dear."

Mom followed me into the kitchen. Bread baskets, jams, pastries, sliced fruit, two coffee cakes, a platter of chocolate-chip cookies, and a quiche covered every square inch of the marbled-gray soapstone island. Three silver urns, labeled "Regular," "Decaf," and "Hot Water," stood tall on a bar cart, along with a carafe of milk, a variety of sugar packets, and an assortment of teabags. At the far end of the kitchen island, Irving was talking to a young woman sitting on a barstool.

Irving edged away from the woman to greet us. "Oh, hi Susan. Vera."

He always reminded me of Harrison Ford—very charismatic and good-looking, full head of stylishly coifed gray hair, an indecisive beard (somewhere between intermittent shaving and deliberate scruffy look), and a deep baritone voice. I heard he still played a mean game of tennis and gave the younger men a run for their money on the golf course. Irving possessed that ageless appeal that eludes women of the same age.

Mom nudged the coffee cake over a few inches, and I placed the lasagna on the edge of the island. "Oh Irving." She threw her right palm up against her heart. "I can't even imagine what you are going through. Our deepest sympathies."

"Thank you, Vera."

"Anything I can do, really anything," she continued.

"Well, it's what your daughter can do—find out who did this and bring that person to justice."

I nodded. "Irving, I will do everything in my power to see that your granddaughter's killer is brought to justice." I glanced over at the tall, slender woman beside him.

"Oh, um, this is Annabelle Pratt. Annabelle worked with Madison." He drew his lips inward, closed his eyes, and inhaled audibly through his nose. The telltale sign of trying not to break down. He turned slightly toward Annabelle. "Annabelle, this is Susan Ford. Her father and I go way back. Now, if you'll excuse me," he said, backing away from the counter. "I'm going to check on Audrey."

"I take it you are *the* Detective Susan Ford I've been hearing so much about," Annabelle said. Soft raven curls framed her lightly freckled face. Her pale blue eyes reminded me of Caribbean waters. She was more adorable than beautiful, but I'm sure she had no trouble in the dating department.

"The one," I responded as Mom elbowed me gently. "Oh, and this is my mother, Vera."

They shook hands and in unison said, "Pleased to meet you."

"If you'll excuse me, I'm going to make myself cozy in the living room," Mom said, narrowing her eyes at me, silently imploring me to behave myself.

"So, you were Madison's business partner?" *This is not an interrogation*, I reminded myself. "Advertising, right?" I tried to say as nonchalantly as possible.

"Advertising, social media, brochures . . . whatever the clients wanted." When she waved her hand, a plume of floral perfume penetrated my stuffed nose. I sniffled at the assault.

"Must have been tough getting in touch with clients, breaking this news."

"Well, we stopped taking on new assignments a couple of months ago. We had just finished our last project two weeks ago and then . . ." She sighed. "This."

I nodded. *This is not an interrogation.* "May I ask, why the breakup?"

"Um . . ." She glanced at her perfectly manicured nails. Bright pink. "We just decided to go our separate ways."

That was a non-answer answer. Evasive. *But this was not an interrogation*, so I let it go. For now.

I shrugged my shoulders. "These things happen."

Rafael poked his head into the kitchen. "There you are," he said, directing his statement to Annabelle. "Camilla's going to be here shortly. You might want to make yourself scarce." He gave a quick wave and departed.

"Shoot." She sniffed derisively.

"I take it you are not fond of her?"

"Have you met her?"

"I spoke to her yesterday."

"That phony British accent. What even is that? Madison once told me that after a high-school spring-break vacation to Jamaica, Camilla came back with a Rastafarian accent."

The kind interpretation of Camilla's vocal affectation: impressionable and quirky. The not-so-kind: a slightly off-kilter attention seeker. "Hmm . . . interesting," I said, searching for a better word but coming up empty.

"I did grad school at Savannah College of Art and Design . . . you don't hear me speaking with a southern twang. She wasn't even in London that long. She merely went for a semester abroad."

"Oh. She made it sound like she did a four-year stint there."

"Of course she did." No eye roll necessary; the sarcasm dripped without recourse to facial expressions. "Even Rafael finds her pretentious. They might be twins, but they are nothing alike."

I made note of these strained family and business dynamics and squirreled them away in the back of my brain for a later discussion. "Did you know Madison was heading up here last Saturday?" I eyed the sliced fruit but reached over the tray and grabbed a cookie off the platter.

"Nope." She smiled coyly, then said, "This is starting to sound like an interrogation, Detective. Are you going to ask me where I was Saturday night?"

"Well, since *you* brought it up."

She threw her head back and laughed. "Well, I have a terrible alibi. I was home alone. Unfortunately, I don't think my cat is going to vouch for me."

Rafael poked his head in again. "Camilla's here."

"Well, that's my cue to vamoose," Annabelle said to me, fluttering her hand. "Adios, Detective. Or as Camilla would say, 'ta-ta and cheerio.'" She dashed out of the kitchen, although her rose-infused perfume lingered a few minutes longer.

Should I stay or should I go? My inclination was to stick around and observe. The DayQuil was still working its magic and there was a nice spread of food here. I noticed the lasagna was still sitting out. Mom walked in and noticed it as well. We simultaneously went to grab it and when our hands knocked into each other, the tin pan flipped over and landed on the tiled floor with a resounding clatter and splat. Tomato sauce and pieces of ground beef sprayed onto the refrigerator and stuck to the stainless-steel door like blood and brains from a gunshot to the head.

Irving and Rafael were the first to appear in the doorway.

"What the—" Irving blurted out.

"We'll just clean this up and be on our way," I said sheepishly.

Irving tore a wad of paper towels off the roll and handed it to me. I sensed he wanted to scold me for being clumsy, but he simply mumbled to himself and swept past Rafael, who gave me a sympathetic nod before following Irving out of the kitchen.

Others who had peeked in peeled away, chattering among themselves.

After Mom and I cleaned up the lasagna mess, I ducked into the first-floor bathroom to wipe off the bits of cheese and sauce that had formed a mosaic pattern on my navy blouse. A black cloth was draped over the mirror. Fine by me—the last thing I needed to see were my itchy, bloodshot eyes, pink-rimmed nose, and ruined blouse.

Mom was standing right outside the bathroom when I emerged. "Susan, your dad is going to be here shortly. We need to leave."

MOM AND I buckled up in silence. These days I felt like I was living in a bleak French farce. My mother walked out of a room, and my father entered—all perfectly choreographed, each beat carefully plotted and rehearsed so as not to run into each other. Eventually they were going to end up in the same place and would have to acknowledge each other's existence. Some intuitive agreement on how to share the space, for the time being.

"I take it that was not just a friendly conversation you were having with Annabelle," Mom scolded. Then eagerly added, "Did you learn anything?"

"Mom, you know I can't talk about an open investigation."

"Ha, I knew you couldn't help yourself." My mom shook her head. "You're just like your dad."

I was about to protest, albeit mildly, when she continued: "Well, I managed to get a tidbit of information you might like to hear."

"Do tell."

"I was minding my own beeswax on the couch when someone—I think a friend of Rafael's by the way they were talking—asked Rafael about a guy named Edward and whispered something like, 'Would he hurt Madison?' And Rafael said, 'Of course not!'" Mom winked. "Just thought this was something you would want to know."

"I thought it's improper etiquette to be investigating during a shiva."

"I didn't investigate. I just listened. Can't help it if things develop as I quietly sit on a couch."

"And this guy actually asked if a person named Edward would hurt Madison?"

"I may be getting up there, but I'm not deaf. I was sitting right next to this guy and definitely heard him say that. But I just played it cool, staring at my phone like I wasn't listening, hoping he would say more. But that's all that was said on that subject."

"You missed your calling as a sleuth."

"Just call me Nancy Drew. Although I guess I'm more like the old broad what's-her-face from *Murder She Wrote*."

"Jessica Fletcher?"

"Yeah, her." She snickered. "So what's your next move?"

"You are asking too many questions, Mom."

Mom leaned forward slightly and turned toward me with a dis-approving glance. "Will you be looking into this Edward character?"

"That's now on my list." I patted Mom's hand. "Thanks to you."

Mom wiggled her shoulders and flashed a contented smile. "Glad I could help."

AFTER DROPPING Mom back home, I drove to South Fallsburg, where Rafael's parents lived. Dad had provided me with a little family history. Rafael's grandparents, Carlos and Josefina Garcia, emigrated from Colombia in the mid-seventies and worked at the Cuttman Hotel dining room from the time they arrived until the hotel shuttered its doors, in 1995. When their son, Luis, was old enough to carry a tray, circa 1985, he too worked the Cuttman dining room. That's where Luis met Rafael's mother, Isabela, who had emigrated from Ecuador in the early eighties. They married in 1987. Camilla and Rafael were born in 1991.

Luis and Isabela were expecting me at two o'clock, and I was right on time, as usual. A therapist once told me that my penchant for punc-tuality was probably an unconscious counterpoint to Mom's constant tardiness. She was wrong about that . . . it was totally conscious. I relished any circumstance in which I could behave conversely to my mother.

At this point in the investigation, I was trying to gather as much intel as I possibly could regarding Madison's life. Sometimes in-laws harbored pretty strong feelings about their children's spouses and could be counted upon to drop both subtle and not-so-subtle hints about what was going on behind closed doors.

Isabela opened the front door and welcomed me warmly. She looked to be about my age, in her mid-fifties. Which means she would have been in her mid-twenties when she had Rafael and Camilla, who were now twenty-eight years old. She was petite, five one or five two, which surprised me, considering how tall Rafael and Camilla were. But like her children, she had those high cheekbones and deep dimples. As I stepped inside, I was greeted by a tantalizing mélange of cumin, onions, garlic, chili powder, and coriander. I breathed in deeply, hoping the spices and aromatics would clear my sinuses.

Isabela must have seen me inhale and said, "Chili."

"Smells good."

"It won't be ready for a couple of hours," she said, perhaps registering my desire for a taste. "But I could give you a small container to take home." Her Ecuadorian accent was faint, washed from her tongue after thirty-five years of living in America.

"If you have enough."

"There's always enough." She smiled and her dimples deepened. "Luis will be down shortly. He was taking a nap. Can I offer you anything? Coffee? Water? I think you could use an old Ecuadorian remedy for that cold of yours—a hot mixture of *toronjil*, lemon juice, and raw sugar."

I smiled politely. "All set, but thank you."

Above us, I heard a door open and close, followed by footsteps. We glanced over at the stairs and watched Luis descend. His shoulders were hunched, perhaps due to the current circumstances, but it could also be a condition of a man who carried a lot of heavy dining-room trays for over two decades. The twins inherited their stature from him. Even with droopy shoulders, he was easily six feet tall. He shook my hand with both of his—warm, enveloping hands that exuded confidence, assurance, and a hint of suave. He was the cliché Casanova: tall, dark, and handsome. They settled on the floral-patterned couch. I took a seat on a chair facing them, a glass-and-brass cocktail table between us. There was an eagerness in their expressions. I've seen that look— they had information they wanted to impart.

I set my elbows on my knees, clasped my hands, and leaned slightly forward. "We are in the early stages of this investigation, gathering information from friends and family. The more we know about Madison, the better our chances of finding out who"—I paused here, as it was always as painful to relay these words as it was for those hearing them—"murdered her."

They nodded.

"I know on some level you might not want to say something disparaging. She is your daughter-in-law, after all. But the more forthcoming you are—"

"We understand," Luis said. His Colombian accent had not faded as much as Isabela's. "We will answer your questions to the best of our ability." He glanced at his wife, and she nodded.

"But we want to make it clear that there is no way that Rafael had anything to do with this," Isabela interjected. "We know it's the husband who always gets the most attention. But there is no way, none whatsoever, that he would do this. He loved her." She paused, then added a bit more assertively, "And she didn't deserve him."

I was a bit surprised by this cut-to-the-chase statement. "Well, then let's start there. Why didn't she deserve him?"

Isabela took a deep breath. "She was selfish. He would do anything for her, and she took advantage of that."

"Can you give me an example?"

"How much time do you have?" She chortled.

"Just a couple of examples . . . so I can gain a better understanding of their relationship."

"Okay. So, Rafael got into a bunch of top schools. Princeton, Brown, Yale. But he went to Boston University. You know why? Madison. Because she pouted and cried how much she would miss him, and how they would drift apart, and he would do better at a less-prestigious school, being that he was a minority. *Pfft.* And he fell for it. Hook, line, and sinker."

Dad had given me a bit of background on Rafael, which helped provide context to Isabela's grievance. Rafael graduated at the top of his class and ended up marrying Madison. Both of those things might not have happened if he went to one of those top-tier schools and attempted a long-distance college relationship. Madison could have just been practical, not manipulative. The issue could merely be that Isabela Garcia did not get an opportunity to boast about her son's Ivy League education to her friends.

"Rafael had this reputation in high school of being a 'bad boy,'" Isabela continued. "But he was an A student. Got a near-perfect SAT score." She squared her shoulders as she defended her son's character. "It was Madison who goaded him into doing the things that got him in trouble. Staying out late. Smoking pot. Drag racing. When Madison's parents forbade her to date Rafael, I hoped that would be the end of it."

"They forbade her? Because of his so-called reputation?"

"No, because he wasn't Jewish." She frowned briefly. "Although I think his . . . his being Latino had something to do with it." She fingered the delicate cross that hung from a gold chain around her neck.

"So you didn't want him dating her and they didn't want her dating him? Very Romeo and Juliet."

"Yeah. And that made things worse," Luis chimed in. "They became secretive, and it probably added a little spice to their relationship. It's exactly the kind of thing you *don't* do if you want a couple to split up. Especially rebellious teenagers. I was of the mind to let nature run its course."

"After Madison's parents died, they didn't have to sneak around anymore," Isabela said. "Her grandparents didn't want to upset Madison even more, so they dropped the issue."

Luis relaxed his shoulders a bit, and his hunch became less pronounced. "By then they were seniors in high school, about to turn eighteen. What say did we really have at that point?" Luis side-eyed

Isabela. "I know Isabela and I don't see eye-to-eye on this, but as time went on, I grew fond of Madison. She was charming and sensitive, and I know she cared deeply for Rafael."

Isabela patted Luis's thigh. "We both want what's best for our children. But I think mothers are just more protective of their sons."

I had neither a brother nor a son, so I had no experience in the truth of that statement. But I was pretty sure Isabela believed it to justify and defend her less-than-stellar relationship with Madison. It was certainly not uncommon for wives to be at odds with their mothers-in-law.

"What can you tell me about Rafael's friend Edward?"

"Edward?" Isabela asked.

Luis knitted his brow. "Do you mean Eduardo Cesar?"

"Hmm. Not sure. I heard he had a friend named Edward."

They looked at each other and shook their heads.

"Rafael went to high school with a boy named Eduardo Cesar. Maybe he changed his name to sound more American?" Luis said, aiming the question at his wife.

"I don't think they remained in touch after high school. It's probably someone we don't know."

Luis tapped his chin. "Actually, now that I think of it . . . Camilla mentioned a guy named Edward once. But I can't remember what it was about."

"Someone she was dating?"

"Camilla doesn't date men," Isabela said matter-of-factly. Luis shifted slightly and cleared his throat, signaling his discomfort with that subject matter.

Isabela eyed him briefly, then shifted her gaze back to me.

"I think it's best you ask Rafael about his friends. Anyone he befriended while in college or after college we wouldn't necessarily know. Madison had a way of keeping him at arm's length from us."

"So would you say she was possessive?"

"That's a good word for it. Yeah." Luis looked at his watch. "We are going to pay our respects this afternoon and need to get going soon. Are there any other questions you have for us?"

"Just the age-old question: How was their marriage? Were they happy? Did they bicker?"

"Like I said earlier, you are barking up the wrong tree if you think Rafael did this," Isabela said. "Sure, they bickered. What couple doesn't? But we have no reason to believe their marriage wasn't on solid footing. I might have had some issues with Madison, but Rafael loved her."

If what Isabela said earlier about Madison keeping them at arm's length was true, would they really know what was happening in their son's marriage? How many wives have the kind of relationship with their in-laws where they feel comfortable discussing the state of their marriage? I doubted Rafael would share an intimate secret of infidelity with his parents; although Isabela might have welcomed this news and hoped that Madison's replacement was worthy of her son.

Isabela leaned forward and made sure she had my full attention. "You may think I'm just saying this because I'm his mother, but I am 100 percent sure Rafael had nothing . . . *nothing at all* to do with her murder."

THUNDER RUMBLED in the distance. I leaned over to the passenger well of my Prius and grabbed the Tupperware container and a small paper bag containing two lemons, a handful of raw sugar packets, and lemon balm. As I stepped out of my car, the first splat caught me by surprise. Then the skies opened up. I dashed to the front door, fumbling for my keys. By the time I made it into the entryway I was soaked through and through.

Moxie cocked her head sideways, her tail wagging furiously. With my hands full, she would have to wait to be petted. She followed me into the kitchen. "Where's Ray?" I asked her rhetorically as I plopped the Tupperware and bag on the counter. I crouched down and rubbed behind her ears. Her tail went into overdrive.

"Right here," he said, poking his head into the kitchen. "What's all this?" he asked, pointing at the counter.

A clap of thunder exploded directly above us and Moxie took cover under the table.

"Whoa!" I glanced down at Moxie, who was now in full whimper. "Hopefully we'll get a break from this insane humidity."

"You still sound like shit. You might have a sinus infection."

"Well Dr. Ray, I have something here that is supposed to cure me," I said, removing the contents from the paper bag. "An Ecuadorian home remedy for treating colds and coughs."

"Grass and lemons?"

"It's *toronjil*, or as we say in these parts, lemon balm."

"And that?" he asked, pointing to the Tupperware.

"Ah, that, my friend, is manna from heaven. Also designed to clear your sinuses. Known in these parts as five-alarm chili—a present from Isabela Garcia."

"Okay then, I guess no need for a doc—"

Another clap of thunder interrupted Ray's sarcastic barb, only this one was now a couple of miles away. Close enough to send Moxie into full cowering mode, however.

My phone dinged. I pulled it from my back pocket and glanced at the screen. The text from Dad simply said, *Call me asap.*

DAD PICKED up on the second ring.

"Hey, what's up?" I asked. I heard chattering in the background. "Where are you?"

"I'm at Madison's shiva. Wait, let me . . . okay, is that better?"

"Yeah."

"I just got an earful from Irving. He's . . . it's not like he doesn't trust you to . . . but . . ."

"Just spit it out, Dad."

"He wants me involved. He thinks your doggedness and my intuitiveness are needed here."

"Does he now?" I tried to sort out whether I was pissed or flattered.

"Hey, we made a great team figuring out what happened to Trudy Solomon last year. Word gets around."

In my best you've-got-to-be-kidding-me voice I said, "I am pretty sure Eldridge is not going to want you anywhere near this case. The Solomon case was yours forty years ago. Made sense you'd get involved. This case, not so much."

"Yeah, I was thinking the same thing. This would be more under-the-radar. You fill me in, I tag along when it makes sense, we put our heads together." He waited for me to say something. "Susan, you there?"

"Dad, this is crazy. I can't just let you tag along and partner up with you. I'm sure there are a whole bunch of rules and whatnot that can get me into a whole heap of trouble. And what if this gets dangerous? There's a fucking killer out there."

"All I'm saying is, involve me a little. Tell me what you got and let's just brainstorm. If you don't, he has every right to hire me as a private detective. I still have my license."

"Is that a threat?"

"Look, I'm just telling you that Irving wants my know-how on this. Honestly, I'm too old for this shit, running around and such, but happy to keep you company . . . when it's safe. And you can't deny we had fun the last go-round. Besides, I know a lot about the families involved— the sordid history, you can say."

"Sordid history. What sordid history?"

"Todd ran with some shady characters."

"What do you mean by 'shady characters'?"

"There were rumors that his business dealings had a whiff of mob involvement."

"And you think that has some bearing on this case?"

"Just saying that I know the family, and I can help you navigate the waters. All I'm asking is that you think about it."

I held my breath for a few seconds, then exhaled slowly. He was relentless, and he knew (and I feared) he was going to worm his way into this case one way or another.

MADISON

Thursday, February 21, 2019

What's my next grievance, dear journal? Or should I say who? That would be Camilla. Where to start with her? A bit of a nutcase. The phony British accent!!! I mean, does she really think she's fooling anyone? She slides in and out of it like a penis penetrating a super wet vagina. "So vulgar," she would probably say, like she was Grace-fucking-Kelly. And her relationship with her brother? Don't get me started. She followed us to BU. Then she followed us to Brooklyn. She's like a wad of old chewing gum that sticks to your shoe. I try. I really try with her. I keep my cool. I play nice (for Rafael's sake). I keep my eye rolling to the absolute minimum. The thing is, I shouldn't dump on her like this. She is genuinely nice to me (or she's the world's greatest actress). She invites me out with her friends (because I'm short on my own friends these days). She cheers me up when I'm blue (she can be very funny). And even though it drives me crazy that she follows Rafael around like a puppy dog, I know she would do anything for him. Which is sweet. So you know what, dear journal, I am going to try harder to be nicer to her. Be less judgy. Ignore her silly

British accent! Besides, I'm going to need her support and understanding when the proverbial shit hits the fan.

And that brings me to Rafael's and Camilla's dear parents. I am quite fond of Luis. In many ways, he is like Rafael. Smart, no-nonsense, handsome. Isabela, well, that's another ball of wax. She dotes on Rafael like he is a toddler. "Are you eating well? Are you getting enough sleep?" I wouldn't be surprised if she asked if his bowel movements were normal. Her questions are laced with the implication that I'm not caring for him properly. She is aloof with me when in the presence of others. Downright cold if no one else is around. Not good enough for her precious only son. Blamed me for all the trouble he got into in high school. But hey, look at him now . . . Mr. Fancy Pants. And I would like to think that I had a hand in that. I've been the love of his life through high school, college, and grad school: the doting girlfriend, the (somewhat) adventurous lover, the trophy wife he could show off at parties. I'm the one who spent many a lonely night while Rafael studied for his finals or worked long hours in the office. So, dear mother-in-law, you can thank me for Rafael's stellar rise.

4

WEDNESDAY | JULY 3, 2019

I REACHED for my phone, which was teetering precariously on the edge of my bedside table, and blinked away the crust from my eyes. A text from Chief Eldridge had come in a half an hour earlier: *The final autopsy report is in.* I stretched and moaned and dragged my ass out of bed.

I downed a DayQuil, then slipped into my black slacks and short-sleeved white blouse, which I was pretty sure would be pitted out by midday.

The humidity did not break after the storm and today was supposed to be another steamer.

"Hey," Ray said when I shuffled into the kitchen. "I boiled up some of that Ecuadorian lemonade."

He had given up trying to persuade me to take it easy and rest. He knew me too well.

"Final autopsy report is in." I poured the hot lemonade into a mug and blew on it. "ME is going to release Madison's body this morning."

"Give any more thought to involving your dad in this investigation?"

"No." That was a lie. I was mulling—big time—but I wasn't in the mood to weigh the pros and cons with Ray. On the plus side, keeping Dad informed meant keeping Irving out of my hair. On the negative side . . . was there a negative side? The guy had been one of the best investigators during his stint as detective—no one closed as many cases as he did. It had been a while since we'd had a murder case this grisly around here, but he was one of the few detectives who had the experience in exactly this kind of case. "I'll sort it out later."

THE CLOSED casket was situated toward the front of the room. About a dozen photographs of Madison—arranged in order from infant to toddler to teenager to adult—graced the black-draped table to the right of the coffin. No flowers. Mom, surprisingly knowledgeable about Jewish traditions and rituals, explained to me the mourning period was more about healing than a celebration of life; flowers were a distraction to this process.

Nearly every chair was occupied. All the men wore yarmulkes; a few women wore coaster-sized lacy head coverings. As was typical when young people died, the attendees ranged in age from those who appeared to be of Madison's generation (Millennials) to contemporaries of Irving and Audrey (baby boomers), with a few Gen Xers thrown in. Being born in 1965 put me squarely between the baby boomers and the Gen Xers—I felt affinity toward neither group.

I took a seat in the back row. I looked around for Dad, then noticed he was sitting directly behind Irving. His yarmulke sat slightly askew atop his distinguishable gray mane. He managed to hold on to nearly every strand of hair, making him appear a good five years younger than his pals . . . and easy to find in a crowd.

Jacob Bowman was sitting one row ahead of me. His presence surprised me. I figured he was *persona non grata*, being that for the last ten years he had been trying to wrestle away Madison's share of the business . . . and I got the sense that many here suspected he had something to do with her murder. The furtive glances tossed in his direction were my first clue. Audrey being visibly shaken by Jacob's entrance, my second. Irving's scowl when he noticed Jacob, my third. Eventually Jacob woke up to the fact he was not welcome and slipped out of the funeral parlor about halfway through the reading of the Psalms.

While Irving delivered the eulogy, I studied the crowd. I scanned the faces of her friends and relatives, looking for a hint of guilt. Was the killer here? I thought again about her call to me the night she was murdered. What if? What if I had answered the phone? What if I knew what was weighing on her mind? What if I had intervened?

"May Madison go to her resting place in peace," the rabbi intoned.

That appeared to be everyone's cue to gather up their belongings. A chorus of murmuring rose as friends and relatives chatted among themselves.

I stayed seated as the procession of mourners passed my row and headed toward the exit. As Dad came up the aisle, I caught his eye. He seemed surprised to see me even though I'd told him I would be attending. He broke away from the crowd and loomed quietly over me.

"You okay, Dad?"

"Funerals for young people suck." Never one to mince words, he nailed the sentiment.

We walked together to the exit and out into the bright, nearly blinding, sunlight. The oppressive humidity was not letting go. It hung in the air, heavy and foreboding.

I felt someone come up behind me. When I swung around, I found myself face-to-face with Irving. "Beautiful eulogy."

He nodded and produced a tight smile. "I meant to ask you something at the shiva, but then the whole lasagna fiasco and, well, my temper got the better of me—" He paused to catch his breath. "Did Madison call you a few months ago?"

"No, but she . . ." I stopped mid-sentence. I wasn't sure how much to divulge about that missed call. "No, but why do you ask?"

"A few months ago, sometime around March or April, she asked me for your number. She knew I was friends with Will and thought I might have it."

"Yeah, yeah. I remember when you asked me," Dad chimed in.

"Why did she want my number?"

Irving shrugged. "When I asked her, she said it was for a project she was working on."

Well, that explained how she got my number. "She didn't call me in the spring. But she did call me Saturday night."

Irving started to blink rapidly. "This past Saturday night. The night . . . I don't understand."

"Neither do I. But I will find out."

Annabelle approached us and tapped Irving on his shoulder. "We're heading over to the cemetery now." The two of them turned and walked toward the parking lot.

When they were out of earshot, Dad said, "Give any thought to what we talked about?"

I had hoped he wouldn't bring this subject up during the funeral, but Dad was not one to sit idly by while I took my time making up my mind. I leaned in closer and lowered my voice. "Well, you certainly made me curious with your out-of-the-blue remark about the Garmins' business dealings. I will admit your knowledge of that family would be useful." I looked at him sternly. "I'm not saying yes, but I'm also not saying no. I'll make up my mind when I get back from Brooklyn."

"Brooklyn?"

"Yeah. To speak with Dr. Samantha Fields, the friend who lent Madison her car. She couldn't make it to the funeral, so I'm heading down there shortly." Dad's eyes widened and his mouth popped open. But before he could say anything, I added, "You need to go to the cemetery and pay your respects."

He sighed and raised his palms in surrender. "Okay, okay. You're right. I can't desert Irving. Besides, I can do some observing . . . be your eyes and ears up here while you're in Brooklyn."

"Sure Dad. But please, please be discreet."

"Discretion is my middle name," he said, turning on his heel with a sly smile pasted on his face.

Why did it always feel like when I gave him an inch, he took a mile?

DR. SAMANTHA Fields was waiting for me in an Italian restaurant (with a Jewish-sounding name, Noodle Pudding) on Henry Street in Brooklyn. Technically, I was on time. But it took me twenty minutes to find a parking spot. I slowly rolled up and down the narrow streets of Brooklyn Heights and finally snagged one down by the Promenade just as someone was pulling out. When I had messaged her twenty minutes ago that I was on the prowl for a spot, she wished me good luck and said she would be waiting inside, at the bar.

By the time I arrived at the restaurant I looked like I had just stepped out of the shower. If I thought the humidity was bad in the Catskills, the sticky-wet air hung like a heavy velvet curtain here in the city. My hair, naturally curly with a touch of frizz on a good day, was now reminiscent of Roseanne Roseannadanna from the early days of *Saturday Night Live*. I slipped the hair band from around my wrist and swooped my hair up into a massive bun on top of my head.

The air-conditioned restaurant was simultaneously refreshing and jarring. I shivered under the layer of moisture that glistened on my skin. I had described my appearance and clothing to Samantha, so when I walked through the door she smiled and waved. She picked up her two-olive martini, swiveled off the bar stool, and pointed to a table in the corner. I followed her.

She held out a delicate hand. I held up both hands like I was under arrest and proclaimed I had a cold and it would be best not to get too close. I could have told her the truth. She is a doctor. She, of all people, would certainly understand. But blurting out I loathe shaking hands because I suffer from palmar hyperhidrosis feels a bit too, well, personal for a first encounter. She smiled politely and took the chair facing out to the restaurant, leaving me the chair with my back to the patrons.

A short, wiry man, nearly bald with a comb-over, appeared at the table. "Dr. Fields! Welcome back. Been a while, no?"

Samantha rose and gave the man a hug, then sat back down. "Sorry, Tony. Work's been a bear these past couple of weeks. But I can only stay away from your baked bluefish for so long. And of course, Tom's martinis," she said, lifting the glass off the table.

"I see you have a new friend!" Tony exclaimed.

Samantha gnawed at her lower lip, perhaps wondering how best to introduce me. "This is Susan."

"Nice to meet you, Susan. Any friend of Dr. Fields is a friend of mine." His eyebrows sprang to life, matching his ebullient mannerisms. "We've got a great special tonight . . . a roasted milk-fed veal loin on the bone with wild mushrooms and potato!" He smiled broadly. "Well, I'll let you two carry on." He turned abruptly, looked around, and shouted, "Larry, Shelly, so good to see you!"

Samantha leaned over the table. "He greets all the regulars. That man is dedicated, with a capital D. I've heard he gets up way before dawn to get to the fish market in the South Bronx. This place has a reputation for its incredible fish dishes. But really everything is fresh and delicious."

I wondered if she got a commission if I showed up without her the next time.

Samantha continued, "Madison came here with me often enough that he knows her. But I haven't said anything to anyone yet. That's why I didn't introduce you as a detective. I didn't think this was the time or place to break the news."

"No worries. Do you mind if I get right to the questions I have?

"No, not at all. Shoot."

A waitress with short brown hair and black-framed glasses suddenly appeared at the table. I was beginning to think this was not the ideal location for questioning Samantha. But she insisted, claiming she finally had a night off and wanted to spend it at this neighborhood restaurant. "Hi Samantha. Whatcha having?"

After we placed our orders (baked bluefish for Samantha, lasagna Bolognese for me), I sensed an opening to get a few questions in until the next interruption, the arrival of the garlic bread. ("On the house," Tony exclaimed when he announced it was coming shortly, fresh from the oven.)

"Did Madison tell you why she needed your car? The purpose for her trip back home?"

"She alluded to wanting to clear up some personal matters."

"Did she provide any specifics? Perhaps this has something to do with her family's businesses?"

"Like I said, she didn't give me that much detail. She never talked to me about any family business. I know her father left her some property, but she told me that someone else runs the business and she was just holding on to it as an investment. Once in a while we would talk about her advertising business. But we usually avoided talking about work when we got together. She didn't want to hear about me cutting people open, and I was not particularly interested in whatever the advertising world was up to."

"Were you aware that she dissolved the advertising business?"

"Yes. But again, we didn't talk much about it. She said she wanted to go in a different direction than Annabelle."

"Did you find it odd that Madison asked to borrow your car?"

"No. I loaned my car to her whenever she needed it. Speaking of which . . . will I be getting it back anytime soon?"

"Your car, unfortunately, is a crime scene. Forensics will release it once they lift all fingerprints and gather up any other evidence they can find. The fingerprints will, hopefully, tell us who was in the car with her."

She slipped an olive off the toothpick and popped it into her mouth before taking a sip of her martini. "She used my car a lot and it's bound to be full of fingerprints from her friends and family, not to mention my family and friends. She and Rafael only had one car, and sometimes they needed it at the same time—especially on weekends when she wanted to get out of the city and Rafael wanted to head into the office to get work done. And there was this one time, pretty recently, when Rafael's car was in service and they borrowed my car. So . . . you are going to find a whole bunch of fingerprints from lots of people she knows. And, of course, from people who have ridden with me."

"Then I'll need you to look at the list we come up with. See if you notice the name of a person who didn't take a ride in your car."

"Of course."

The garlic bread arrived with the glass of iced tea I ordered. My nose was mildly stuffy, but the pungent garlic, butter, and parsley managed to sneak its way in, reminding me that it had been since this morning that I had something substantial to eat. I picked up a slice and polished it off in two undainty bites.

"Oh my. That is good." I wiped my greasy butter fingers on my napkin. "Speaking of friends, do you know a friend of Rafael's named Edward?"

"Edward Moore?"

"I don't have a last name. Just looking for an Edward."

"He's the only Edward I can think of. He was Rafael's roommate sophomore year at Boston University. Not sure how he would be involved, or even know anything. They got in a huge brouhaha a year or so ago."

"About?"

"He accused Rafael of poaching a big-money client. Rafael claimed he never even met this client and said the guy called him out of the blue."

"I heard that Edward might have had some kind of beef with Madison."

Samantha swirled her martini with her finger before taking another sip. "If he did, I don't know anything about that. But then again, I'm so buried at the hospital, I'm not really in the loop these days." She slid the second olive from the toothpick and popped it into her mouth before polishing off the rest of the drink. "Are you thinking Edward had something to do with Madison's murder?"

"Right now he's just another person in their circle I would like to chat with. The more I get to know the victim"—Samantha's pained look made me correct myself—"the more I know about Madison, the better my chance of bringing this case to a close quickly. I need to understand the angles, that's all."

"Well, Rafael can tell you more than I can. I have no idea where Edward is nowadays. He cut ties with all of us—he's a bit of a grudge holder. Me, I'm not one to hold grudges—life's too short. I see it in my line of work every day—people hurting each other." She downed her martini. She breathed in deeply and slowly exhaled, then wiped a tear midway down her cheek. "Sorry."

"No need to be sorry."

As if perfectly timed, the waitress arrived with our main courses.

"Thank you, Amy," Samantha said to the waitress, picking up her martini glass and handing it over. "Another one of these, when you get a chance."

"Is it okay to ask a few more questions? Feel free to answer between bites."

She nodded.

"Are you friends with Camilla too?"

She sucked in her lips and nodded. "Yes and no. Or should I say on-again, off-again. She's hard to take in huge quantities—a little of her goes a long way. She has a way of consuming all the oxygen in the room." She titled her head. "Have you met her?"

I laughed gently. "Well, I met her once, but I got a sense of that."

"Then you're very observant. She can be very . . . I don't know . . . exhausting . . . with her need to be the center of attention. But don't get me wrong. Camilla's fun to be around and she'll give you the shirt off her back. She'll do anything for family, especially Rafael. I guess because they're twins they have a special bond."

The waitress placed the martini with two olives in front of Samantha, smiled, and walked away without comment. Samantha took a rather large gulp.

"I have twin grandsons—identical—so I know what you mean."

"Grandsons?" she asked, clearly doing math calisthenics in her head trying to figure out how young I must have been to have a kid who has kids.

"Yeah, a high-school necking that got out of hand," I said, swooping my hands around my belly.

She leaned across the table and whispered: "Me too. But I didn't go through with it."

I found her confession quite startling. I have never met anyone who so freely admitted that to me. Let alone someone I met barely an hour earlier. Maybe it's because she's a doctor. Or perhaps it's the second martini.

I nodded, in that knocked-up-in-high-school sisterhood kind of way.

We finished our meals in contemplative silence. No sooner than I took my last bite of lasagna, Tony swooped on over to our table. "Tiramisu?"

"I'm full," I said, patting my stomach.

"One tiramisu, two spoons," Samantha said to Tony, then turned to me. "Trust me, you'll want half."

"Is there anything else you can think of that might be helpful to me? An argument she told you about? A sense that something was amiss?"

"I don't know if this is relevant . . . but I did sense she was a little depressed. Nothing monumental, but yeah, she seemed a bit stressed these past couple of months. I chalked it up to her having to start a new business from scratch."

"And her relationship with Rafael? Was that on solid footing?"

Samantha turned her head slightly to the side, then shrugged. "As far as I know."

The eye aversion. The shrug. The hesitation. Was she hiding something? "You're sure of that?"

She pursed her lips and nodded before taking another swig. "Like I said, as far as I know."

With waiters flitting about and Samantha now a bit inebriated, this felt like neither the time nor place to push further. "Okay, last question . . . this place is called Noodle Pudding, but there is no noodle pudding on the menu."

Samantha laughed. "Well, wasn't expecting that question. Tony's last name is Migliaccio. Migliaccio translates to 'black pudding' in Italian."

"And the noodle part?"

She smirked. "Well, Detective, you're going to have to interrogate someone else at this fine establishment to get to the bottom of that."

MADISON

Wednesday, February 27, 2019

Annabelle. Hmmm. *Here's my advice to anyone who stumbles upon my journal . . . never, and I mean never, go into business with your best friend. Sure, at first it seems fun. It was her idea. After grad school, she approached me with the idea of working together. I was not happy at my copywriting job at a tech startup (boring!), so the timing was perfect. And so we became Mad Bell. Great name, huh! I came up with it, even though she claims we came to it together after a night of drinking and brainstorming. Whatev. But then our relationship got blurry. Arguments over creative decisions bled into our friendship. Where it used to be fun to get together with her, now it felt like an extension of work. Instead of gossiping about friends and celebrities, conversations would inevitably drift to project deadlines and pain-in-the-ass clients.*

I get the sense she feels the same way. She's been acting strange lately. Can't quite put my finger on it. But something is definitely up with her. She isn't dating anyone, but she's been secretive. Maybe she's trying out a new boyfriend. But she'd tell me, wouldn't she? Maybe there's a reason that she can't. Or maybe she too is thinking about parting business ways so we can find a way back to our madcap days.

On the other hand, this might have nothing to do with her, and everything to do with me. Maybe she is perfectly happy with our partnership, and I simply need to blame someone else for the dissolution of our agency. In all honesty, I am the one who wants to call it quits. And yet, I will convince myself and everyone else that it was Annabelle who couldn't make it work. This is how I operate—nothing is ever my fault. I do what I think needs to be done and never hold myself responsible when things go south. That's the old Madison.

A new & improved Madison would shoulder the blame, take the wrath, and hold herself accountable. Will there ever really be a metamorphosis? Am I like that zebra . . . unable to change its stripes? Or am I a caterpillar who has the ability to shed its ugliness in order to live a freer and unencumbered life? For inspiration, maybe I'll get a butterfly tattoo.

5

WHEN I stepped through the elevator doors into the lobby of the Brooklyn Marriott, I couldn't believe who I saw lounging on a couch near the reception desk.

"What in the world are you doing here?" I asked.

Dad jumped up. "Okay. Susan. Don't be mad. A couple of the guys came down to Brooklyn wanting to watch the fireworks tonight and I hitched a ride. I knew you were headed over to Madison's place this morning to have a look-see and I told you, Irving wants me involved, and I thought this was an unobtrusive way to insert myself. You can just think of it as keeping you company."

"Keeping me company? That's an interesting way of putting it." I kept my annoyance in check, although clearly some amount of irritation leaked through. "When did you get down here?"

"Last night."

"And you stayed here? At the Marriott?"

"No, the guys got an Airbnb—"

"Airbnb?"

"Yeah, it's this—"

"I know what it is, Dad. I'm just surprised you do."

He ran his hands through his hair. Overdue for a haircut, it reached the lower part of his neck and hung carelessly over his ears. "C'mon Susan. It's this or me getting involved in a more official capacity as his hired private detective."

"I don't know . . ."

"It's not like I'm entering some drug den. We're simply going over to a lovely brownstone in Brooklyn Heights to get a glimpse into Madison's life." He grinned, then gently elbowed me. "C'mon, it'll be fun. We make a good team. Like Nick and Nora Charles."

"Well, more like Veronica Mars."

"Who?"

"Never mind." I rolled my eyes. He had won this round. "Let's just go."

※

RAFAEL AND Madison lived in a brownstone on Schermerhorn Street, a ten-minute walk from the hotel. I had told Rafael I would stop by at ten o'clock. My objective was to find the journal, or letters, or something that would hint at some trouble in Madison's life. Of course, Rafael could have purged his quarters of incriminating evidence, but sometimes suspects don't even know what they're looking for and overlook the items of interest to investigators. He insisted he had not gone through her things, knowing it would just make him look bad . . . and feel worse.

"Dad, you are accompanying me as an observer. Got it?" I said as we climbed the nine steps to the front door of the four-story edifice.

He raised his hand, palm down, to his forehead. Then saluted. "Aye, aye, Detective Ford."

I turned away and privately scowled before ringing the doorbell.

We were buzzed into the hallway. We climbed the stairs to the second floor and knocked on a door with a golden number *1* affixed above the peephole. Rafael flung the door open and led us down a short hallway into a spacious living room. The focal point of the room was a whitewashed brick wall that housed a long, narrow, rectangular gas fireplace. Although the interior was completely refurbished, the original 1920s decorative touches—the ornate ceiling medallion and prominent crown moldings—were preserved. The furnishings were mid-century modern pieces in light woods and muted hues. An impressively large Persian rug provided a burst of color, crimson and gold, to offset the quieter tones of the space. On the far side of the room, a pair of French doors led to a cantilevered balcony overlooking a garden patio below, accessible by a metal spiral staircase.

Dad knocked into my arm as he scooted past me to check out the view. He nudged me just enough to raise my ire. Giving him access like this was crazy. In that slight shove, I felt an escalation from mere presence to giant pain in the ass. Instead of me doing him a favor, I was starting to believe I got snookered. Was he Irving's obedient servant—hired expressly to keep an eye on me? Which was pretty insulting, come to think of it.

A black cat with a white belly and white paws slithered out from under the sofa. I recognized it immediately. It was Madison's Facebook profile picture.

Rafael scooped up the cat. "This is Penguin. She's Madison's, but I guess she's mine now." His eyes watered, but he pursed his lips to control his emotions. Or maybe it was allergies. "I was never much of a cat person. I'm just getting used to taking care of her. Thank goodness Madison bought one of those automatic feeder gizmos. I fill it up, program it, and it dispenses food at set times."

"Cats don't require much attention," Dad said, like he was an expert, which he was not. "Now, dogs, that's a full-time job."

I was going to correct him in that caring for dogs is more like a part-time job, but this whole exchange seemed so pointless and off-course.

Rafael gently lowered Penguin to the parquet wood floor and gazed around the room. "There aren't too many personal items on this floor. Our bedroom is downstairs on the first level and Madison's office is on the basement level." He bent his head and stared at his shoes. When he looked up, he sighed deeply. "Sorry. Still processing all this."

"Let's start in her office, shall we?" I said.

Rafael led us down to the first floor and pointed out the master bedroom. Told us to feel free to head there after we rummaged through her office. Then he led us down another flight of stairs to the basement level. But because the first floor was well elevated from street level, this lower level, with the windows high on the wall, offered an abundance of natural light.

"If you find something, anything that sheds light on any of this, will you please let me know?"

"I guess that depends on what we find," I said, then quickly added, "I will keep you informed on all pertinent matters as long as it doesn't jeopardize the case."

Rafael glanced at Dad. Dad cocked his head in my direction. "What she said."

"Okay, then. If you need me, I'll be on the patio."

"I've had my fair share of cases where the husband is guilty as sin," Dad whispered. "I'm just not getting that vibe with Rafael. Not to mention, he's giving us free reign of his house without a warrant."

"Vibe, huh?" I said, handing Dad a pair of blue latex gloves.

"Yeah, vibe. This is why I can be useful to you. My Spidey senses never fail me."

"Okay, Spider-Man. You take the file cabinets over there. And I'll start with the desk."

"So, what are we looking for?" Dad picked up the guitar resting in a stand. He played the opening riff to "Stairway to Heaven."

"Notes about disgruntled clients. Secret love letters. That journal Rafael mentioned. Bank statements. You know, the typical shit."

As Dad crouched down to thumb through the lowest drawer in the gunmetal file cabinet, I opened the center drawer of the mission-style oak desk. We did our work silently, opening drawers, sifting through papers, moving items, reading documents, closing drawers. Rinse and repeat.

Next to the desk was a small wooden file cabinet. When I opened the top drawer, I audibly gasped.

"Find something?" Dad asked.

"Well, I heard that Madison was a weed smoker, but there is quite a bit of paraphernalia in here. Bongs, papers, vape pens, grinder, dab ring." I snapped a picture.

"Dab ring?"

I held it up. "It's like a bong, but used to smoke hash oil or wax rather than the flower. People use it to consume concentrates. Think freebasing. The user heats up the concentrate until it becomes vaporized and then inhales it. It's extremely potent. Not exactly something the casual toker would be into."

"Maybe her death is tied to her drug use? Beef with a dealer?"

"For all we know, she was the one doing the dealing. So could be a beef with a customer." I pulled several evidence bags out of my backpack and laid them on the desk. "I'll be packing all that up to take with me. You find anything enlightening?"

"She kept meticulous records of her monthly income statements from Shangri-La and New Beginnings. The payments vary from month to month, so it's hard to make head or heel of the revenue situation. But look at this . . ." Dad said, handing over one of the Shangri-La statements. "In the margin she wrote 'doesn't make sense look into.'"

I scanned the paper and then took a picture of it.

"It's dated February 1 through February 28, 2019. Is this amount larger or smaller than the same period last year?"

Dad leafed through the statements. "Larger, by quite a bit. And there are other statements that have question marks next to the expense entries."

"What about her computer?" Dad said pointing to the Apple on Madison's desk. "Maybe something on there can shed some light."

"It'll have to be sent to the tech lab. They need to pull everything off the drive and then we . . . *I* can take a look at it."

"We can't just start it up? Take a quick look."

"No!" I said sharply. Perhaps too sharply. Dad had been out of the game for quite a while now and he wouldn't necessarily know procedure for handling digital evidence. "Our technicians will mirror this computer and the phone we found at the scene. These days, computer innards are treated like physical crime scenes . . . we don't want to taint—or even worse, lose—the evidence. Besides, if Rafael doesn't give us permission to take it, we are going to have to get a search warrant. He only consented to letting us search the premises." I glanced at the desk. "The drug paraphernalia and the couple of ounces found in the drawer will help us obtain it."

Dad opened the top drawer of the file cabinet and dug back in. I walked over to the sparsely filled bookcase—mainly books about graphic design, copywriting, and advertising—and leafed through several of them looking for hidden notes and whatnot.

"Find anything?"

With my back turned to the door I jumped slightly, startled by Rafael's sudden appearance. When I turned, I noticed him staring at the open drawer of the file cabinet exposing Madison's stash. "We were—"

"What the hell?" He breathed in deeply, clearly trying to control his anger. "She told me she was done with this shit."

"So I take it you never came down here, poked around?" I asked.

"No," he said firmly. "Madison asked me to treat this space like a private office and I respected those boundaries."

"I'm going to have a tech come by and take the computer."

"Don't you need a warrant for that?"

"Not if you grant us permission to take it."

He looked over at the pot drawer, then back at me. "Sure, take it." He glanced over at Dad, who was holding the financial statements. "Are those Madison's business records?"

"Yeah," I said before Dad could answer. I wanted to make sure Rafael knew I was in charge. "We . . . I just have a few questions."

"Okay. But not in here." He bit his lower lip while surveying the room. "It's hard to be in here."

We followed Rafael up the stairs and through his master bedroom, where sliding doors led to the patio garden I had spied from the upper level.

He motioned us toward the wrought-iron chairs on the far side of a matching table shaded by a large sage-colored umbrella. Once seated, he laced his fingers together and placed them on the table. With a tilt of his head and a quick eyebrow raise, he silently prompted us to ask our questions.

"Before we delve into what we found in Madison's office, quick question about a friend of yours." I clasped my fingers together and placed them on the table, mimicking his posture. I leaned forward. "I heard there was an issue between your friend Edward and Madison. What can you tell us about that?"

"Where did you hear that?"

"Does that matter? I just want to understand the issue between them."

"Edward accused me of poaching a client of his. Turns out it was Madison who did the poaching, unbeknownst to me. She met the guy at a party and convinced him to walk away from Edward and set up his portfolio with me. Guy's worth millions, so that did not sit well with

Edward. Madison claimed she was merely joking with the guy—told him I could do a better job. But I guess he took her seriously."

"Do you think Edward would kill Madison over this?"

"No. I don't. Besides, if he was going to kill her, it would have been a year ago, which is when this happened. I can't say that we're all friends again, but he has certainly moved on. Hedge-fund trading is a competitive, cutthroat business. If everyone killed the person who poached an account, you'd have a bloodbath on your hands every day."

"Well, we'll be talking to this guy Edward," Dad chimed in. "Hear his side of the story. Check out his alibi."

I shot Dad a look. The "we" in his statement bothered me.

"So you're working with the police on this?" Rafael said to Dad.

"Not officially. But Irving asked that I stay close to the case, that's all."

Rafael nodded. "The more the merrier, I guess."

"Not to mention, two heads are better than one," Dad added, then winked at me.

I ignored their banter and reached down to my backpack, pulling out the folder containing the monthly financial statements. I handed the top sheet to Rafael. To counteract Dad's congeniality (which felt incredibly inappropriate), I adopted a more serious tone and curtly asked, "What do you make of Madison's note in the margin?"

He silently read it, then looked up shaking his head. "I don't know. She didn't say anything to me. We didn't talk much about her father's businesses. All I know is that Jacob would send over her percentage of quarterly earnings along with these monthly statements. She wasn't that into the business, and in my opinion, she held on to her portion out of spite. She did *not* like Jacob."

"Was the feeling mutual?"

"I'd say so. And he was really putting on the pressure for the last six months." Rafael placed the financial statement on the table. "To sell her shares and give him 100 percent ownership."

"Did you think she should have sold her shares to him?"

"As a matter of fact, no. I thought she should hold on to them. The area is turning around and now isn't the time to—"

"Yoo-hoo!"

In unison, we all looked up and saw Camilla standing on the balcony, waving.

"O Romeo, Romeo, wherefore art thou, Romeo?"

Rafael rolled his eyes. "She does that every time she's up there looking down at me."

"And do you respond?" I asked.

"No."

Camilla raced down the stairs and pulled out the chair beside Rafael and plopped down. "Inside joke," she said. "We used to call Rafael and Madison Romeo and Juliet because our parents had forbidden them to date."

Rafael shot her a shut-the-fuck-up look. She coyly smiled back.

"Maybe you can help us, Camilla," I said. I slid the paper over to her side of the table. "Do you know why Madison might have written that in the margin?"

Camilla picked up the document and read it. "Nope. But maybe . . ." She turned to Rafael. "Does Henry know about Madison?"

"No, I haven't told him yet."

"Henry?" Dad asked.

"Our upstairs neighbor, Henry Lamont." We all looked up again. "Owns the third and fourth level. Finance law professor at NYU. Well, recently retired. Madison sometimes talked to him about the properties."

THE FOUR of us stood outside Henry Lamont's door. Rafael knocked. I heard a faint "I'm coming." We waited in silence for another two minutes until the door swung open. Henry was clearly surprised to see four people standing on the other side of his threshold.

"Good morning, Henry," Rafael said. "May we come in?"

"Sure, sure. What's this about?"

Henry had an aristocratic air about him. He stood tall at six foot two or three. Somewhere in his seventies, he still had most of his hair, silver and wavy, slicked back as though he had just gotten out of the shower. His facial features were sharp—long nose, pointed chin, chiseled cheekbones. He wore a long-sleeved flannel shirt and brown corduroy jeans, as though it was the middle of January.

He ushered us into his chilly living room, the air conditioner set somewhere in the low sixties. But the room projected warmth. Intricately spun, multicolored tapestries hung on the wall, along with oil-painted portraits, still-life charcoal drawings, and watercolor landscapes. Antique oriental rugs covered almost every inch of hardwood—when one ended, another begun. Dark mahogany end tables flanked a maroon velvet sectional.

A pleasant mustiness filled the air. Four magnificent abstract sculptures, one made of wood, one of clay, and two of bronze graced each corner of the room. A crystal chandelier hung from an intricate ceiling medallion.

"Not the original, I'm afraid," he said when he saw me staring up at it. "I found this one in another brownstone, restored it, and had it mounted." He turned to Rafael. "So, what's going on?"

Rafael started to cry. Henry looked at me, his expression caught between concern and confusion.

"Mr. Lamont," I began. "My name is Susan Ford. I am a detective with the Monticello, New York, police department. This is my dad, retired detective Will Ford."

"Monticello? As in the Borscht Belt?" He looked over at Rafael and Camilla, confused. "Where the two of you grew up, right?"

Rafael simply nodded.

"I'm afraid we have a bit of bad news," I said. "Madison was killed Saturday night."

Henry lowered himself onto the velvet couch and cradled his head in his hands. Camilla sat next to him and wrapped her arm around his back. Rafael lowered himself onto the lounge edge of the sectional. Dad and I remained standing.

Henry wiped away his tears, then pointed to the open seating to his left, inviting us to join the semicircle. We obliged.

I laid out what had happened. What we found. And why we came to see him. I handed him the bank statements with the scrawl in the margin.

"Yeah, Madison did come to talk to me about this," he said, handing the documents back to me. "Back in March, she asked me to look at the financial statements dating back a few years. I found some irregularities. Or as we call it in the law profession: monkey business." His last two words were accompanied with air quotes.

"What kinds of irregularities?" I asked.

"For starters, the increase in revenue that didn't make sense to Madison. The extravagant purchases of artwork, which Jacob described as property improvements. The seedy bar in Ellenville. This has all the earmarks of a money-laundering scheme."

"Bar?" Dad and I said in unison.

Henry nodded. "Madison told me Jacob had a third business, J & T Tavern. Her father and Jacob Bowman shared it fifty-fifty. But unlike the other properties, Todd bequeathed *all* his shares to Jacob. So Jacob became the sole proprietor of J & T."

"So what if he owns a bar?" Dad asked.

"There's no better place to wash money than through a cash-driven business, like a bar," Henry explained. "Well, unless he also ran a casino."

Was this the real reason Jacob applied for a gambling license for electronic table gaming? Not to bring a bit of Monte Carlo to the place, as he put it, but to set up a cover for his money-laundering operation?

I turned to face Henry. "Jacob recently secured a gambling license for electronic table gaming." I clutched the financial statements and held them up. "Do any of you know if Madison confronted Jacob about any of this?"

Rafael and Camilla, both looking genuinely shocked at this revelation, shook their heads.

Henry cleared his throat. "She did question him about it." All heads spun in his direction, like we were in one of those old E. F. Hutton commercials. "In early March, before she came to me. She asked him to explain the increased revenue and pricey investments. Madison told me he had a logical explanation for all of it. He explained that—"

"I'm going to kill that son of a bitch," Rafael seethed. Then he stood up and stormed out of the apartment.

Camilla followed on his heels.

Dad and I hung around to hear what Jacob had explained to Madison. Then, before we headed back home, I warned Rafael to stay the fuck away from Jacob.

MADISON

Friday, March 15, 2019

I visited our upstairs neighbor Henry today. Such a sweet, sweet man. And brilliant. Oh, and his apartment. Where ours looks like a page straight out of a Pottery Barn catalog, his has that homey, eclectic vibe going on. Rafael thinks it's stuffy and suffocating, but I'm in awe of the place.

Well, it was a very enlightening visit, to say the least! But also a bit frightening. Turns out something weird is going on with the properties. Call me naive, but it never crossed my mind that Jacob might be up to no good. If what Henry suspects is true, Jacob is no ordinary asshole; he's a criminal asshole. This is just crazy, really. I have my own shit to deal with and now this. Henry suggested I set up a second meeting with Jacob to probe a little more, hint at possibly selling my shares to him to make it sound legit. Which, who knows, I might do anyway! But I think I'm going to hold off talking to Jacob—wait a few months and see what shenanigans we might find on the spring statements. "Build a case," like they say in police jargon.

Besides, I got other fish to fry right now, dear journal. I've got to get my head on straight. I contacted a friend of a friend who says she knows a woman who can help women like me kick the habit. This weed habit of mine is a bone of contention between me and Rafael. I started in high school, got stoned at parties and loved the sensation. I could feel myself relaxing in ways I never had before. Anxieties magically lifted. Problems dissolved with each toke. Petty arguments I had with my parents forgotten. I felt free of woe and despair. So I thought, why only feel this way at parties? Pretty soon I took a bong hit in the morning. Snuck out between classes for a quick smoke. Finished my homework and celebrated with a fresh doobie. And, voila, my problems receded into the background. My insecurities seemed less pronounced. Under the influence, it was easier to let shit roll off my back. So, wasn't pot making me a better person? I had it under control. Until I didn't.

My parents blamed Rafael. Of course they did. Maybe that's where I inherited the "it's not my fault" gene. To blame Rafael was ludicrous. He rarely imbibed. Sure, he projected this bad boy image, but it was mostly a facade, a role he played well that made him popular. It didn't matter what I said to them in Rafael's defense, they would come up with any excuse to keep us apart. They even had the gall to throw "religious differences" in my face. This from two people who only practiced Judaism twice a year—on Passover and Rosh Hashana. And that was only to appease my grandparents.

I'm an adult, so, in hindsight, I can understand their concern, even give them the benefit of the doubt. They were just trying to help. I'm sure they were pretty freaked out. I know that now. I also know that I have a problem, and that I am the only one who can do something about it. A few months ago I told Rafael I was weaning off the stuff. But that was not entirely true. I tried. I failed. But I know if my marriage is to survive— and it must—this is a necessary step . . .

So much to do to right my ship before it sinks completely.

6

FRIDAY | JULY 5, 2019

RAY PLACED a bowl of Cheerios in front of me.

"I picked those blueberries this morning," he said. "Lots of antioxidants for that cold of yours." He sat down beside me. "That's one hell of a turn of events. Money laundering?"

I had gotten home late the night before and regaled Ray with the highlights of my trip. Told him we could discuss it over breakfast in the morning, when my head was clearer.

"Well, suspected money laundering. All we have now is the conjecture of a finance law professor based on what he calls monkey business."

"What does he think, this professor?"

"Madison noticed that revenue had been creeping up slowly for the past three years, despite a pretty dismal couple of years prior to that." I scooped up a spoonful of Cheerios and two blueberries and shoved them into my mouth. "In early March, she questioned Jacob about it. According to Henry, Jacob told Madison he raised rates, added more services, made upgrades to the place, and this strategy boosted revenue. But Henry still thought it was strange that the revenues for December 2018 and January 2019—typically slow months—were substantially stronger than the previous year's numbers. And when she saw the February numbers jump even higher, she started to suspect something wasn't kosher.

"She was convinced Jacob was fudging the numbers in some way, although she thought it odd that he would fudge them up, not down, to convince her to sell her shares."

Ray nodded. "A 'get out while you can' kind of ploy?"

"Except he was making the business look great."

"Isn't it possible the business *is* doing great?"

"Well, perhaps. But then there's also the expense side of things. Jacob was buying art for the lobbies and guest rooms, a couple of motorboats for waterskiing, and three sailboats." I held up my phone and scrolled through the pictures I took of the expense statements. I handed him my phone. As Ray read, I finished off my bowl of Cheerios and placed the bowl and spoon in the sink.

He looked up. "Again, if the place is doing well, aren't these merely sound investments?"

"Perhaps, but there is one other notable addition to this story."

"I'm listening."

"Did you know Jacob owns a bar in Ellenville?"

Ray shook his head.

"Yeah, news to me too. And that he just got a gambling license for Shangri-La?"

"Yeah, I did hear about that."

"Bars and casinos are ideal businesses for money laundering. The bar is obvious, as many people pay cash for drinks. A bank wouldn't find it odd for him to be depositing sums of cash, what's called *smurfing* in laundering lingo. It's the part of laundering called *placement*."

"Placing ill-gotten gains into the financial system."

"Right. As for the casino, someone—say, an accomplice of Jacob's—can buy a shitload of chips with dirty cash, play a few games of roulette, then return the chips for a clean check."

Ray let out a slow whistle. "So you've got all the ingredients of a money-laundering scheme. Cash flowing into a business that normally takes the Benjamin. Once in the bank, shift it over to Shangri-La to look like increased revenue in a thriving business. Then use that money to purchase high-ticket items that can eventually be sold legitimately. Goes in dirty. Comes out clean."

"Rinse and repeat."

"So, Madison brought her concerns to Jacob in March and he justified the revenue and expenses. But Henry wasn't buying it." Ray's eyebrows shot up. "Did Madison confront Jacob more recently and threaten to expose him?"

"Henry didn't think so. He's pretty sure Madison would have told him if she had confronted him. Maybe she planned to bring it up to him when they were supposed to meet last Sunday."

"Or perhaps they met on Saturday night, and he took care of this little problem right then and there. What's your next move?"

I mulled over that question. I would need a subpoena to delve into Jacob's bank records, but I didn't want to show my cards just yet. And I wasn't even sure I had enough justification to obtain a subpoena. If I tried and failed to get it, I would surely spook Jacob, and he might cover his tracks—or run. "I'm going to talk to Jacob again. Friendly-like. Try and get some insight on his business. Perhaps catch him in a lie."

"What about this Edward character you mentioned?"

"He's also on my list. Even if he had nothing to do with her murder, he might be a fountain of information on the dynamics of the Garcia marriage. He's known them since college."

"So you're heading back down to the city?"

"Nope. Boston. He moved back to the Boston area after his fallout with Rafael." I removed the carafe from the coffee machine and filled my mug. "But I have another thing I need to tend to today. I think I've figured out a way to get my dad and mom in the same room and get them talking."

"Good luck with that."

I PULLED into the parking lot of Horizon Meadows. Dad mentioned he had a bocce ball tournament today. But the humidity bordered on torturous and I wondered if they had postponed it. If I was having a hard time, I could only imagine that the older geezers were not handling this torment of nature particularly well.

I followed a concrete path around the side of the brick apartment complex to the expansive outdoor recreation area. This main residential building was connected, via a second-floor skywalk, to a dining hall for the independent-living residents. I crossed under the bridge and continued along the walkway to the bocce ball court. Dad and three of his ex-cop friends were standing in a clump, gesticulating wildly, probably arguing about who gets to throw the *pallino*. The rules call for a coin toss, but they have this crazy system based on answering some stupid trivia question. When Archie looked up toward me, the others stopped talking and waved.

"Good. Someone to settle our argument," Dad said as I approached.

"Whatever it is, keep me out of it," I said.

"Pick a number from one to four," Archie said.

"Three," I replied.

"That's me," Ralph exclaimed. "Give me the jack."

Archie plopped the *pallino* into Ralph's hand. Ralph positioned himself at the head of the sixty- by twelve-foot playing field and tossed the *pallino* about thirty-five feet. It landed with a soft thud then rolled another few inches along the packed-dirt runway. I watched as they took turns throwing the red, green, blue, and yellow bocce balls. Of course, Dad successfully *kissed* the *pallino* on his last turn and scored the winning point.

They were all sweating profusely.

"Iced-tea time," Ralph said. "This shit is unbearable," he added, wiping his brow with the lower half of his T-shirt.

They all mumbled in agreement as they placed the balls back in the bag.

Dad separated from the group and steered me toward the footpath. "So, what's up, Susan? Any new developments in the case?"

"No. But I have a proposition for you. A kind of win-win."

"There's no such thing. But shoot."

We reached the building entrance and Dad opened the door for me. Always the gentleman. Unlike most places, the air-conditioning was not on full blast. It was just pleasantly cool. Perhaps a consequence of complaints from the residents about it being *too cold*. We settled in a little seating nook in a corner of the lobby.

"Okay, maybe not a win-win, but a little tit for tat." I was afraid neither of us was going to be a winner in this little scheme of mine.

Dad glanced up and waved to a woman who walked through the lobby, then looked back at me. "I'm listening."

"I will be happy to include you in this investigation . . . as long as I am certain there is no danger to you . . . in exchange for you having a conversation with Mom in a professional setting with a mediator. Clear the air once and for all."

"Are you off your fucking rocker?"

"Perhaps. But I'm pretty sick and tired of the two of you avoiding each other like the plague."

"What she did was worse than the plague. And I'm having none of it. Done. *Finito. Caput.* And don't threaten me with my role in this investigation." His shoulders slowly rose to his ears, which were now a bright pink. "Irving has made it clear that he wants me involved, and he will hire me without the condition of speaking to your mother."

"You know you can't do this as a solo PI. And I'm offering you a fine deal here. I'm asking for two, maybe three, sessions with Mom to clear the air. And in exchange, you get to pal around with me—when it's safe to do so—and offer up all the advice and wisdom you want."

Dad leaned forward in his chair, his shoulders still hunched. "This is extortion, y'know. I'm not keen on being forced into a corner . . . especially by my own flesh and blood."

"That's why I'm asking you—"

"You're not asking, Susan. You're telling me what I have to do."

He was right on that measure. And maybe I was being a bit of a bully, but damned if I wasn't going to try every trick in the book to re-solve the animus between Mom and Dad. "I know you, Dad. You're not a grudge holder. I know there is a way forward with the two of you. I'm just giving you a little incentive. Tell me you'll think about it."

He stared down at the ground, poking the dirt with the tip of his sandal. "I don't know. And I don't like the way you sprung this on me." He glanced up, a scowl on his face. "But sure, I'll give it some thought."

"Thanks, Dad. I sure could go for an iced tea," I said, hoping to lower the temperature.

"I'm not thirsty," Dad said as he stood and walked away.

WHEN I got back in my car, my phone dinged.

Eldridge: The fingerprint report is in. From the doc's car.

Everyone we had spoken to so far had agreed to give us their prints—Rafael, Camilla, Samantha, Annabelle, Irving, Audrey, Luis, Isabela. Even Benjamin Worsky, the guy who stumbled upon Madi-son's body and touched the door handle. We already had Jacob's in the system because he'd applied for a gaming license. I texted Eldridge to let him know I was heading back to the station. As soon as I heard the swoosh, my phone rang. *Eldridge* flashed on the screen.

I hit the answer button on my console. "Yeah?"

"Just thought I'd give you the bottom line."

"Okay. Shoot."

"As the doc told you, a lot of people in Madison's circle were in that car. Of all the prints we were able to identify, the doc confirmed that every single one of them could have had an innocent reason for being in the car. Of those we collected—" He paused and I could hear paper rustling. "We got a hit on Rafael, Camilla, and Annabelle. But they all admitted to being in that car prior to the night of the murder. There were prints from one of the doc's friends who was in the system, but he had a solid alibi for the night of the murder—open heart surgery."

"How many unidentified prints did you lift?"

"There were four fingerprints we didn't have a match for. One could be our guy, but they could also just be valets or more friends."

"Were Jacob's prints in the car?"

"Nope."

"When I go see Edward Moore, I'll get his prints." I glanced at the clock on my dashboard. "I'll meet you in an hour to review this. Got a quick errand to run."

WHEN I arrived at my mother's house, I let myself in. Mom was prone on the tartan sofa watching *Schitt's Creek*. I lingered in the archway a few moments. She bolted upright when she saw me and hit pause on the remote.

"How long were you standing there?"

"Not long."

"Well, you scared the bejesus out of me."

"Sorry. Hey, I just want to tell you that I spoke to Dad and he might be game to talking things out."

She slapped her knees and blew out air. "Really? Did you trick him somehow? Or is he really on board?"

"Well, he's not exactly on board. Not yet. But he will be. He wants something from me and if this is the price he is willing to pay—"

"So you're extorting him?" Mom slowly stood and bent sideways at the waist to the right, then left. She limped over to where I was standing. "Don't bring me into your little schemes. If he doesn't want to talk to me ever again, I get it. Maybe I deserve it. But don't get yourself in the middle of this. I don't want it blowing up in your face. Right now he's just mad at me. I'd like to keep it that way."

My phone rang. "Gotta take this," I said, swiping. Mom breezed by me and disappeared into the kitchen. I heard the refrigerator door open and shut. "Detective Susan Ford."

"Hi. Detective Ford? This is Samantha Fields. Um, there's something I didn't tell you when we met, and it's been bugging me. Do you have a moment?"

"Yes." I moved a few throw pillows and sat down on the edge of the couch.

"I'm sorry I didn't mention this . . . but, well, I just . . . I just didn't want to . . . sully Madison's reputation. I know it's stupid." There was silence. "You there?"

"Yes. Go ahead."

"When Madison asked to borrow the car last weekend, I pushed back a bit. Thought I might need it to run errands. But she insisted. Even said she would reimburse me for Zipcar or Uber if I had to use that. You know how I told you she had some personal matters to attend to. Well, she said something else. She went on to say that she was going to do something she should have done years ago. Something that would clear her conscience and set the record straight."

"Clear her conscience? Do you know what she meant by that?"

"I asked her. She told me I would find out soon enough. I really . . . I really feel bad about not saying anything. It's not like me. I just—"

I waited a few seconds for Samantha to finish her sentence, but the word "just" hung in the air.

"No worries. You're telling me now. Is there anything else that I should know?"

Again, silence filled the void for a few moments.

"You know when you asked me if their marriage was on solid footing. Well, I may have not been entirely forthcoming." She cleared her throat. "I think Rafael was having an affair."

"SHE THINKS?" Eldridge bellowed. "What makes her *think* that? And why in hell didn't she tell you this when you met with her?"

I doubted Eldridge would understand the bond between girl-friends that forces them into the murky world of absolute secrecy. You keep a friend's secrets. It's sacred.

"Who knows?" I replied, not in the mood to explain girlfriend etiquette. "But she did say *think*. She couldn't be sure, but said Madison suspected as much. That he had been aloof lately. Distant. Secretive. And other telltale signs."

"This certainly puts Rafael back in the suspect's circle."

"Or the woman . . . or man . . . he was allegedly having an affair with."

"Man?"

"Just covering all bases, sir."

"Jeez. I'm such an old fart. My mind would never go there." Eldridge spun his wedding band. "What's your take on Rafael?"

"Honestly, the guy seems pretty shook up. Genuinely heartbroken. Even my dad thinks—"

"Wait, Will spoke to Rafael?"

I hesitated. "At the shiva." I chewed at the edge of a fingernail. "And at their apartment in Brooklyn."

Eldridge's eyebrows shot up.

"He was down there with a few buddies to watch the fireworks and I invited him along. He knows the family. I figured Rafael might feel more comfortable in his presence. Besides, the guy has great observational skills and I'm riding solo on this case right now."

Eldridge made a fist, then stabbed the air with his index finger. "The department gave you a lot of leeway last year allowing Will to join you on the Trudy Solomon case. But I don't see that happening again." He relaxed his fist and dropped his hand to the table. "From what you told me about a potential laundering scheme, this one could get dangerous. This case is getting a lot of attention. Internally and externally. Don't add to my already existing headaches."

"I hear you loud and clear, sir, but there's a chance Irving might hire him on the side and that would be worse. I'd like to keep an eye— and a leash—on him. Include him just enough to keep everyone happy and out of my hair."

Eldridge groaned. "A very short leash."

MADISON

Sunday, March 17, 2019

L unch with Samantha today! Now, she's someone I can confide in. Should I tell her about my big, bad secret?

Will she sway me to do the right thing or sweep it under the carpet? So much time has passed, what difference does it make, she might say. Or . . . that's a big burden to be carrying around, you should come clean. But really, I can't tell her.

Hell, if I can't even bring myself to write the story of what happened in this magnificent, leather-bound journal, how the hell am I going to tell a real human being!?

A part of me was hoping someone would figure this out and out me. Instead . . . crickets. I got away with it! But now that silence is deafening and no matter how hard I press my palms to my ears, I can hear the voices in my head goading me to exorcise this overwhelming guilt. Guilt that has blossomed from a tiny seed to an insidious weed. And here's the thing about weeds—if you don't get the root, it will emerge again and again, destroying all the good things around it.

I think I will merely tell Samantha I am dealing with a personal crisis, that I've done something that weighs on my soul, that I need to clear my conscience. It would be wrong to involve her in this . . . she's so busy these days. At the hospital day and night, hardly has the time to get together anymore. But she'll give you the shirt off her back, even if she's freezing. Hell, she gives me her car whenever I ask! She's a friend, in the truest sense of the word. And when push comes to shove—when it's time to yank out that weed—I am going to need a true friend.

7

SATURDAY | JULY 6, 2019

I DECIDED to head to Boston to speak with Edward Moore before meeting with Jacob. At this juncture, I thought it more important to exclude or include Edward as a suspect than to lean on Jacob. I needed a fuller picture of what was going down with Jacob's businesses, and that would take a bit more time.

Edward agreed to meet me at his apartment in the South End, a gentrified area of Boston with a Whole Foods, funky new condo buildings, and trendy restaurants.

"There. There!" Dad yelled, pointing to a space between two parked cars.

"Finally. This is worse than Brooklyn." I parallel parked into the spot. "You up for the walk? I think we're like five blocks away."

"Yeah. I need to stretch my legs after five hours sitting in the car."

Dad caved to my proposition. But I had a few conditions. He could join me for casual questioning (no precinct interrogations) of Madison's friends and family, but Jacob was off limits. Money laundering usually meant dangerous players, and there was no way he was going to be involved in that aspect of the investigation. I told him I would keep him apprised, but he was to keep his distance. He agreed (after a lot of hemming and hawing). I wouldn't say things were 100 percent fine between us; he was still mildly pissed at this arrangement. Hopefully this little trip would get us back to a better place.

"What did Eldridge say when you told him I was joining you on this road trip?" Dad said as we walked briskly up Harrison Avenue.

"He didn't say anything, because I didn't tell him."

Dad stopped. "I thought you said he said—"

"He said I can talk to you about the case, get your advice. He didn't exactly say you can tag along with me. So let's just keep this between us, okay?"

"Your call, Susan, but I'm happy to talk to Eldridge about—"

The scowl on my face stopped him mid-sentence.

We walked the last three blocks in silence.

EDWARD MOORE looked like he would be more comfortable in a lifeguard chair than in an office of a hedge-fund trading firm. His sun-drenched blond bangs hung casually over his forehead, threatening to fall in his eyes, a dusty shade of blue, similar to mine—cornflower (as Mom would say). He was lean, muscular, and tan. Definitely had the physique of someone who could thrust a knife with force and precision.

He led us into his living room, where a white sectional with white throw pillows awaited us. He motioned for us to take a seat and inquired about our need for a beverage. Dad asked where the bathroom was.

I glanced around at the icy white-and-silver decor. White walls, white couch, white pillows, a white-and-silver rug. White lacquered coffee table with matching television console. A chrome etagere housed a few books, some small metal sculptures, and a couple of sterling-silver vases. On the walls, silver frames encased bland abstract art. I couldn't imagine anyone drinking red wine in this room without experiencing an anxiety attack.

"I'll have a water or club soda," I said, scrambling for safe options.

"I'll have a glass of milk," Dad said, casing the room. "Kidding. Water will be just fine." I could barely suppress a chuckle. Edward didn't seem to notice the snide remark and swiftly disappeared to get the drinks. Or perhaps he was just a good sport. Dad scooted down the hall to the bathroom. "Be right back," he called to me over his shoulder.

I fished my pad and pencil out of my bag and leaned back against the white cushion. Granted, it was a very comfortable couch. If I closed my eyes, I might have fallen asleep. Dad shuffled back into the room and sat next to me on the sofa. He leaned back and patted the cushions. If he closed his eyes, he would have fallen asleep.

Edward reappeared holding two glasses. He shifted his view to the white coasters in a silver holder and raised his eyebrows ever so slightly . . . my cue to remove two from the stack and place them in front of us. He smiled and placed the glasses on the square coasters. Then he took a seat to the left of us.

"I totally get why you're coming to see me," Edward offered. "If anyone wished harm to Madison, I guess I'm on the top of that list." Edward lowered his head and trapped his hands between his thighs. "But I had nothing to do with this. Sure, I wanted something bad to happen to her—karma, you know—but I would never wish her dead."

"I'd like to eliminate you as a suspect. And to do that, I'm going to need three things from you," I said, unzipping my backpack. "Your fingerprints, your DNA, and an alibi." I pulled out a mobile fingerprint scanner and a DNA swab kit. I saw Dad's eye widen at my gizmo collection.

"Oh man, what I wouldn't give to have those back in the day."

Edward swatted his bangs away from his forehead. "Uh, I'm not prepared to do that." He cleared his throat. "I mean, I'm happy to help in your investigation, but that's a bridge too far."

I couldn't force him to comply, not without a warrant. I smiled in my best I-come-in-peace face and tried again. "It's just standard procedure . . . and it would really help us move the case forward."

He shook his head and his bangs fell back over his eyes. "I'm sure you'll move the case forward just fine without trampling on my rights."

I sipped the water, giving myself a few seconds to decide if it was worth forcing the issue. Without a warrant, the answer was obvious. "Okay. Let's move on. Where were you the weekend of June twenty-ninth?"

"The entire weekend?"

"Saturday and Sunday, and—for good measure—let's throw in Friday."

"So I know this isn't going to sound good, but I was here." He waved his hand in circles. "By myself, all weekend. I've had a stressful few weeks and needed to take a breather." He sighed. "Alone time."

"Certainly someone saw you. Grocery delivery? The doorman?"

"I stopped at Whole Foods on Friday and got everything I needed for the weekend. You can ask the doorman if he saw me sneak out. And there are security cameras in the lobby. If you watch them, you'll see that I entered the building Friday night and didn't leave until Monday morning when I headed out to work."

"That's not really something we can rely on. Slipping by cameras, either in disguise or knowledge of camera placement is done quite often."

Edward shrugged. "Well, then I don't know what to tell you."

"You can tell us about the incident with Madison," Dad chimed in, putting air quotes around the word *incident*. "Your side of the story."

"I'm not sure how that will help your case."

"To know how someone died, you have to know how they lived," I said. "The more we know about Madison—her quirks, her foibles, her fears, her dreams, her secrets—the better we understand what might have happened to her. We merely want to hear your perspective on the *real* Madison. The things her friends and family won't necessarily tell us."

He ran his fingers across his forehead, swooping his blond bangs out of his eyes.

"I was Rafael's roommate our sophomore year in college. Boston University. That's how I met Madison. I started dating Annabelle and the four of us were pretty inseparable. Rafael's sister, Camilla, hung around with us as well. She's a bit of a strange bird—a few loose screws—but she was fun, and you could always count on her to make a night . . . eventful." A half smile appeared suddenly, then vanished. "It all went to shit after moving to New York."

"Because of what Madison did to you?"

"No, it started before that. If I had to describe Madison in one word I'd use *controlling*. She would get miffed if I got together with Rafael for drinks after work. And Annabelle started to complain that Madison was micromanaging her graphic designs. Then she pulled that stunt at a cocktail party."

"When she poached one of your clients?"

"Yeah. But what really steamed me was that Rafael didn't turn the guy away. He could have done the right thing."

"The right thing?" Dad asked.

"Yeah. Tell him I was a terrific money manager and to stick with me." He paused, then added, "I would have, if the shoe was on the other foot."

"Were they faithful to each other?" I asked.

He scrunched his face, seemingly baffled by my question. "Well, I don't know anything about their relationship since . . . but before that, I can't imagine either of them cheating. They were devoted to each other. Rafael's only issue with Madison was her weed habit."

"You know about that?" Dad asked.

"She started smoking pot in high school and—although they say it's not an addictive drug—Rafael told me she had become dependent on it. He said she claimed to need it to relieve her social anxiety."

"Do you know if she dealt?"

Once again, Edward swept his hair away from his forehead. A nervous habit? A tell? Was he hiding something about her drug use? "Again, I don't know what she was up to in this past year, but I find that hard to believe. They certainly didn't need the money. She was just a hard-core recreational user. I do know that it pissed off Annabelle."

"In what way?" I probed, hoping to better understand if her drug use had any role in her death.

"It was beginning to influence Madison's work. In fact, it might be one of the many reasons they went their separate ways."

"You know about that too?" Dad asked. From Dad's incredulous tone, I suspected he too was curious about how Edward seemed to know what was going on in Madison's life despite their falling-out.

"Um, yeah." Edward cleared his throat. "Annabelle and I still chat once in a while—we had a pretty amicable breakup and we've remained somewhat close."

"You said, 'one of many reasons.' Was there something else going on between Annabelle and Madison?" I asked.

Edward's eyes darted around like he was looking for an escape hatch. He suddenly stood. "It's not my place to say. And I'm sure it has nothing to do with what happened to Madison."

"This is a murder investigation." Dad stood to face him. "If you don't answer Detective Ford's question, that could be construed as obstruction. If you know something, it's not your place to decide whether or not it has a bearing on this case. Let us be the judge of that."

Edward sat back down. His gaze settled on the lacquered coffee table, which he held for ten seconds before looking up. "A few months ago, Madison found out that Annabelle was having an affair."

"With Rafael?" Dad blurted out.

"Rafael? No. I already told you . . . he would never."

"Then with whom?" I asked, tapping my pen against my thigh.

"With Irving. Madison's grandfather."

※

"YOU KNOW this makes Irving and Annabelle suspects?" I said to Dad as we rode the elevator back down to the lobby.

"What? I know no such thing. That's crazy. Why on earth would he murder his granddaughter?"

"Really Dad? This is what I was afraid of. You're too close to these folks to look at this objectively." The elevator doors opened and I stepped out. "People with secrets sometimes do crazy-ass things to prevent those secrets from coming out."

Dad hopped out of the elevator just as the door started to close. "Knowing these people is what makes me pretty damn sure that Irving would never do such a thing."

I gnashed my teeth. "Well, you might know Irving, but you don't know Annabelle."

"I trust my gut. Always have. Rarely steers me wrong."

He stormed ahead of me to the front desk, where a security guard was seated behind a large counter. I flashed my badge and informed him that there would be a formal request for the CCTV tapes for the weekend of June twenty-ninth.

Dad put on his reading glasses and leaned over a stack of flyers piled on the counter. "What's this?" he said, pointing to the paper pile.

The security guard stood up slightly to see what Dad was pointing at, then sat back down. "Oh that. Every month, one of our residents holds a seminar on a topic they have expertise in. This month has something to do with finance."

"Did Edward Moore drop these off?" Dad said.

"As a matter of fact he did . . . this morning."

Dad lifted the stack of flyers, carefully slid out the bottom paper, and gripped it by its corner. He held it that way until we got out on the street.

"What was that all about? Planning to come back and take a seminar about money management?"

"You got a baggie in that backpack of yours?" Dad asked. The flyer waved in the breeze. I reached for it, but he pulled away. "If Edward brought these down to the front desk this morning, his fingerprints might just be on this paper." A mischievous grin spread across his face. "Abandoned property in a public place. And ours for the taking."

I riffled through my backpack and pulled out a clear evidence baggie.

Dad deposited the flyer into the bag. "Someone might have already taken the top copy—the one that would have revealed his thumbprint." Dad lifted his hands and pretended to hold an imaginary stack of papers. "But if he held the stack like this—"

"Then it's quite possible his four other fingertips touched the bottom piece of paper."

Dad tapped the side of his forehead. "Bingo!"

Too close to the players in this case or not, Dad had just earned his keep.

MADISON

Friday, March 22, 2019

Sometimes I can be an evil bitch. I've never told anyone the truth behind the "Edward Incident." But to you, dear journal, I will tell. Perhaps starting small by telling you about this act of malevolence will give me the courage to tell you about the other incident.

First it must be said that Rafael is truly a master at making money for his clients. A genius, really. He's got great instincts and a knack for picking winners (and even picking losers if it serves a client's tax purposes).

I was introduced to Mr. Phillip Johnson at a fundraising gala to raise money for private-school scholarships for "kids at risk," a lovely euphemism for black and brown children. Side rant: The rich love feeling philanthropic, as though the mere act of tossing a few dollars (which they can write off) to the poor is the way to fix the ills of the world. They understand there is a need, but they would rather throw money at the problem than get involved in any meaningful way. That would mean having to take sides on justice and equity issues. And that is the third rail of the well-to-do. These folks are not going to join a protest or write to their *congressmen. No fucking way. They are going to pull out their checkbooks and their Venmo apps and give enough to ease their conscience. Rant over.*

Back to Mr. Phillip Johnson. CEO & President of Johnson Freight & Shipping. Inherited the family-run business from his dad (originally Johnson & Sons) and turned it into an international conglomerate. He's a charismatic guy with a George Clooney vibe. The guests flitted to him like moths to a flame. Although many of the women looked like rare butterflies with their sequined dresses and sparkling jewelry. I might not have been the prettiest, but I have a figure (if I do say so myself) that turns heads—both men's and women's. Perhaps that's the reason why motherhood's siren call is quiet. Do I really want to ruin this? That might sound shallow. But I find it hard to believe that other women don't harbor such vain thoughts.

Anyway, back to my story. While Rafael schmoozed and boozed, I found myself next to Mr. Phillip Johnson at the bar, where we simultaneously yelled out an order for Glenlivet neat. We clinked glasses and, well, one thing led to another, and I casually mentioned Rafael's trading prowess. So, what's so bad about that, you might ask? It was a serendipitous meeting where you casually tossed out your husband's financial wizardry and he took the bait.

But alas, that is not what truly happened. Insert dramatic pause here!

I planned it. I learned of his favorite drink from a Forbes *article. I stalked him around the room until he headed toward the bar. I wore his favorite color, red (gleaned from a men's magazine "Bachelor of the Month" article). I knew he loved horse racing and the Indy 500, so I studied up a bit on these subjects . . . just enough knowledge for cocktail party banter. And I knew he was Edward Moore's wealthiest client. But I had to be sure to win him over, and so what I did next was pretty despicable. I hinted that Edward was being investigated for "something." He pressed for more about Moore, but I swatted away his questions, claiming I had said too much already. That's all it took. That seed. And the next morning, Rafael gets a call from Mr. Phillip Johnson's personal assistant to arrange a meeting.*

I do this thing where I make contracts with myself. If I do this good thing . . . it will make up for what happened . . . and my guilt will somehow magically dissipate. But then I do something like this—and it becomes clear that I am not a good person. Why did I do this to Edward? Because this is who I am—a manipulator. A selfish, conniving, self-centered manipulator. And it's time to stop. It's time to pay my penance, to wipe the slate clean. Tabula rasa.

8

SUNDAY | JULY 7, 2019

"**HOW OLD** is Irving?" Ray asked when I finished telling him what I learned on my road trip to Boston. He set a plate of scrambled eggs on the place mat in front of me. "Ketchup?"

I nodded. "I asked Dad that same question when that bombshell landed in our laps. He's sixty-eight, ten years younger than Dad."

Ray whistled between his teeth. "So, a May-December thing."

"More like a February-December thing, if you ask me. That's exactly a forty-year difference between Irving and Annabelle." I swooshed my eggs in the ketchup, took a bite, then slyly asked, "Would you do that?"

Ray shrugged. "I plead the Fifth."

I gave him my best hairy eyeball.

"Would your Dad date someone that young?"

"I don't think so. And we almost came to blows after meeting with Edward, so I didn't push the subject."

"Blows? About what?"

"Okay, not blows, but he's got blinders on when it comes to Irving and family. And if I hear one more word about his magical gut, well . . ." I sighed. "I'm just trying to walk a fine line between appeasing Dad and not getting into trouble with Eldridge, and it's making me grouchy."

"Well, it sounds like Irving and Audrey are not as happily married as they pretend to be."

"Dad told me Irving and Audrey got married young. High-school sweethearts. Like me, she got pregnant at eighteen. He went to college; she stayed home to raise Robin. They've been together fifty years. I guess the thrill is gone. Obviously he sought excitement elsewhere. Same old story."

Ray nodded slowly and squeezed his left eye shut, his telltale sign of working through a theory. "If Madison knew, this might explain Madison's and Annabelle's falling-out. I can certainly see why she wouldn't want to work with Annabelle. I can just imagine a conversation that starts, 'So, how's my granddad in the sack?'"

I smacked Ray on the upper arm. "Jesus, Ray."

"So, how did your dad react?"

"Not well. He's insisting that Irving would never harm his granddaughter. And therefore having him involved in this case is now a clusterfuck." I caressed my temples in a feeble attempt to stave off an impending headache. "He's way too close to the players involved, he'll never be objective."

"Your dad has great instincts." He rubbed the scruffy whiskers on his unshaven chin. "That's what made him such a good cop back in the day."

"Yup, he reminded me of that too."

Ray whisked away my empty plate and placed it in the sink. "Boy, I'd like to be a fly on the wall when you confront them today."

"Might not be today. Annabelle is in Brooklyn, and according to Dad, Irving is in New Jersey. Something to do with his work. But he'll be back up here tomorrow. I don't want to tip my hat, so I need to get Annabelle up here on some other pretense."

"Well, I have to agree with your dad."

I opened my mouth to object but stopped myself and let Ray have his say.

"I find it hard to believe that Irving would kill his granddaughter in such a gruesome manner." Ray chewed his lip and closed that left eye again. "What if Madison threatened to expose the affair and Annabelle *stopped* her?"

That thought had crossed my mind as well. If Annabelle was hell-bent on keeping her relationship with Madison's grandfather a secret, that would certainly give her motive. But they were friends and business partners, and as much as Dad's gut told him that Irving would never hurt his granddaughter, my gut told me Annabelle wasn't capable of such a brutal stabbing.

But then again, in the Trudy Solomon case, the glamorous and gregarious Rachel Cuttman had had no qualms about steering a knife into the man who was blackmailing her husband. People are very adept at erecting facades when it suits their purposes.

I picked up on his thread of reasoning to play it through. "Dr. Fields did mention that Madison wanted to clear her conscience of something. Maybe this was it. Maybe she didn't think it was right to hold this back from her grandmother. That it was unconscionable to keep such a secret."

"Sounds plausible."

I steepled my fingers and rested my chin on the point. "Except for one thing. Dr. Fields said that whatever was bothering Madison went back a few years. According to Edward, Madison only recently found out about the affair. Doesn't mean Annabelle didn't kill her over this, but I don't think it's related to whatever was keeping Madison up at night. I'll find out soon enough when I question those two."

The doorbell rang.

"Expecting someone?" we said in unison.

"Jinx," I said as the doorbell rang again.

I parted the window curtains in the living room and spied my mother's car on the gravel driveway. Curious, I activated my phone and searched for a missed text or phone call as I made my way to the front door. Nothing. She never just pops in. When I opened the door, Mom quickly stepped inside. I could see the gleam of sweat running from her biceps down to her wrists. Her hair was matted against her head as though she had gotten caught in a rain shower.

"Fuck, it's hot out there. The car's air conditioner is on the fritz and Johnny can't get to it until Friday. Probably time to trade in that old heap of crap."

I glanced over her shoulder at the old heap of crap—a 2008 Toyota Corolla she bought used in 2015.

"Sorry for barging in. Got a minute?"

"Yeah, a few minutes. But I gotta get to the station."

"Your dad stopped by last night. I thought you should know." She hesitated for a moment. "And I just wanted to tell you my side of the story before you speak to him."

"Your side?"

"I told him that I knew you bribed him to reconcile with me and that he didn't have to follow through if he wasn't up for it. I really don't want him feeling forced into this. It just makes things even more awkward." She lifted her cane slightly off the floor and wagged it at me. "And I don't want you getting mad at him or excluding him from this case, because it's not his fault I deceived him. He has every right to be pissed, and you can't just wave your magic wand, Susan, and make everything hunky-dory again."

"And what did he say?"

"He said he'll think about it. But here's the thing. I don't want you talking to him about this. Besides, he kept his side of your bargain. He came to see me. I'm the one who's giving him an out."

My phone dinged and I reached for my back pocket and glanced at the locked-screen pop-up notification. *Eldridge.* When I looked up,

Mom opened the front door and slipped out with a quick wave. My phone dinged again as she started the car's engine. I swiped. Two messages greeted me.

The first: *Get here now. Feds just showed up.* The second: *Seems you're not the only one interested in Jacob.*

❋

THE WOMAN seated across from Eldridge pivoted her neck when I entered the chief's office. The few seconds of silence were broken when Eldridge introduced me.

"Agent Ginger Larson," she replied, as she stood and extended her hand.

I held up my palms. "Bad cold."

She nodded and backed up a few inches.

Eldridge cleared his throat. "Seems we stumbled into the briar patch. Agent Larson is from the US Treasury's Financial Crimes Enforcement Network."

I nodded and turned to Agent Larson. "We have reason to believe that Jacob Bowman, a suspect in a local murder, might be running a money-laundering operation. Is that what this is about?"

Agent Larson adjusted the barrette that scooped up her curly hair, a rich auburn with copper highlights. She appeared to be about my age, give or take a year or two in either direction. She wore standard federal government garb—black slacks, white blouse, black blazer—that appeared to be one size too small. Perhaps she had recently gained a few pounds and, instead of buying new clothes, she hoped to lose the weight and keep the outfit.

"Yes." She pointed to the chair next to the one she had just been sitting in. She sat down and waited for me to join her. When my butt was firmly planted in the chair, she continued: "We received a Suspicious Activity Report from a bank in November of last year . . . pertaining to a bank account held by Jacob Bowman. That's all we need to subpoena bank statements and financial records without the knowledge of the customer."

"Patriot Act," Eldridge chimed in.

"Exactly. Allows the Feds to look into potential funding of terrorist activity. But it's used more widely to find all kinds of malfeasance associated with money laundering without tipping off the criminals."

"So what did you find on Bowman?" I asked.

"I'll get to that. Let me just back it up a bit." She leaned forward and put her elbow on Eldridge's desk. "The FBI has been keeping tabs on a guy named Oliver Finch. Mob-connected. Mostly drugs and prostitutes. Keeping it old school. He's got a few seemingly legit business-es—four dry-cleaning shops in Brooklyn and Queens and a couple of garages on Long Island. Also owns a sub shop in an area called Southie in Boston. Ever hear of him?"

Eldridge and I both shook our heads.

"Well, I'll get to him in a minute. But let me set the stage first. So this bank issued an SAR—"

"SAR?" I asked.

"The acronym for Suspicious Activity Report."

I nodded.

She continued: "So this bank issued an SAR when it noticed an unusual amount of cash being deposited into a business account for J & T Tavern."

"J & T Tavern?" Eldridge asked. "What does that have to do with—"

"That's Jacob Bowman's bar," I said.

Eldridge raised his eyebrows in a way that indicated he was not aware of the connection. Nor pleased to be hearing about it for the first time.

I cleared my throat. "I recently learned about this bar from Madison's neighbor."

Eldridge admonished me silently with knitted eyebrows, then turned his attention to Larson. "As you were saying."

"This bank, like all banks, monitors large deposits of cash, and the algorithm caught some sort of anomaly associated with the J & T Tavern account." Agent Larson removed her elbow from the desk and sat back in her chair and crossed her legs. "The bank brings it to our attention, then we conduct a forensics audit."

"Follow the money," I said.

"Exactly."

"So, where did it take you?"

Agent Larson smiled ever so slightly, producing a tiny dimple on her left cheek.

"Every month, for years, varying amounts of money from this J & T Tavern account were transferred—via cashier's check—to a company called OF Holdings."

"OF. Oliver Finch?" I asked.

"Yeah. Super clever, huh? You can name your shell company anything in the world and he comes up with his initials." Agent Larson snorted derisively. "From here it gets a bit more complicated."

"Go on," Eldridge said, enraptured like a child listening to a bedtime story.

"Business checks issued from OF Holdings were then made out to an entity called Mountain Investments, another company registered to Oliver Finch."

Eldridge blew a low whistle.

"This is where things get exciting." She paused, perhaps for dramatic effect. "Once we had a bead on Jacob Bowman, we subpoenaed bank records for his other bank accounts. Turns out his businesses are all set up at different banks. That in itself is somewhat of a red flag. One for J & T, the second for Shangri-La, and a third one for New Beginnings."

Eldridge and I nodded like bobblehead dolls.

"There was nothing particularly fishy about New Beginnings. At least nothing we could find. But Shangri-La . . . that's a whole other kettle of fish. In this account, we saw money flowing in *from* Mountain Investments. And shortly after the money comes in, checks are made out to art dealers and boat companies. Both the Shangri-La and New Beginnings accounts also pay out quarterly checks to your victim, Madison Garcia."

"Madison's neighbor told us that she received quarterly payments based on some kind of profit formula," I said.

Eldridge stood and started to pace. "So, let me get this straight. Jacob Bowman set up accounts in three different banks for his businesses. Unexplained cash into his J & T Tavern account triggered an SAR. You followed the money to a company called OF Holdings, a shell company registered to Oliver Finch, who you've been monitoring for some time for mob-related criminal activities."

"And some portion of this money was transferred from OF Holdings to Mountain Investments, also owned by Oliver Finch," I added.

Eldridge picked up the thread. "So then you looked into Jacob's other business accounts. New Beginnings appears to be legit. But you traced money flowing *from* Mountain Investments *to* Shangri-La, most likely to purchase high-end items that can later be turned into cash."

"That about sums it up." Agent Larson picked up a pen from Eldridge's desk and started scribbling on a piece of paper. "This might make it easier to explain to others. It's pretty classic." She handed the paper to me as she continued. "Smoke and mirrors. Mingling of legit and illegitimate money. Cashier's checks issued from a bank to another entity and then onto another entity. High-end purchases that will later be converted to cash. Jacob owns a bar that doesn't take credit cards. In an undercover operation, we discovered that many of the patrons use an ATM on premises. He even offers to pay the service fee if they buy drinks."

Did she notice my jaw drop as I looked at her drawing?

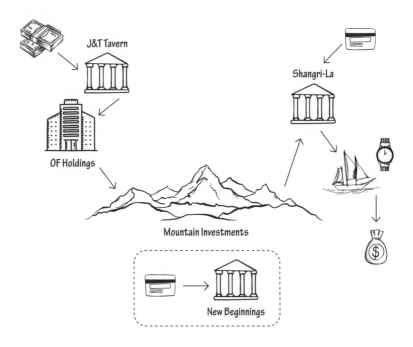

"So that's how he can explain an all-cash business," I said.

"Exactly. But the bank monitoring system is sensitive to changes in deposits and must have triggered an alert. And we just learned he obtained a license for table gaming, which opens another door to all forms of cash-to-chips-to-cash manipulation." She smiled and pointed to the sheet of paper. "I was a fine-arts major before switching to criminal justice."

I had so many questions swirling around in my head, but one rose to the top of the pile. "Do you think Madison Garcia was involved?"

"Hard to say. She was the recipient of quarterly payments, her share of profits, based on her percentage of ownership. Whether or not she knew these were from ill-gotten gains is yet to be determined. She was on our list of people to look into—"

"We have reason to believe she was in the dark about this but had become suspicious." I went on to explain what we learned from Madison's upstairs neighbor. "We have no idea if she went digging further into this, perhaps attracting the attention of someone who would prefer this stay quiet."

"Hmm," was all Agent Larson offered up.

"Anything else we should know?" I asked, staring at her detailed drawing.

"Well, there is something else that might have bearing on both our cases . . . but it could just be a coinci—"

Without warning, I violently sneezed. Looking up at their stunned faces, I whispered, "Sorry."

Eldridge yanked three tissues from the box on his desk and shoved them in my direction. "As you were saying, Agent Larson. This coincidence."

Agent Larson cleared her throat. "Oliver Finch attended Boston University at the same time as Todd and Robin Garmin . . . your murder victim's parents."

"WHERE ARE you?" Chief Eldridge's voice echoed around the stall.

I switched the audio off speaker mode and held the phone up against my ear. "Little girls' room."

"In the station?"

"Yeah. I never left."

"Annabelle Pratt is at the front desk. Madison's friend. She's looking for you."

Definitely wasn't expecting that. What the hell was she doing here? Had she gotten wind of what we'd learned? Was Dad leaking info to Irving? Or was it something else, unrelated?

I greeted her in the lobby. "Wanna grab a coffee?" I asked. My strategy with Annabelle was to make this as nonconfrontational as possible. Play it cool. See what she was willing to impart voluntarily. "Miss Monticello Diner is a short walk from here."

On our walk to the diner she peppered me with questions about growing up around here. Asked me the question everyone does when I tell them I'm from the Catskills—was it just like *Dirty Dancing* and *The Marvelous Mrs. Maisel*? This area is hard to explain to outsiders. Yes, it was a vacation wonderland for Jewish families in the fifties, sixties, and even into the seventies and eighties. Some people say that air-conditioning, assimilation, and airplanes—the Three A's—killed the Catskills, but it was way more complicated than that. Atlantic City, the fourth A, a shiny new gambling mecca on the East Coast, also had a hand in this area's demise. The appeal of the hotels and bungalow colonies waned as the Four A's took hold, and gambling, which was supposed to revive the area, got snared in political wrangling. In the mid-eighties, the decline steepened and, as bookings dwindled, many of the hotels were unable to afford the cost of modernizing their properties. The sons and daughters of the elderly owners weren't interested in taking over the reins of these crumbling resorts. By the mid-nineties, only a handful of hotels remained and most of the bungalow colonies were bought by the Hasidic. Now, especially in the summer, you were more likely to see men in long black coats and fuzzy hats and women in long sleeves and wigs than teenagers in halter tops and cutoff jeans.

The gambling referendum finally did pass, and old properties are seeing new life these days. Would the area ever become the mecca for Jewish families again? I doubted it. The hope now was that casinos and spas and cultural attractions would revitalize the area. The Hip Catskill Mountains. Rebranded for the Instagram generation.

We settled in a booth and ordered coffee and Danishes.

Annabelle dumped two creamers into her coffee. "I spoke to Edward," she said, stirring her coffee. "He told me he told you about me and Irving."

I blew on my coffee and took a sip. "When did Madison find out?"

She drew in a quick breath. "I'm not sure when, or even how, she found out, but she confronted me about it in April. That's why we dissolved the business. Well, that and other issues." Annabelle tapped her spoon on the edge of the coffee cup. "But here's the thing. I wanted Madison to tell Audrey. I wasn't planning on stopping her. I was tired of sneaking around. This was the make-or-break moment. Either Irving left his wife . . . or he left me." She took a small bite of her pastry. "The truth has a way of setting people free."

"I've heard that."

She snorted. "Once the cat was out of the bag, I'd find out once and for all if I was just a fling or, as he put it, the love of his life."

"So I guess Madison never got the chance to tell Audrey."

"Nope. So, now I'm left to either do it myself, break it off, or continue as is. Call me chicken, but Madison being the tattler took a lot of decision making off my shoulders." She leaned back against the red Naugahyde. "I loved Madison. Sure, she got on my nerves occasionally, but I would never, ever hurt her. At the shiva you asked me where I was the night of the murder and I told you home alone." She lifted the cup to her lips, obscuring her face. "I was with Irving."

"Did Irving know that Madison knew about the two of you?"

A fly landed on the lip of the sugar bowl and circled the rim. It stopped momentarily to rub its hands together, a movement that insinuated it was planning something evil. Although I had read somewhere it was simply a grooming practice. I shooed it away.

"I don't think so. And even if he did, there is no way—and I mean no *fucking* way—he would kill her."

"So . . . how long have you been together?"

She squinted and nodded in that way people do when they try to remember dates. "Since Labor Day. So a little less than a year."

"Did you tell Irving that I know about the affair?"

"Not yet. But I plan to today. It would be cruel of me to let you ambush him."

"And if I asked you to not tell him?"

She fingered the crumbs on her plate, contemplating the question.

"I know our age difference makes it hard for you to believe that we are compatible, let alone in love, but we are. And I have every right to let him know what's coming down the line."

There wasn't much I could do, short of arresting her. I wasn't sure I could even convince her it would be in her best interest not to discuss this with Irving. But I gave it the old college try. "It would really be in your best interest not to discuss this with Irving," I said sternly.

Annabelle shrugged. "I'll take it under advisement."

We each took a sip of our coffees. Neither of us said anything for a couple of minutes.

"I'd like to ask you about something else. Did Madison ever speak to you about Shangri-La and New Beginnings? Do you know if she had any intention of selling her shares?"

"We never talked about it much, but she mentioned a few times that she wanted to cut ties with those places. She thought it would be a betrayal to her parents if she sold her shares, seeing that they left them to her. But she really wanted to be free of it. And she didn't like her dad's business partner."

"Jacob Bowman?"

She scrunched her face. "Yeah. Him."

"Was she afraid of him?"

"If she was, she said nothing to me about that." She took the last bite of her Danish, then licked the tips of her fingers. "I've been so spooked about what happened to Madison, I've enrolled in a self-defense course."

"Yeah? That's a good idea."

"It was Camilla's idea, actually. A friend of hers got mugged earlier this year, so she enrolled at SD and SD in the spring . . . it stands for Self Defense and Spanish Daiquiris. After class, everyone learns how to make daiquiris. Leave it to Camilla to find a women's self-defense course that offers bartending lessons. But trust me, it's a great marketing gimmick. Sealed the deal for me."

I laughed. Then caught myself. This wasn't a get-together with a pal. But Annabelle was easy to talk to. She exuded confidence—but not in that pompous way that made you feel inferior. It was more like she wanted everyone to enjoy life the way she did, so she unabashedly shared her exuberance. I think under different circumstances we could have been friends. I frowned slightly to offset the laugh. "What does the course entail?"

"In the first few classes the instructor teaches evasive maneuvers and a little hand-to-hand combat, and for those who are interested, he also offers weapons training. But that's too hard-core for me. I'll stick with mace and some basic defensive techniques."

"A knee to the balls. A poke in the eye."

"Exactly." Annabelle checked her watch. "Well, I appreciate you hearing me out. I gotta head back to the city. Clients, ugh." She winked. "They expect their work to be done on time."

I watched her slink out of the booth and out the door. I thought how grand it would be to be a fly on the wall when Annabelle broke the news to Irving.

MADISON

Sunday, March 24, 2019

Damn Annabelle. Are you fucking kidding me? This is just insane on so many levels. Just think . . . she could be my step-grandmother. Ha! Does she really think this is appropriate? I haven't told her I found out. Wanna know how I found out? I saw them together at Boqueria. It was serendipitous that I was even on the Upper East Side (doing a little shopping).

Now what? Do I confront her? My grandfather? Ignore the whole thing and let it fizzle out when Annabelle comes to her senses? This ain't Grandpa's first dalliance. The first time I witnessed his infidelity was when I was in middle school. Mom took me to the mall in Middletown to go shopping and we saw him in a restaurant canoodling some young woman. Mom saw too . . . steered me in another direction and told me to ignore it. "It's probably a business meeting, but let's keep it to ourselves, okay?" she insisted. Did she think I believed that? I can't imagine Grandma doesn't know.

Does she not care? Does she have her own "diversion"?

Do they have an understanding?

What to do with my knowledge of Annabelle and Grandpa? Even writing their names together in the same sentence is so icky. On one hand, it is truly none of my beeswax (as Grandma would say). But the age difference—what is she thinking? Doesn't she want to get married? Have kids? She's always talked about that. We're going to be thirty in two years—she needs to be finding Mr. Right, not Mr. Too Old to Have Babies. I wonder what people think when they see them together. Probably how sweet it is for a granddaughter to be out with her grandpa. Until they see them cuddle, or kiss. Then what do they think? I really have to stop dwelling on this. It's none of my business. I repeat, it is none of my fucking business. I've got my own fish to fry. My own woes to contend with. My own life to get on track.

And who am I to judge anyway? There was that almost one-night fling a few months ago. Okay, it was just a kiss. But that was a mistake. It was foolish. One time. One regretful time. And what was my rationale . . . Rafael was spending more time at work than with me. So, poor me, I was feeling neglected. Stupid. Stupid. Stupid. Why would I risk our marriage? To punish myself? To show the world what a horrible person I am? Is it possible that in seeking absolution I am deliberately trying to sabotage my marriage because I married the man my parents disapproved of?

If I clear my conscience and confess, would it even make a difference? Whatever wrong I right will not change the past. No punishment will assuage the shame. (Or am I trying to make myself believe this so I can justify my silence?)

And if I stay silent, can I simply expel this guilt from my mind, my heart, my lungs, my stomach—all the places it has taken hold, boring in, growing like a tumor?

9

MONDAY | JULY 8, 2019

I AWOKE to a relentless drumbeat in my left sinus cavity. I gently pressed my index and middle finger against my left cheek and felt the swell of fluid trapped in there.

Ray must have turned the air conditioner off. The room was as stuffy as my nose. My skin was moist. The outside humidity had wafted in through the open window and the air was clammy, wrapping itself around me like an unwelcome hug. My hair was plastered to the edges of my face. When I slowly lifted my head, the drumming in my sinuses intensified. I plucked out the bottle of Advil I kept in the drawer of my bedside table and downed two tablets with the remaining two inches of water from the glass I'd brought to bed with me last night. I lay back down, hoping that in fifteen minutes the boom-boom-boom below my cheeks would subside enough to get on with my day.

Ray poked his head in the doorway. "You up?"

I moaned.

"Jeez. It's warm in here."

"That's what happens when you turn off the air conditioner during a heat wave," I murmured.

"I wanted to open the windows. Get some fresh morning air circulating through the house."

"Uh-huh," was all I could muster.

Ray sat down on the bed, causing me to roll slightly to his side. He placed the back of his hand on my forehead. "I'm calling the doctor. You've got a fever."

"And a rock band playing in my sinuses."

"Soft rock or hard rock?"

"Led Zeppelin-level." I sat up. "The Advil is working," I lied. Although those two ibuprofens did manage to take the edge off.

"You seem to forget I'm a trained interrogator and you are clearly not telling the truth. You, my dear, are seeing a doctor for what I think is a sinus infection. No ifs, ands, or buts."

"I've got a shitload of stuff to do today. I'm meeting Camilla at Shangri-La. And I plan to stop by Irving's office this afternoon." I plucked a tissue out of the box and blew my nose. "I'll pick up a neti pot."

"I know you, Susan. You ain't going to be doing that weird shit twice a day. Besides, you have a low-grade fever. You need antibiotics."

"All right," I mumbled.

"That's the spirit!"

I picked up my phone and called Dr. Regina Low, my primary care physician. Ray lingered in the room, probably to make sure I followed through. After some time on hold, I finally got through and scheduled an emergency appointment for eleven o'clock.

"Happy?" I said as I bounded out of bed and headed toward the bathroom.

"As a pig in shit."

AFTER MY twenty-minute appointment with Dr. Low and a quick stop at the pharmacy, I drove to Shangri-La to meet Camilla.

Camilla had emailed me while I was sitting in the waiting room to let me know she had escaped the city heat and ensconced herself in Serene Scene for the upcoming weekend. Attached was a spreadsheet of Madison's friends and acquaintances. The first column listed the person's name. The second column indicated their relationship to Madison (high-school friend, college friend, work friend, neighbor). The third column represented the intensity of the relationship based on the number of stars she assigned: one star for an acquaintance, two stars for a friend, and three stars for a confidant—all of which was explained in a legend at the bottom of the chart. The only friend designated as a confidant was Dr. Samantha Fields. The majority were acquaintances. The next column listed a phone number. The next an email address. The subsequent columns listed their social-media handles for Facebook, Twitter, Instagram, TikTok, Snapchat, and LinkedIn. The next column revealed their political leaning, the text color-coded red for Republican, blue for Democrat, and purple for Independent. The final column displayed sets of letters. I scanned down the list of about twenty names and all but one had one set of letters assigned to them: JB, PB, BS, EW, KH, DT, or AY. The majority were EW. The next most popular was BS. A smattering of JBs and PBs. One DT and one AY on the list. *What the hell?* The legend didn't explain the significance of the letters.

In eight days, she'd amassed this information and laid it out in this insanely detailed Excel document. And I was on my way to meet with her because she requested I come see her so she could explain in even greater detail.

I parked in Lot A. Before stepping out into the oppressive heat, I unscrewed my water bottle top and popped my first antibiotic. Then I lowered the visor and peered into the little mirror. Ugh.

As I came over the knoll from behind the main building, I could see Sackett Lake shimmering in the distance. To my left, a group of guests—garbed in body-hugging yoga attire—were forming human triangles . . . head down, backsides up. In unison, they dropped to the ground, arched their backs, and stretched their faces to the hot sun. A young woman sitting cross-legged next to the instructor played a round steel tongue drum. Namaste.

The air was so heavy and still that the wind chimes, hanging from a hook that had been screwed into the eave, hung motionless like a mobile over an empty crib. A swarm of gnats acted as gatekeepers, blocking the steps that led to the cottage door. I swatted them away and proceeded up the stairs.

Before I could knock, the door opened slightly.

"Quickly," Camilla whispered from behind the four-inch crack. "I don't want those nasty bugs in the house." She opened the door a bit wider and ushered me in. The door slammed behind me. "Those things give me the creeps."

"The gnats?"

"The dragonflies." She shuddered. "Anyhoo. Safe and sound in Serene Scene. Tea?"

"Sure."

She led me to the kitchen and pointed to one of the stools nudged up against the granite island. "There's a printout of the spreadsheet I sent you on the counter."

I picked it up. "What do the two letters connote?"

"Guess!" she exclaimed as she placed a mug of steaming tea in front of me.

I really did not want to play a guessing game, but I needed to stay on her good side. She was someone who could be helpful; pissing her off by telling her to pound sand and grow up would probably not work in my favor. I tilted my head slightly and tapped at my chin. "Initials?"

"Yes."

I waited for her to explain. But instead she sipped her tea.

"Are the initials associated with the schools they went to?"

She scrunched up her face, then let out a haughty laugh. "Good one. Nope." She remained silent.

How long was she going to make me guess? "Does BS stand for bullshit?"

She clucked her tongue emitting a tsk sound, then said, "You are really bad at this."

"Well, you got me. I'm probably not going to figure it out," I said with a hint of disappointment to try to avoid sounding annoyed.

"I'll give you a hint."

I sighed. "Okay. One hint and if I don't get it, I lose."

"I'll give you two hints. It's something I figured out from reading everyone's posts on Facebook. And it has to do with something that is going to happen in November 2020."

I squinted as it dawned on me. "The contenders for the Democratic ticket? BS for Bernie Sanders, EW for Elizabeth Warren, and so forth?" I thought another moment. "DT for Donald Trump?"

"Ding. Ding. Ding."

"And you included this info because . . .?"

"To show you what a good sleuth I am."

Facebook had become a dumping ground of misinformation, and people were sharing dubious stories and pontificating on falsehoods meant to scare fellow citizens about immigrants! BLM! socialism! capitalism! antifa! You didn't have to be Sherlock Holmes to figure out what camp people belonged to.

But if she wanted to pretend she was Colombo, who was I to tell her otherwise?

"Well, I appreciate you pulling this together. Good work." I studied the sheet. One name jumped out at me. Sarah Steinberg. I was pseudo-friendly with her mother, Patty Steinberg, who had moved away from the area years ago. Sarah got in all sorts of trouble, ran with a rough crowd, and was expelled from school because she had stabbed a classmate at a party.

As if reading my mind (or perhaps noting my gaze landing on her name), Camilla said, "Have you gotten in touch with Sarah Steinberg? She once stabbed someone. I listed her as a friend, but she and Madison had a falling-out the beginning of junior year. Sarah accused Madison of stealing Rafael from her. Said she would get back at her one day."

Twelve years was a long wait to seek revenge over a high-school spat. But as the saying goes, revenge is a dish best served cold. "I'll talk to her. Any other folks on this list have a backstory I should be aware of?"

"I really don't know these people well. And I wasn't super friendly with Madison in high school. I'm sure she had friends back then I was unaware of. We ran in completely different cliques." Camilla removed a hair band from around her wrist and in one deft move cinched a perfect ponytail high on her head. "We hung around more when we got to BU. I did a year here at the community college and got to BU my sophomore year. That's when we all met Annabelle and Edward. I was always the odd girl out with those four—the fifth wheel. That's why I went to London to study." In that last sentence she ratcheted up the British accent. "Rafael told me you spoke to Edward."

I nodded, then glanced at the spreadsheet. "Just reaching out to everyone in Madison's circle."

"Yeah. That was nasty business between the two of them. I probably should have told you about him and Madison when we first met, but I plumb forgot about that. I listed him as an acquaintance, but I guess he's more like a frenemy." She lifted the mug to her lips and blew gently. Before taking a sip, she frowned and said, "Guess I'm not that great of a sleuth after all."

"A good sleuth keeps her cards close to her vest," I said. I had an ulterior motive for seeing Camilla, and she had just given me a good entry point to bring up what I wanted to convey to her—to keep her from blabbing what Henry had told us about Jacob's possible involvement in money laundering. "You know the conversation we had with Madison's neighbor, the professor? Let's just keep that between us."

"Oooh. I get it." She winked, and with her right hand she zipped her lips and tossed the imaginary key into the air. "Mum's the word."

※

DAD DIDN'T utter a single word until I finished relating what Agent Ginger Larson had told me and Chief Eldridge. Then he said two words.

"Fuck, man."

Then three words.

"Excuse my French."

I stifled a laugh. "Larson thinks they have enough on Jacob to haul him in for questioning, but she's convinced that Oliver Finch is the mastermind. The Feds want the whale, not the guppy. They're hoping they can get Jacob to turn on Oliver by offering him some sort of deal. She also said Madison's murder has been mucking up the works. She's not convinced her death has anything to do with Jacob and Oliver."

"Did she ask you to back off on your investigation of those two?" He opened the refrigerator, then peered back over his shoulder. "Beer?"

I held up my hand. "I'm on antibiotics." I tapped my sinuses. "She hinted at it. I made it clear to her that this is a murder investigation first and foremost, but I'll stay in my lane as much as possible. I also told her I would let her know if I uncover anything related to her case."

Dad's phone dinged with a text message. He ignored it. "I bet she's afraid that if you start rattling cages, you'll force both Jacob and Oliver to start covering their tracks."

"Yup. But, to her point, Madison's murder could be totally unrelated to Oliver and Jacob's shenanigans. Sure, there is motive in offing her if she was snooping around and threatening to expose their scheme. But I also get the sense there were other things going on in her life that put her in danger. I don't want to get single-minded about this so early in the investigation. I still think there are plenty of avenues to explore."

"But that part about Todd and Robin being at Boston University at the same time as Oliver Finch. That could be something." Dad's phone rang. He glanced at the caller ID and tapped the decline button.

"You told me that Todd ran with shady characters. Perhaps Finch was one of them. That's why I came to see you. Perhaps you can do a little digging on that front. Locate their college friends and suss out if there was a connection between Oliver and Todd. Just be discreet about it, okay?"

"Aye, aye, captain," Dad said with an enormous grin on his face.

My doorbell rang.

"Expecting someone?" Dad asked.

"Nope." I stood up and hurried to the front of the house. Before opening the door, I edged aside the curtain that covered the cut-out window. Shit.

I opened the door. Irving stepped inside. "We need to talk. I know Will is here. I've been texting and calling, and I really need to clear the air here."

Dad entered the foyer, palms facing out. "Irving, now is not a good time."

"It's fine," I told Dad. "Let's hear what Irving has to say." I shot Dad a look, hoping he understood that he was not to interfere. I turned to Irving. "Were you aware that Madison knew about you and Annabelle?"

Irving squeezed his eyes shut and rubbed his temples. He strode into the living room and started pacing.

We followed him. "Did you?" I asked, this time more forcefully.

Dad touched my arm, signaling I go easy. I yanked my arm away and glowered. A headache was taking form in the back of my skull.

Irving stopped pacing. He collapsed on the couch. "I had no idea that Madison knew. And even if she did know, what does that have to do with anything?"

"Really Irving? You're smarter than that. If Madison told your wife . . . well, y'know. Game over."

"Jesus, Susan. I would prefer my granddaughter was still alive even if it meant Audrey finding out." He started to weep. He wiped his eyelids, took a few deep breaths, then regained his composure. "So would Annabelle." He pulled a hanky from his pocket and blew his nose. "Sorry."

"No need to apologize. Let's just be straight with each other."

Irving nodded, although he refused to look up and meet my eyes.

"Annabelle told me that she was with you the night of June twenty-ninth," I said. "Can you confirm that?"

He cradled his head in his hands for a moment, then dropped his hands back to his lap. "Yeah. Yeah, of course. We were together that night."

From behind me I heard, "Irving, we're not accusing you—"

I whipped around. "Dad! Stay out of this or I'll ask you to leave."

Dad's hands shot up and he stepped back.

I sat on the chair facing Irving and leaned in. "A friend of Madison's told us that she wanted to 'clear her conscience' about something. Let's assume for the moment that it's not related to your affair. Any idea what it could be instead?"

Irving scrunched his face, seemingly puzzled. "'Clear her conscience'? Honestly, I have no idea. She wasn't in any trouble that I know of in recent years. Annabelle might know, though. Did you ask her?"

I ignored his question. "How about a few years back? Anything come to mind?"

Irving shrugged. "She was definitely up to a lot of mischief in high school, but Audrey and I were beside ourselves, grieving the death of Robin and Todd, and didn't pay much attention."

"Do you know any of Madison's high-school friends?"

"She didn't have a lot of friends. She mainly hung out with Rafael."

"The incident report regarding Todd and Robin's deaths states she was with a girlfriend the day her parents died. Do you know who that was?"

He cocked his head and squinted. "That would be . . . um, Crystal. Crystal Booker." Irving sighed. "Wait, are you saying that something she did years ago might be connected to her murder?"

"We're just covering all the bases. And one of those bases involves your son-in-law's business associates."

"Todd's associates? Are you talking about Jacob?"

I ignored his question again. "Do you know of any other partners or investors in Shangri-La?"

"No. I wasn't really privy to any of that . . . but Robin did complain to me once in a while that Todd owed money to some guy who helped him out of a jam. But she said it was eventually settled and everything was copacetic. She certainly didn't make it sound dire or dangerous. Just a minor problem they were dealing with." Irving scratched at his chin. "Do you think that's related to Madison's murder?" He pursed his lips and squinted. "Wait. If that's the case, is it possible Robin and Todd's deaths were not an accident?"

That thought had crossed my mind when Agent Larson connected the dots between the Garmins and Oliver, but I wasn't about to get into that with Irving. "We're exploring any and all connections." I pulled out a photograph of Oliver Finch. "Recognize this guy?"

He stared at the picture and shook his head. "Should I? Is he a suspect?"

I had to tread carefully here. The last thing I needed was Irving knowing this guy's name and hiring some private eye to smoke him out.

"He's a person of interest. Someone we just want to talk to."

Irving nodded, seemingly lost in thought. I thought he would press further, but instead he asked, "Are you going to tell Audrey about, about—?" He couldn't even bring himself to say "me and Annabelle." He merely lifted his eyebrows slightly to infer the affair.

"No. That is between you and *your* conscience."

Irving glanced at his watch and abruptly stood. "I gotta go."

Dad led Irving out onto the porch, where they exchanged good-byes.

No sooner than Dad returned, he lit into me. "Jeez, Susan, you were a little harsh on him. For God's sake, he just lost his only grandchild."

"A little harsh?" I grunted. "You've got to be kidding me. I handled him with kid gloves." I clenched and unclenched my fists. "You're too close to this to be impartial."

"Being close to this gives me the proper perspective. My judgment is not clouded by my relationship to Irving. I'm an experienced police detective. These are people who can help us crack the case—Irving, Annabelle, Camilla, Rafael. We have to trust them."

I shook my head and snorted. "Trust them? My job is to be suspicious of them, not let them off the hook so easily."

"We're going to have to agree to disagree, Susan."

"Really? That's your answer to this."

Dad crumpled onto the sofa and cradled his head in his hands. It was clear he didn't like this feuding any more than I did. When he finally looked up, he held up his palms and whispered, "Truce?"

That back-of-the-skull headache had migrated to my forehead over the course of this confrontation. I exhaled. "Sure." My acquiescence was half-hearted, but I wasn't in the mood or condition to make more of a stink.

My phone rang. It was Eldridge. "Hold on, gotta take this." I walked out of the living room.

When I reentered the living room Dad was snoozing on the couch, his shoulders slouched, his head bent downwards. I gently touched his forearm to rouse him. He mumbled softly.

"Dad," I whispered. "Eldridge just told me that one of the unknown fingerprints in the car matched Edward's fingerprint lifted from the flyer." He straightened his back. I had his full attention now. "Samantha bought that car earlier this year, so for someone who claims he hasn't seen Madison in a year, he has a lot of explaining to do."

"Man o'mighty," Dad exclaimed, jumping up from the couch. "Does Edward know?"

"Not yet. Fingerprints in a car might not be enough to arrest and extradite him. Eldridge is dealing with that now." I pressed my fingers into my temples. "Shit, Sarah Steinberg."

"Who's that?"

"A high-school friend of Madison's who agreed to talk to me. I told her I would drive down to the city tomorrow and meet with her at her apartment."

"About what?"

"I'm hoping she can shed some light on Madison's past. And get this . . . Camilla said Sarah held some sort of grudge against Madison . . . and she knows how to use a knife."

MADISON

Thursday, March 28, 2019

I did it! I confronted Annabelle. Her face! I wish I had my camera at the ready. Her eyes widened in disbelief, shock really. Then her face crumpled. She burst into tears, almost inconsolable. Thank goodness we were tucked away in our office. I thought about confronting her in public, at our favorite restaurant, but I'm trying to tick off more boxes in the "good" column. We aired a lot more than her dalliance with my grandfather. She complained about my weed habit and how it was affecting my work. I ripped into her about her inability to separate work life from personal life. She accused me of micromanaging projects. I accused her of making decisions without my input. It was not pretty. Not at all. But at least we aired our grievances. And you know what, dear journal, it felt good. Like we ripped off a Band-Aid, and the healing between us can begin.

Maybe my fight with Annabelle has taught me something: just say what needs to be said, be honest and truthful. But here's the thing, the fallout for Annabelle and me will simply be the dissolution of our business. But if I come clean and own up to what I did, I could lose everything.

10

ELDRIDGE CALLED this morning with good news. Edward was willing to drive to Monticello and "explain everything." The bad news . . . he was coming with his lawyer, so this wouldn't be a freewheeling interrogation. His arrival was set for four o'clock this afternoon. That gave me just enough time to hustle down to the city, meet with Sarah, and get back upstate.

Sarah lived in a section of Manhattan called Alphabet City, a neighborhood in the East Village. Driving around these streets brought back a rush of memories. In 1987, when I was living in Brooklyn and working as a location scout for a production company, I dated a photographer who lived on Avenue C. His specialty was taking black-and-white photos, then hand tinting them with transparent oil paint. It was pretty cool. And he made enough money to keep the lights on.

The neighborhood was way sketchier back then. In broad daylight, someone had crawled into his bathroom window and stolen all his camera equipment. For those who needed a fix, scoring drugs was easy—just head on over to Tompkins Square Park (or as it was in my case, avoid that park like it was a leper colony). Day or night, street dealers were easy to spot. But it wasn't all bad. The music scene in this section was thriving at that time, with bands like Nirvana and Red Hot Chili Peppers playing over at the Pyramid Club.

In some ways, the neighborhood had maintained its bohemian, artsy vibe. But there was no denying it, gentrification was on full view. Trendy restaurants and beer gardens had replaced dilapidated storefronts and crumbling buildings. And these days, students, artists, young families could stroll through Tompkins Square Park without clutching their purses.

I parked on Avenue B and walked two blocks to Avenue D.

Sarah led me into her living room, where hundreds of photographs covered nearly every square inch of the grayish blue walls. Groups of musicians stood positioned in front of amps and speakers and drum sets, holding their instruments or striking silly poses. No one recognizable. But this was not my era of rock music.

"These are all the artists we've met on tour," Sarah said as she watched me take in the room. "I try to document the entire experience."

I had done a little research on Sarah before this meetup. While in juvie she learned how to play the guitar. Unbeknownst to anyone, she was a gifted singer. She befriended a guy who knew how to play piano, and they performed for their fellow delinquents. Upon release, the two of them picked up a bass player and a drummer. They called their band Venetian Blinds. When asked in an interview why that name, they said that they'd had no reason and that was the reason. It meant nothing and therefore made sense to them, as life to that point had meant nothing. They gigged around Brooklyn and Manhattan and built a fan base. They'd been on the worldwide festival circuit for a couple of years now, and their music—what music blogs called post-punk pop—was a staple on indie rock stations. *Pitchfork* gave their last LP, *Doomed from the Start*, an 8.2 rating, praising Sarah's haunting vocals and clever lyrics. "It's clear that her bandmates know when to hang back and let her vocals act as the lead instrument," the reviewer wrote. In another review, she was compared to Natalie Merchant with a hint of PJ Harvey. Nowhere in any of the articles I read was there a reference to Sarah stabbing someone in high school—although you'd imagine that this would give her punk-rock cred. She obviously chose not to reveal that incident in her interviews (or perhaps her publicist advised against it).

"I was planning to get in touch with you," she said. "We got back from Germany three weeks ago. I always need a few weeks to clear my head before getting on with life." Sarah poured coffee into a mug and handed it to me. She sat down on the couch and slipped the calf of one leg under the thigh of the other. She blew gently on her coffee.

I sat down on the couch next to her. I was not sure what to expect, but this wasn't it. Sarah was soft-spoken. Her strawberry-blonde hair fell in layered waves to her lower back. Her skin was smooth and pale, in fact so pale you could see tiny blue veins around her nostrils and below her lower lashes. Her almond-shaped eyes were hazel with green flecks. A hint of makeup accentuated her natural beauty. Black leggings covered her long, thin legs. A T-shirt, two sizes too big and emblazoned with another band's logo, hung down to her thighs. She looked like the consummate "girl next door," not a punk-rock singer.

After taking a sip of coffee, she sighed. "I was heartbroken to hear about Madison. Back in April, I reached out to her to make amends." She paused. "Step nine."

I nodded to show I understood. Mom was on step eight—making a list of people she hurt and building up the courage to approach them.

"I had a feeling you would seek me out, being that Madison was stabbed. I get that. But I'm not *that* person anymore."

"Camilla told me you threatened Madison back in high school for stealing Rafael."

"Camilla said that? She's a drama queen, y'know. Has to be the center of attention. Always sticking her nose where it doesn't belong. Sure, I was mad at Madison when she started dating Rafael, and tried to win him back, but revenge over a stupid high-school jealousy, really?" She snorted. "Life isn't like a YA thriller. Besides, I wasn't the one who stabbed Joanna. I just got blamed for it. Someone planted that knife in my locker."

"Why didn't Joanna tell the police who stabbed her?"

"Because she didn't know. We were at one of those big, out-of-control, booze-flowing high-school parties at someone's house whose parents were out of town. Joanna had passed out on a pile of coats in the master bedroom. When someone went to retrieve their coat, they found her there in a pool of blood. Joanna had blacked out and had no recollection of what had happened to her."

I thought about Madison's hankering to clear her conscience. "Is it possible Madison stabbed Joanna and planted that knife to set you up? Perhaps you getting in touch with her triggered her desire to come clean. Did she say anything about that incident?"

"Neither of us brought it up." Sarah tilted her head slightly and tugged at her ear. "It's all a bit fuzzy, but I don't think Madison was at that party—I think she and Rafael were with a bunch of kids on a class trip to Washington, DC. But I could be mixing up weekends with some other booze-fueled party."

I squirreled away this tidbit of info. Perhaps Rafael would remember when that DC trip took place. "So you did time for a crime you didn't commit?"

Sarah swept her hand toward the photos hanging on the wall. "Maybe it was a blessing in disguise—I found my passion for music in that place." She shifted slightly. "Look, I did things I'm not proud of, and although Madison broke the girlfriend code by going after Rafael, I'm the one who pressured her into using drugs. That's why I initially reached out to her. To apologize for that." She stretched her legs, then tucked both feet under her butt. "In fact, Madison and I started talking again, a phone call every other week or so—I think she was happy to have a friend to talk to. I got the feeling she didn't have many girl-friends she could confide in."

"Did she say anything that would lead you to believe she was in danger?"

"No. Absolutely not."

"You say she confided in you. Did she tell you something she didn't want anyone else to know? Even something that sounds innocuous can help here. I'm just trying to get a handle on her life, anything that might shed light on whether she was a target or random victim."

She slid her tongue over her teeth. She was mulling.

I let her.

She raked her fingers through her strawberry blonde mane. "She told me about something she was ashamed of, but honestly I can't imagine it has anything to do with what happened to her."

"I know this is hard, betraying her trust. But every snippet of info I collect gets added to other snippets. Like a jigsaw puzzle. With more pieces, a clear picture might emerge."

She gnawed at her lower lip and gently rocked back and forth. More mulling. "Do you mind?" she asked as she opened a silver ciga-rette case.

"Um, I would prefer if you didn't."

She slid the cigarette back in the case. "It's the one habit I can't seem to break."

"About this secret . . ." I nudged.

"Yeah, it's just that I promised her I would take it to my grave."

"Look, I can't promise anything. If it turns out this secret has noth-ing to do with her murder, then mum's the word. But—"

She didn't wait for me to finish, and her words landed hard and fast. "Madison kissed a client. She was going through a rough patch. Rafael was buried in work and traveling a lot and this guy was a shoulder. They were working late one night and one thing led to another and—" She stopped abruptly.

"And?"

Sarah turned away and swiped at her cheek. "She said she regretted it."

"Did she mention his name?"

Sarah turned back to me. "She did. David Cox."

"And when did this affair happen?"

Sarah squinted and tilted her head, calculating. "Eight months ago. And it wasn't an affair. It was a kiss. A mistake, she said. Like I said, they both regretted it and went about their lives like it never happened." She hesitated, then added, "Well, for her it was over. A couple of months ago, he called her out of the blue, said he couldn't stop thinking about that night. He even left his wife and called her several times."

"Harassing her?"

"She said it wasn't like that. He was just feeling her out."

"And this 'rough patch' you mentioned. What was that about?"

"She wouldn't tell me. Just that she needed to clear her conscience about something that happened a while ago."

Again with the clearing of conscience. "A while ago meaning when? A few years ago? College days? Or high-school days?"

Sarah shrugged. "She said I would find out soon enough. Once she took care of the matter."

"And you're sure this wasn't connected to the stabbing incident in high school?"

"I truly think if it was related to that stabbing, she would have said something to me. And even if she did stab Joanna, I probably would have talked her out of going public with it. Water under the bridge. I wouldn't want all that dredged up again."

I reached into my backpack. "One last thing." I pulled out my fingerprint scanner and DNA kit and placed them on the coffee table.

Sarah raised an eyebrow. "Sure."

AFTER LEAVING Sarah's apartment, I called Sally and asked her to dig up contact information on David Cox. I was sure Annabelle would know who he was, but I didn't want her wondering why I wanted to talk to him. Besides, I did promise Sarah I would be discreet. If Sally didn't come through, I would simply ask Annabelle for a list of all their clients.

"I'm heading back to the station soon. Just finishing up detail," Sally said. "I'll call you back when I'm in front of my computer."

As I sped up the Palisades Parkway, Sally finally called back. "Hey. Are you on your way back up here?"

"Yeah."

"Well if you're not too far along in your journey you might want to turn around. David Cox lives in Hoboken, New Jersey."

I glanced at the clock on the console. It was eleven o'clock. Edward Moore wasn't due at the precinct until four, so I had plenty of time, but I was beat. My sinuses were pounding like storm-driven waves crashing against a sea wall. I just wanted to crawl into bed. "You sure it's the right David Cox?"

"Yeah. He runs a start-up—some kind of tech product called an SAS, whatever that means. Anyway, he is LinkedIn to Madison and sung her praises on her recommendation page."

If David left his wife, he would no longer be living at home. And even if he was back with his wife, probably best not to show up and raise the suspicions of his wife—who might or might not know what transpired between her husband and Madison. There was also the possibility, albeit remote, that his wife had known about the infidelity and had sought revenge. "Where's his office?"

"Also Hoboken. I'll text you all his info."

I took the exit and reentered the Parkway, now heading south.

❋

"HOW CAN I be of help?" David Cox asked.

"We are speaking to all of Mad Bell's clients, Mr. Cox. Seeing if anyone has any information that can shed light on this case." Not exactly true, but come to think of it, not a bad idea.

David Cox shifted slightly in his mesh-backed ergonomically designed chair. My chair, situated on the other side of his desk, was a standard-issue gray swivel chair.

"So, Mr. Cox—"

"David, please."

"David, is there anything you can think of, perhaps something Madison said, that might be relevant to this case?"

He dropped his head and shook it slightly, exposing a small round bald spot on the crown. When he looked up, his eyes were glassy. He sniffled slightly. He coughed into his sleeve. He was clearly trying not to break down in tears. But then the floodgates opened, and he sobbed. I reached into my backpack and offered him a couple of tissues, which he accepted.

"I'm sorry. I don't know what came over me. I mean, I know what came over me. I just can't believe Madison is . . . is gone."

"No need to apologize. I imagine the two of you were close, seeing that she did a lot of work for your company?"

He cleared his throat and regained his composure. "She did a lot of projects for us. She was very good at what she did."

"I've been speaking to a few of her friends. Girlfriends she confided in." I let that last sentence hang in the air for a few seconds. "But best to hear these things straight from the horse's mouth . . . if you know what *I* mean."

He opened his mouth slightly, then closed it, pursing his lips.

His gaze darted around the room and landed on a photograph on his desk. I couldn't see it but assumed it was the kind of photograph most people have on their desks—their spouse or kids. The picture that shows him what is at stake for lying.

"Obviously you know what happened between us, but I swear I had nothing to do with Madison's murder, Detective."

"Why don't you tell me exactly what happened between the two of you?"

EDWARD ARRIVED at the station at four on the dot. His pricey lawyer was at his side: starched white shirt, diamond-crusted cuff links, tailored suit, silk tie, manicured fingernails, perfectly coiffed black hair with flecks of gray. Straight out of central casting.

Edward's bangs no longer hid his forehead. Sometime between Saturday and today he had gotten a haircut. He was now sporting a military look, close cut on the sides with a short spike of gelled hair shooting skyward. He unscrewed the top of a fancy-looking water bottle and took a sip.

I planted one elbow on the table, leaned forward, and cupped my chin in my hand. "So, Edward, you told me that you hadn't seen Madison in a year, yet your fingerprints were in a car that is six months old. A car that Madison borrowed from Dr. Samantha Fields on the night of her murder."

Edward slowly inhaled through his nose, exhaled through his mouth. "I can explain. It's just that, well, I didn't quite tell you the truth because it's . . . it's embarrassing." Edward paused and turned toward his lawyer. The lawyer nodded. "I might have also done something illegal. But obviously I've got to come clean about that in order to clear my name of . . ." He took a sip from his water bottle. "In May, I had a meeting with a client in Manhattan who asked if I knew where he could score some first-class weed. But I don't do drugs." He must have seen my eyebrows shoot up, and added, "Believe what you may, but I don't. Anyway, the first person I thought of asking was Madison." He shrugged. "Figured she owed me. The very least she could do was help me score for this guy. So, I called her and she agreed to part with some of her stash. She even said something about finally kicking the habit, so I was doing her a favor. And that is why my fingerprints are in Samantha's car. Madison stopped by my hotel and, because she couldn't find a place to park, she told me to come down to *her* car to pick up the weed. So when you told me she was found dead in Samantha's car, I had no reason to believe you would find my prints in that car."

"You do understand that just because you're now telling me that you were in that car in May doesn't mean that you were *not* in the car the night of her murder. Prints don't come with a time stamp."

"Well, that's the embarrassing part." He ran his tongue over his lips, swallowed hard, then took another swig of water. "On the night Madison was murdered I hired an escort. She was with me all night." He glanced over at his lawyer. "And that's the truth."

The lawyer reached into his attaché case and pulled out a folder. He slid it across the table. "Here's everything you need to follow up and confirm my client's story."

MADISON

Tuesday, April 2, 2019

Y*ou will never believe who showed up on my doorstep today. I still can't believe it. Sarah Steinberg. At first, I didn't even recognize her. In high school she was all goth—died her hair black and some other bizarre color, wore black clothes, sported Hot Topic jewelry, had that whole Avril Lavigne smeared-black-makeup look going on. Once bleak. Now chic. Talk about a transformation. Her hair a shiny reddish blonde. A touch of makeup. Pastel cable-knit sweater (she might have quit booze and drugs, but I detected a hint of stale cigarette smoke lurking in those cable-knit threads). And she's a rock star. I listened on Spotify after she left. Not my cup of tea, but she does have a great voice.*

Anyway, she stopped by on her "Making Amends" tour. That's what she called it. Which, I will admit, is pretty funny. She asked if I still used (was she trying to recruit me into AA?). I told her I dabbled here and there. So I lied. I wasn't about to lay my shit on the table with someone I haven't laid eyes on in twelve years. I thought she was going to apologize for ghosting me when we got to high school. But her apology confused me. She apologized for "introducing" me to drugs and alcohol, and that she "pressured" me when I said no. I have zero recollection of this, but if she says it happened that way, who am I to argue? When I told her I was sorry for stealing Rafael, she just waved her hand and said they had been on the outs anyway. I thought she might bring up the stabbing incident (a journal entry for another day), but she didn't, so neither did I. Camilla once told me that she saw Sarah and Joanna fighting that night. Maybe Joanna is a stop on her "Making Amends" tour. But here's the thing, dear journal, I really like her. She seems like a good person, someone I can talk to and trust. I think I found a new friend. Well, an old new friend! Yay for me!! We've already made plans to get together in a couple of weeks before she heads out on her Europe tour.

11

WEDNESDAY | JULY 10, 2019

DAD SQUATTED to pet Moxie, who was splayed out on the tiled entryway. She turned onto her back, exposing her belly.

"Such a good girl. You like that, huh?" Dad said, rubbing her underside. He looked up at me. "Ready to swap notes?"

He'd told me in a quick text that he had dug up some information on a connection between Oliver Finch and Todd Garmin and was eager to share. I had some interesting updates to share as well. Our conversation would be like a pissing contest—the winner, the one with the juicier story. Mine was good, but I suspected his was better.

We settled in the living room. I went first. I explained why Edward's fingerprints were on the glove compartment latch and how a high-priced escort alibied him out. I also briefed him on my conversation with rocker Sarah Steinberg.

Then I filled him in on what had transpired between Madison and David Cox.

"Did Cox seem like the spurned lover out for revenge?"

"He wasn't exactly her lover. According to both Sarah and David, it was just a kiss. Of course, I don't have Madison's version of events. He admitted to calling her a few times to see if a future relationship was in the cards, and she made it clear it wasn't. He said it stung, but he pretty much accepted that she wasn't going to leave Rafael. He went on to say that although he was attracted to Madison, he knew the problem resided with his loveless marriage."

"Do you believe him?"

I shrugged. "He seemed genuinely bereaved. I'd like to think that I can suss out a liar . . . but for all I know, he could've been giving me an Oscar-worthy performance of grief and innocence."

"So you're trusting your gut?" Dad asked with a wink, knowing full well it wasn't the way I typically operated.

"Perhaps. But I've got Sally running down his alibi. Claims he was at a tech conference in North Carolina that weekend." I glanced at my notepad to see if I had left out any details. "I asked him if his wife would exact revenge if she found out. He said she's wheelchair-bound with a broken leg due to a waterskiing accident, so highly unlikely."

"So that's it?"

"Nope. David and Madison had a coincidental connection. When Madison told David she grew up in the Catskills, David told Madison his mom worked in the Catskills. And from there they figured out their moms knew each other. David's mother, Sheryl, worked at the Cuttman Hotel as a counselor in the seventies with Madison's mother, Robin."

"So?"

"Hold your horses. I'm getting to the good part. David told me that his mother was one of the last people to see Madison's parents alive, so I decided to call Sheryl Cox on my way home."

Dad nodded, rapt, and I continued, "Their friendship waned through the years, and like most relationships found renewed life through Facebook in 2006. By 2008, they had gotten quite chummy again. Turns out, she visited the Garmins two days before their deaths."

"Whoa."

"Yeah. And when she arrived at their home, she was introduced to another visitor, a man named Oliver. While she and Robin remained in the kitchen chitchatting, she said she heard raised voices in the den, like a heated argument. Alarmed, she asked Robin what that was all about. But Robin shooed away the question and said it was a tiff between old friends."

"Whoa again."

"When she first heard that Todd and Robin had died, her immediate thought was that they were killed and wondered if that guy had something to do with it. She'd found him *menacing*. Her word. But when she learned it was carbon monoxide poisoning, she felt somewhat relieved they weren't murdered. She attended their funeral, but she doesn't recall seeing Oliver there. She said she wasn't exactly looking for him, so she can't be sure whether he was there or not." I grinned, believing my story would be hard to top. "Okay, your turn."

Dad's grin was wider. "Okay. That was good, but mine is better." He rubbed his hands together. "After you die, Facebook does not take down your profile page, unless someone specifically requests it. Robin Garmin's page is frozen in time. Todd never had one. Anyway, back in 2008, Robin was planning a reunion of a few college friends and posted an invitation . . . like a Save the Date-slash-RSVP kinda announcement."

"And Oliver replied?"

"No. But I did reach out to the people who commented on her Facebook post."

"Clever."

Dad tapped the side of his forehead. "Computer King of Horizon Meadows, remember?"

"Yeah. Go on."

"The first guy I reached . . ." Dad flipped open a small pad and scanned the page. "Daniel Masters. He said he barely knew Oliver Finch and didn't like the guy. The next guy . . ." Dad looked at his notepad again. "Mitchell Bloom also remembered Oliver and reiterated what Daniel said. Not a nice guy. Kept his distance."

"Okay, so you established that Todd and Robin knew this guy, and no one liked him. Is that it?"

"C'mon Susan. I'm getting to the good stuff. I'm just laying it out for you."

"Well, can you lay it out faster?"

"Okay, okay. I got in touch with one of Robin's friends, a . . ." Dad once again scanned his notes. "Carol Beringer. From this one, I got an earful. But she said she didn't want it getting back to Oliver Finch. Anyway, Carol told me she and Robin were roommates freshman year, and that they lived next door to Todd and Oliver, also roommates freshman year. That's how Robin and Todd met. When they started dating, they would invite Carol and Oliver to come along . . . y'know, like a double date."

"So this Carol dated Oliver Finch?"

"Yeah. But not for long. She said he was intense and could go from sweet to belligerent in zero to sixty."

"Was he violent with her?"

"She said he wasn't. More like mind games. But here's the thing. No one liked the guy except Todd. And although others pleaded with Todd to cut the guy loose, Todd wouldn't."

"Okay. So now we know that Todd and Oliver were friends in college. We also know no one really liked the guy. So?" I kept my impatience in check. Dad had this habit of rolling out a story slowly, burying the lede.

"Yeah. So I spoke to a few more folks and got the same story. But then I found someone who ran into Oliver a few years after college and, man, he was quaking in his boots when I started pressing him about the guy."

Dad stood and started pacing, as was his habit when he got to the climax of the story. He stopped abruptly, then said, "Seems Oliver was dealing cocaine in college. His uncle, Charlie Finch—who was a bigwig mob guy in South Boston—hooked Oliver up and he was like a fucking Mary Kay Cosmetics salesperson, going door to door in the dorms selling the shit. After college, Charlie set Oliver up in a sub shop, which was probably a front for drug dealing. Seems Oliver had a knack for this line of work, and quickly rose in Charlie's organization."

"So, he would have won the pink Cadillac?"

Dad made a quizzical face.

"Mary Kay Cosmetics . . . pink Cadillac. The top salespeople got them."

"Oh right. Funny," Dad replied with an exaggerated eye roll.

"And you learned all this from this guy you found?"

"Yeah. He said he'd tell me what he knows if I kept his name out of the equation."

"And is there a connection to Todd in all this?"

"Getting to that." He sat back down. "In college, Todd was like a scout for Oliver. As was this guy. They wouldn't sell the drugs, but they sussed out who was looking to buy. And the two of them would get a kickback."

"Which explains why he wouldn't cut ties with Oliver. Was Robin aware of all this?"

"The guy I spoke to said she was. There was no way she wouldn't know."

"So, did this arrangement continue after they graduated?"

"According to this source, no. They seemed to have gone their separate ways . . . until 2002. Apparently Oliver invested in Todd's Shangri-La project." Air quotes around the word *invested*.

"By invest, do you mean put up cash as a way to launder his money?"

"Bingo."

"And this guy knows this how?"

"He stayed in touch with Todd through the years and Todd confided in him. Probably thought he could trust him with this info because of what they did in college. But this guy wanted to be like those three monkeys—hear no evil, see no evil, speak no evil—so after Todd told him he was back in business with Oliver, he cut ties with Todd. Claims he has no idea what transpired between Todd and Oliver after that year."

"So you're not going to tell me who this is *and* you want me to treat him like an undercover informant? I don't know, Dad."

"Look, the guy was forthcoming, and I'm not inclined to upend his life by dragging him into this investigation . . . and possibly getting him killed. I did a little research on him—he seems to be on the up-and-up. He's a children's-book illustrator. Married. One kid."

I was just going to have to trust Dad's instincts on this, at least for the time being.

We sat quietly for a few minutes before I offered up my assessment. "This money-laundering scheme goes back decades. I can't shake the feeling that the Garmins' 'accidental' death was not accidental . . . and that Oliver was somehow involved. And just maybe this is tied to Madison's murder. She might have kicked a hornet's nest with her inquiries about the unexplained revenue and expenses."

"Yeah. Thinking the same." Dad slapped his thighs. "So, what's your next move?"

I rubbed my hands together like that fly on the sugar bowl, then cracked my knuckles. "It's time to lean on Jacob."

"WAS IT really necessary to haul me down here?" Jacob asked, looking around the windowless interrogation room. His eyes came to rest on the two-way mirror. "Do I need a lawyer?"

"Do you? If you had something to do with Madison's murder, then that might be wise."

Jacob slumped in his chair. This is where the suspect knew they were trapped by their own question.

If he asks for a lawyer, he just answered my question in the affirmative.

"I had nothing to do with Madison's murder. Nothing. So get on with it, so I can get back to work."

"Okay, then. Just a few quick questions and you can be on your way." I hit the record button. "Detective Susan Ford interviewing Mr. Jacob Bowman. July tenth. Four o'clock p.m. Mr. Bowman has declined legal counsel."

He looked up at the two-way mirror again.

"Mr. Bowman, can you tell me where you were the evening of Saturday, June twenty-ninth, and into the early-morning hours of Sunday, June thirtieth."

"I already told you. I was working, getting ready for the July Fourth weekend. And I have a list of guests and staff who saw me." He reached into his leather briefcase, pulled out a piece of paper, and slid it across the table. "Go ahead, contact them. They'll tell you I never left the grounds."

I glanced at the paper.

There were four names.

Next to each name was a phone number and an email address. "You mentioned you would provide the email exchanges and texts between you and Madison regarding her intent to sell her shares to you. Any chance you got that in your briefcase?"

He lifted the briefcase and placed it on his lap, then pulled out a manila folder. "They're all in here," he said, handing over the folder.

"Okay. We'll see if they match up to the emails and texts our tech guys pulled from Madison's devices."

His nostrils momentarily flared. "Are we done here?"

"Not quite."

I had spoken to Agent Larson before bringing in Jacob for questioning. I told her my murder case and her money-laundering investigation appeared to be connected and it was time to confront Jacob.

After some back-and-forth, she agreed to let me have a go at him, but she insisted on being present.

She was now standing behind the glass.

Jacob shifted slightly, then glanced at the closed door. Sweat glistened on his forehead. Did he think he could make a run for it?

I leaned forward, getting as close to Jacob as I could. "It seems Madison caught wind of your little money-laundering scheme."

Jacob started blinking. Rapidly. About fifteen seconds went by before he spoke. "Um, money laundering?"

On cue, Agent Larson entered the room. She grabbed the chair leaning against the back wall, dragged it over to my side of the table, then sat down.

She tilted her head slightly toward Jacob and squinted, her expression stern and intimidating with a you-better-not-shovel-me-bullshit look.

I checked my watch, cleared my throat, and leaned into the recording device. "Four fifteen p.m. Joined by Special Agent Ginger Larson, Federal Bureau of Investigation, US Treasury Department."

Jacob's eyes widened.

"What can you tell me about Oliver Finch?" Larson asked.

"What? Who?"

"Oliver Finch. Seems you and him have some shared financial interests."

"What does this have to do with Madison's murder? And who are you?"

"As Detective Ford just stated, I'm a federal investigator with the US Treasury Department."

Jacob opened his mouth. Then shut it quickly. Sweat droplets formed above his upper lip.

"Seems Madison knew what you were up to." I paused, taking note of the tremor in his hands. "Did you silence her? Or did you get Oliver Finch to do the dirty work?"

Jacob swiped the back of his hand across his lips, then tucked his hands under the table. "I had nothing to do with Madison's murder," he whispered.

"What about Finch?" I asked.

His shoulders slumped and he pursed his lips tightly to thwart what he had a natural tendency to do . . . blather.

"We know about Todd Garmin's relationship with Oliver Finch," I continued, "and Finch's continuing business arrangement with you. Maybe you had no choice, or maybe you were a more-than-willing participant, but either way, you are in a heap of trouble."

"With the bank evidence we have, you're looking at some substantial jail time, Mr. Bowman." Agent Larson waited two beats. "But that can be reduced . . . depending on your level of cooperation."

Jacob sat up straighter, regained his composure. "If Madison knew what I was up to—as you purport—she said nothing about it to me. And I'm pretty sure there is no way you can link me to her murder because, as I keep telling you, I am not involved in any way, shape, or form." Jacob crossed his arms like a petulant child and leaned back in his chair.

Agent Larson clasped her hands and placed them on the table in front of her, giving her the air of a principal admonishing a student. "I'm not investigating Madison's murder. That's Detective Ford's jurisdiction." She leaned in closer to Jacob. "I'm here to tell you that we've subpoenaed yours and Finch's bank records and have enough evidence to charge you with money laundering, wire fraud, tax evasion, and a whole host of other related crimes. But today is your lucky day. Today, and only today, I'm willing to make a deal—ratchet down the charge from first-degree money laundering, a Class B felony, to a second or third. I want Finch. And you are going to help me get him." She paused, then added, "And my offer expires when you walk out that door."

He glanced at the door. "I'm a dead man if I talk to you."

"You'll be in the clink for twenty-five years and facing a fine that is equal to twice the amount of the money involved in the illegal transactions if you take the fall for this guy. The alternative, should you choose wisely . . . sixteen months to four years and a two hundred and fifty-thousand-dollar fine. Take your pick." Agent Larson crossed her arms and leaned back in her chair.

Jacob dug the heels of his palms into his forehead. He held that pose for about two minutes. "I need to talk to a lawyer," he mumbled.

"That's fair. Tell you what. I'm feeling generous. I'll give you the day to chat with your lawyer, think things over." Agent Larson smiled. "See, I can be flexible."

"Am I free to—" He belched slightly, grabbed his briefcase, and emptied the contents of his stomach into the leather satchel.

MADISON

Friday, June 7, 2019

M*an, it's been two months since I've written. To tell you the truth,*
dear journal, I was too depressed to write. I've just been so dis-
tracted lately. So many decisions to make. Decisions that will not only
affect my life, but the lives of those around me. Which secrets do I share,
which do I keep to myself?

Speaking of decisions . . . I decided I won't tell Jacob about my sus-
picions until we meet later this month. And what if I find out something
illegal is going on indeed? Do I go to the police? The FBI? Do I just keep
my mouth shut, sell him my shares, and never look back? My plan right
now is to let him think I am finally ready to sell my shares (and maybe
I will). I've already sent him a few emails informing him that I am con-
templating such a move . . . that should buy me some time. If Shangri-La
is a money laundering operation, even more reason to put that place in
my rearview mirror. And what about New Beginnings? Henry was confi-
dent that New Beginnings was completely legit. My shares revert to Jacob
when I kick the bucket. Although I'm damn sure he'll be in the grave long

before me—I wouldn't be surprised if he suddenly dropped dead from a heart attack or stroke. He can barely make it across the lobby without gasping for air like he just ran a marathon.

Rafael thinks I should hold on to the businesses as an investment. But is it worth the headache? Why Dad set up this crazy arrangement is a mystery to me. Grandpa thinks Dad hoped I'd end up running the places. But I was such a fuck-up then. Did Dad see promise in me? Promise I couldn't even see in myself? Was I blind to how they were only looking out for my best interests? Dad probably thought that Rafael and I would no longer be a couple after high school and so he was handing me my future.

But no one and nothing was going to come between me and Rafael.

12

THURSDAY | JULY 11, 2019

I GLANCED at the clock on the microwave: 6:56 a.m. I had gotten in touch with Rafael the night before to ask him about the high-school stabbing incident and to confirm Madison's whereabouts, but he was attending an awards function. From the string quartet and the clatter of dishes in the background, I pictured a garish event honoring unscrupulous hedge-fund managers who made the rich—and themselves—even richer. Would a husband in mourning even attend an awards banquet? Would a truly bereaved man be backslapping and whooping it up with fellow sharks?

Rafael agreed to a video call this morning before heading into the office. I wanted to *see* his reactions to my questions. Facial expressions, body language, even hesitations have a way of betraying (or confirming) what comes out of a person's mouth. At first, he pushed back on making this a face-to-face meeting, but he eventually relented when I told him the alternative was hauling his butt up here to Monticello.

I yawned as I poured my first cup of coffee, then made myself comfortable at the kitchen table. Rafael said he would jump on Zoom at 7:30. That gave me just enough time for two cups and a browse through my notes.

At 7:27, I logged on and Rafael's face filled my screen. Unshaven and bleary-eyed, he appeared to be adjusting his laptop to get himself into the center of the screen.

Was he hungover?

"Hold on a sec," he murmured. He stood up and padded away from the monitor. About two minutes ticked by until he returned holding a cup of steaming tea, the string of the teabag still hanging over the edge. He cleared his throat, then coughed into his fist.

"You okay?"

"Awards banquet ran late. Drank more than I should have. But I'm fine." He sipped his tea. "What did you want to ask me about?"

"Madison mentioned to a couple of friends that she wanted to clear her conscience about something that happened a while ago. Do you have any idea what that might be?"

He tapped his scruffy chin. "Like how long ago?"

"Not sure. Madison didn't reveal any details, which is why I'm asking you."

"I see." He nodded, perhaps expecting me to say something. "Well, I'll give that some thought. But nothing comes to mind immediately."

I observed Rafael's movement for some clue to the veracity of his answer, hoping to see him squirm, or clear his throat again, or blink, but he remained statue still. "I find it interesting that she told a couple of friends that something was bothering her, but she didn't say anything to you."

His jaw muscle tightened. "I don't know about your friendships, Detective, but there are things I tell my buddies that I don't—didn't— tell my wife. Not saying it's right, just saying it's pretty typical of most married couples I know."

"Is it possible Madison was involved in that stabbing incident in high school?" I flipped through my notepad. "On October fourteenth, 2007."

He scrunched his face and narrowed his eyes. "You mean the one with Sarah and, and . . ." he paused and dropped his head. When it came to him, he jolted upright and said, "Joanna?"

"Was there more than one stabbing?"

"Uh, no. It's just that your question came out of left field. Haven't thought about that in years." He rubbed his bottom lip. "It was Sarah who stabbed Joanna. Madison had nothing to do with that." He paused, then added, "And I wasn't even at that party. I remember my friend Matt telling me about it the next day."

"If you weren't there, how can you be sure that Madison had nothing to do with it?"

"'Cause she wasn't there, either."

"And you know that how?"

He scratched his head. "Wait, hold on a sec." He got up and walked away. Madison's cat, Penguin, slinked past the laptop camera. When Rafael returned, he was holding a small photo album. "Madison's teacher gave out disposable cameras to document the trip." He leafed through the album. He peeled back the plastic, removed a photo, read what was written on the back of it, then turned it toward me. 10/15/07 was scribbled in ink. "Yeah, just as I thought. She was in DC that weekend. On a class trip." He glanced at his watch. "Look, I gotta go. Is there anything else?" he asked impatiently, as though finding out who killed his wife (and why) was an inconvenience.

"All set . . . for now. If you think of anything . . ."

Rafael disappeared from my screen. No good-bye, just whoosh, gone. I stared down at my empty cup. Two was usually my limit, but the way that call ended irritated the hell out of me. At least I established that Madison did not stab Joanna. So what was causing her so much consternation?

And did it have anything to do with why she was murdered?

Another crazy thought came to me. Maybe Rafael *was* at that party. What if Rafael stabbed Joanna and pinned it on Sarah . . . and Madison knew. And it's not out of the realm of possibility that the visit from Sarah triggered Madison's desire to clear Sarah's name. But, and this was a big but, would Madison actually throw her husband under the bus for a woman she hadn't had any contact with in years? Nobody died. And Sarah found her calling. So happy ending, right? I glanced at my watch. Too early to call Sarah, so I made a mental note to check in with her later—see if she recalled Rafael being at that party.

As I poured my third cup of coffee, my phone rang. "Hey Chief. I'm on my way in."

"Afraid not. You're needed at Shangri-La. Jacob Bowman is dead. It appears he hung himself."

GLORIA NODDED in my direction when I entered Jacob's office. She was focused on photographing the body. Mark Sheffield handed me the suicide note, enclosed in a plastic baggie.

"I compared the handwriting to other notes around his office," he said. "We'll do further analysis, but eyeballing it, I'll say it's a match." He glanced up. "I was just about to take him down."

"Who found him?"

"Ryan Joyner. General manager of this place."

"Where is Joyner now?"

"He was escorted to his office and told to wait there."

"All yours," Gloria said, stepping away from the hanging corpse.

I circled the body carefully so as not to disturb the knocked-over chair to Jacob's right. He was hanging by a sheet that was secured to the rafters. A folded five-foot step ladder leaning against the wall provided the clue to how he got the sheet up there.

Or at the very least, provided a reasonable answer.

I held up the baggie and read out loud:

I'm a coward. I'm damned if I do and I'm damned if I don't. I either take my chances in jail or at the hands of a gangster. No thank you. I've lived a good life. Tried to balance the bad with the good. Perhaps not a morally upstanding existence, but when I meet my maker, he will decide. I proclaim my innocence in the murder of Madison Garcia. If she knew something and was going to report it, her murder does not surprise me at all. Madison's death is a reminder that no good deed goes unpunished. And I would have certainly met the same end. By taking my own life, I get to do it my way.

"Hmm. No mention of Oliver Finch," I said. "You would think, to be in better standing when he meets his maker, that he would at least have given us a name."

Chief Eldridge, donned in a crime-scene jumpsuit and booties, appeared in the doorway. "Holy crap."

Mark unfolded the step ladder and set it up next to Jacob's dangling body. Eldridge stepped forward and helped Mark lower Jacob to the waiting body bag. Gloria snapped close-ups of the now exposed neck.

"Is there any indication that he was murdered before he was hung?" I asked Mark.

He squatted next to Jacob's body for a few minutes, then looked up. "Based on a cursory examination of his neck, it looks like the sheet is the culprit. I don't see signs of strangulation by hand or ligature. Nor are there signs of a struggle. But I'll know more when I get him back to the morgue." He groaned as he stood. "Shit, my knees."

Eldridge stepped away from the body. "Let's get a team in here to go through this office. Which, pardon my French, is a fucking mess and smells like a goddamn gym locker. And get the computer forensics team to pick up the computer. Let's start connecting some dots between Jacob's business dealings and Madison's murder."

I CALLED Dad and brought him up to speed about Jacob's demise.

"What about the guy who found him, the general manager of the place . . . Ryan Joyner?" Dad pressed. "Maybe he's involved somehow."

I had taken Ryan's statement. The guy was a wreck. Completely freaked out. His incredulous reaction to the possibility that Jacob was laundering money through Shangri-La and J & T Tavern seemed genuine enough. He even offered up his alibi, fingerprints, DNA, bank records—the whole megillah—to clear himself of any financial and criminal mischief. Unbeknownst to Ryan, Agent Larson had already subpoenaed his bank records and failed to find anything tying him to Jacob and Oliver. She explained to me that, in a lot of these cases, the scheme holds together better if there is an innocent, in-the-dark person in charge of the operation. It's those guys that usually end up dead when they stumble upon something they shouldn't have.

I laid this all out for Dad.

"Hmm. So what's next?"

"Gotta wait for the autopsy report on Jacob. I'm also looking into who inherits Jacob's business interests. In the meantime, I called Crystal Booker—the girl Irving mentioned, Madison's friend from high school—and she's agreed to see me tomorrow morning. Perhaps she could shed some light on Madison's guilty conscience."

"Where does she live? Around here?"

"New Paltz. After seeing her, I might take the afternoon off and do the Lemon Squeeze at Mohonk Mountain House. She asked that I come alone because her daughter gets anxious around strangers, but you're welcome to hike with me afterwards."

"I'm getting too old for the rock scramble. But happy to keep you company on the drive. I can explore the Preserves while you traipse about on some boulders."

MADISON

Monday, June 10, 2019

R afael has been acting strange lately. It's like he's plotting something. If he's on the phone with someone, he immediately gets off. If I walk in on him while he's on the computer, he promptly switches screens.

Are we drifting apart? Our lives have become so complicated. His work is demanding. I'm having second thoughts about my own career. Am I going to write advertising copy my whole life? God, I hope not. Our five-year wedding anniversary is coming up in a few months. I turn thirty in two years! Shouldn't I be thinking about having kids? Isn't this the age where those feelings come on strong? Where is my urge? Why am I ambivalent? Maybe it's the weed? Gotta kick the habit before getting pregnant. It's been two months since I thought about contacting that woman who could help me, and I still haven't called her. Why am I procrastinating? I don't need a shrink to answer that question . . . it's as clear as spring water . . . I'm afraid. I have convinced myself that the weed quells my anxiety, quiets my mind, relaxes my body. Without it . . . well, I don't want to think about that right now.

I want to put all my energy into repairing my relationship with Rafael. I need to be the best wife, no, make that the best person, I can be. The person he fell in love with. The person who stuck by his side when everyone was against us, pulling us apart, telling us we weren't "right" for each other. He needs to be reminded of everything we went through to be together. That I love him so much that every sacrifice I made was worth it. Because in the end, we got what we wanted. Each other.

13

FRIDAY | JULY 12, 2019

"THANK YOU for seeing me," I said to Crystal as we settled onto her sofa. I had leafed through Madison's yearbook before paying Crystal Booker a visit, and the woman sitting before me hadn't aged much since high school. The only change was that her iron-straightened hair was now an exuberant afro, pulled up on top of her head with a bright green velvet scrunchie, her corkscrew curls pointing straight up.

In the corner of the living room a toddler just shy of three silently played with blocks. She would stack four or five, then knock them down and start again.

"Kelly is autistic," Crystal said. "She'll come over to greet you when she's ready."

"She's adorable," I said.

"Not when she is having a tantrum. It's quite scary, actually." Crystal closed her eyes for a moment, her shoulders rose as she inhaled deeply, perhaps envisioning a tantrum, then she slowly exhaled through puckered lips. "So, I'm not sure how I can help you. I was shocked when I read the news about Madison." Crystal glanced over at Kelly, who was still stacking and knocking over blocks. "I haven't seen or heard from her in ten years. I've caught glimpses of her life on Facebook and Instagram. But I'm not on social media much these days." She smiled in Kelly's direction. "I have my hands full with Kelly. I can't even remember the last time I checked my Facebook page."

"Well, I'm actually trying to determine if there was some kind of incident that might have occurred when you were teenagers, in high school."

"Oh. Okay."

"She told a few of her current friends that she wanted to 'clear her conscience.' Can you think of anything Madison might have done that she would later come to regret? Or perhaps she was keeping a secret that, if told, would have negative consequences for someone else?"

"Wow. I would have to think about that. I mean that was ages ago." Crystal scratched at the dimple on her right cheek. "Honestly, we did a lot of things that could've led to regret."

I picked up a wedding photo from the cocktail table. "Your husband?"

Crystal smiled. "Yeah. Ray."

"My boyfriend's name is Ray."

"And what does your Ray do?"

"He's also a detective."

"Oh boy. That must get interesting. My Ray and I don't share the same line of work. I'm a videographer. Weddings mostly, but I do pick up commercial work and some music videos. Ray owns a recording studio. He's also a session drummer. We met at a music-video shoot five years ago. Got married a year later. Then had Kelly three years ago." She glanced over at Kelly and smiled. "She's challenging, but I believe God gave her to us for a reason."

Kelly stood and padded over to us, her chin tucked into her neck. She was still in her pajamas, which she tugged at as she walked. Her complexion was darker than Crystal's, a closer match to her father's skin tone. Her curls were kinkier than Crystal's but free from any hair bands or barrettes.

She glanced at me, and I was briefly mesmerized by the color of her eyes: a vibrant jade.

"We named her Kelly because of her eyes," Crystal explained when she saw me staring.

Kelly lay down on the carpet at her mother's feet and curled her lithe body around Crystal's legs.

"Her favorite position," Crystal whispered. "This way she can be close to me without actually being touched . . . which she doesn't like."

I nodded in understanding. "My daughter, Natalie, works with a few autistic children in her psychology practice, and she's told me about the tactile and sensory issues."

Crystal glanced down, then spoke in a hushed tone, "I'm not sure I can help you with anything specific Madison might have felt guilty about. She misbehaved in many ways. Teenage rebellion, I guess."

"Because they wouldn't let her date Rafael?"

"Yeah. She thought her parents were hypocrites for telling her Rafael wasn't good enough for her, while her father ran with shady characters and her mother barely practiced Judaism." Crystal cocked her head to the side. "It's so funny. I haven't thought of this in ten years. But now, as an adult, looking back, we did some pretty crazy shit. As a mom, I would be beside myself if my daughter did half the things we did. Y'know, on the day her parents died, she was at my house. She was high as a kite."

"Can you tell me about that day?"

Crystal gently patted Kelly's head. She winced and rolled away. She stomped back to her blocks and starting building and knocking them down again. Crystal shook her head, but it was hard to discern if it was a reaction to her daughter's refusal to be touched or a reluctance to tell me what happened that day.

She sighed. "There isn't much to tell. I lived about fifteen minutes' walking distance from the Garmins, and Madison came over quite often. She showed up at my house that day and—"

"What time?"

"Oh, um, not sure. But it was an hour or so before the storm, so probably around eleven?"

"Okay. Just trying to understand the time line."

"Gotcha. So she came over . . . around eleven . . . and we just hung out. Her mom called her at some point—and I have no idea what time that was—and asked what she wanted for dinner. If I recall, her mom was trying to get to the supermarket before the blizzard hit. But what I do remember is that Madison said, 'meatballs and spaghetti,' then started singing that silly meatball song to annoy her mother."

"The one where it rolls off the table and onto the floor?"

"Yeah! We were pretty stoned by then. And still, Madison wanted to make hash brownies, but her stash was at home. So she attempted to make her way back to her house. But by then the storm was bearing down, so she turned around and came back. But when Madison got an idea in her head, she didn't let it go. She called Rafael to ask if he would go to her house and get it and he, of course, said he would." Crystal's shoulders shuddered. "I think if she'd made it home, she might have saved her parents. As we know, Rafael got there too late."

"Did she feel guilty about that?"

"I don't know if guilty is the right word. It's not her fault there was a storm. But she refused to talk about it. Can you blame her?"

I nodded. "According to her grandfather, Rafael was the one who called Madison to tell her what happened."

"Yeah. But Madison being Madison, she had broken into my parents' liquor stash, downed a fair amount of vodka, and was passed out in my bedroom. So Rafael ended up calling me. He was frantic, claimed he'd been trying to reach her all afternoon. Something about a flat tire.

The rest is a blur to me. It just got kinda crazy. My mom drove Madison to the hospital. I didn't see Madison for days after that."

"Obviously Madison had a drug problem. Do you think 'clearing her conscience' is somehow tied to that—snitching on a dealer? Or maybe she dealt herself?"

"No way she dealt. At least not in high school. I would've known. We just got it from other kids at school. It wasn't like there was a shady dealer on a corner. Most of us would just buy twenty dollars' worth of pot. Roll four or five joints. We're not talking big bucks here."

"Twenty for five joints? In my day, we could get five joints for five dollars. A nickel bag, we called it." I had no idea why I was telling this to her.

"My dad said the same thing when he found out what I was spending my allowance on. He was like, 'Man, that's some serious inflation.' Then I was grounded for a month." She laughed. "I quit the shit after Madison's parents died. It's why Madison and I drifted apart. I straightened out. She didn't."

"I think I knew your dad. Well, I knew his older brother, Sam. We were in the same grade."

"Yeah? Sam is doing good. But my dad died three years ago. Colon cancer." She sighed and looked over at Kelly, who was still playing with the blocks. "Kelly would have adored him."

Kelly started taking off her clothes. "Itchy!" she screamed. "I'm itchy. I'm itchy. I'm itchy," she persisted.

"I hope we're done," Crystal said as she stood. "Unless you want to hang around for the meltdown."

I stood and handed Crystal my card just as Kelly started screaming at the top of her lungs.

DAD TOOK the wheel for the drive home.

I twisted my right ankle just as I was finishing up the rock scramble and pressing my foot on the accelerator was mildly painful. It probably would have hurt worse, but a woman on the trail handed me a Vicodin like she was offering me a stick of gum. ("Want one?" she said, holding up the vial.) I was going to protest, let her know I was the law, but the thought of hobbling down the remainder of the Lemon Squeeze with a throbbing foot swayed my moral compass.

"How was your hike?" I asked Dad as I hoisted my right foot onto the dashboard.

"Less treacherous than yours," he said, pointing at my wrapped ankle. "Really Susan, you should have joined me in the Preserves. You ain't no spring chicken anymore."

"Jeez. Thanks Dad."

"So, how did it go with Crystal?"

I filled him in on the conversation.

"So, no real light shed on what was gnawing at Madison's conscience?"

"No, but I'm getting to know Madison. She was quite rebellious in her youth, and some of those bad habits carried on into adulthood. Hard to say if her past is related to her murder. But that girl harbored secrets."

"Speaking of secrets . . ." Dad tapped the steering wheel. "I'm not too keen on this little tit-for-tat shit you've concocted to repair the damage caused by your mother's betrayal. You including me *unofficially* in this case in exchange for having some come-to-Jesus talks with your mom is over. Either you want my two cents, or you don't."

I wondered how long he'd rehearsed those lines. Probably in the time it took him to hike the Preserves.

"Well, Mom is with you on that. She came to see me and told me to butt out. She isn't keen on me engineering a kumbaya moment between the two of you."

Like Madison, I too carried bad habits from childhood into adulthood. This desire to be the peacekeeper between my warring parents.

This strong impulse to create harmony, when, quite frankly, neither of them showed any hankering to be harmonized. What my mother did was unforgivable, if you look at it with an unbiased eye. While my father toiled for years trying to solve a missing-persons case, my mother knew all along where that missing woman was (and why she disappeared). That woman—Trudy Solomon—was my father's white whale. He was obsessed with the case until the clues diminished and resources dried up. That case made him feel like a failure. And obviously Mom didn't give a shit. Yeah, she was dealing with her own demons—alcoholism, loneliness, a disappointing life—but still! Was she so blind to see that her decision to hold back key information about a missing person was incredibly hurtful to Dad? I forgave her. But for Dad, I'm not so sure there is really a way forward to forgiving her. Mom was right, I had no right to butt in and bribe him to talk to her.

We sat in silence for a while. Dad was probably stewing about me meddling in his life. I was mulling my next move on the Madison case. And there was really just one move . . . it was time to confront Oliver Finch.

MADISON

Friday, June 14, 2019

Yesterday I was at Bloomingdale's, and I saw a woman with an ador- able little girl, and for a moment, I got that twinge for motherhood. But that sensation lasted a hot minute until the girl, seemingly out of nowhere, threw herself down on the floor and pitched a tantrum. The mom scooped her up and dashed out of the store. Then it dawned on me who she was. Crystal Booker.

Crystal was my best friend in high school. (Although, can you really have a best if she is your only friend?) I think our friendship was based on one shared activity: smoking pot.

Crystal's house was my refuge: an easy walk from my house to hers and a place to escape when my parents were bickering. Their fights were not knockdown drag-out events. There was just this constant tension that hung in the air between them like a fumigant. Sometimes they argued about me when they thought I was out of earshot. Looking back, I will admit that my behavior was concerning, but they blamed each for my rebellious nature. Mom would tell Dad that he wasn't around enough.

Then Dad would tell Mom she was too hard on me. Then Mom would tell Dad she was sick of being the disciplinarian in his absence. Then Dad would tell Mom that everything he does, he does for the family. And on and on it went. Instead of finding common ground to try and fix the dynamic, they retreated to their separate corners and left me to my own devices. Except when it came to Rafael. On this, they were a united front. However much they blamed each other, they blamed Rafael even more. They refused to get to know him. They refused to believe we were madly in love.

I was at Crystal's house the day it happened. There are a lot of "what ifs" associated with that day. The biggest being: what if Rafael didn't get a flat tire? He would have made it to my parents' house in time. It's like that movie Sliding Doors . . . *one little blip in time changes the trajectory of your life.*

Rafael pleaded with me to cut ties with Crystal afterwards. He blamed her for my predilection for marijuana. That was a bit unfair, since I was in much deeper than she was. But Crystal avoided me as well. I heard she stopped smoking and boozing after that day.

I was a screwup. Making bad decisions left and right. Maybe this is the sign! I think seeing Crystal has strengthened my resolve to "do the right thing." Because I can't move forward until I rectify my sins from the past.

14

SATURDAY | JULY 13, 2019

AS I crossed the George Washington Bridge from the Jersey side to the New York side, I got a call from Sally confirming Jacob's alibi. I had asked her to follow up with the list of people Jacob claimed could vouch for his whereabouts on the night of Madison's murder.

Turns out one of the women on his list, Jane Smith, was also his lover. Jane told Sally that he came to her cottage at 10:15 p.m. and didn't leave until 7:30 the next morning. She went on to say he took a sleeping aid at midnight, rendering him out cold by 12:30. The other three people, two employees and one guest, all recall seeing Jacob between eight o'clock and ten o'clock, either working in his office or heading off to Jane's cottage.

Jane, quite distraught when questioned, told Sally that their relationship was purely sexual. ("He was into S and M, and I played the dominatrix role," she offered up.)

"People never cease to surprise me," Sally said. "Who woulda thunk that guy was into that?"

"As long as they're not hurting anyone, what they do behind closed doors shouldn't cloud our judgment."

"Well, his alibi is rock solid and his fingerprints were not found in the car. And I can't picture him stabbing someone with such precision . . . he's a somewhat sloppy kind of guy. I don't think Jacob is your doer. But that's just my take." Sally cleared her throat. "Did you hear back from Sarah Steinberg? Y'know about whether Rafael was at that party?"

"Yeah. Sorry, forgot to tell you. She's pretty certain he wasn't there. She said she was so mad at Madison, that if he was there alone, she would have seduced him just to get back at her."

"Jeez. Talk about teenage drama. So glad those days are behind me." Sally groaned.

"Speaking of drama, how about that other line of inquiry you're chasing? With that redheaded Fed that showed up a few days ago."

"I'll fill you in on the deets when I get back," I replied as I merged onto the West Side Highway heading in the direction of the redheaded Fed.

AGENT LARSON felt she had enough to bring Oliver Finch in on money-laundering charges, and I certainly had a fair amount of circumstantial evidence to connect him to Madison's murder. Well, at least enough to warrant a face-to-face. I was still waiting on the final autopsy results to confirm Jacob's death was caused by the sheet, not human hands or some other kind of ligature. Of course, someone could have coerced him to take his life.

"Without Jacob, we have no one to roll over on this guy, so normally I would say it's premature to even bring Finch in," Agent Larson said to me as we headed over to the bureau's office in lower Manhattan. "So, the purpose of this interrogation is to rattle his cage. Let him think we got enough to nail him . . . on both charges. Then we watch what he does in his attempt to cover this up. That's where these guys always fuck it up." She tapped the side of her forehead. "They think they're smarter than we are."

I limped up the stairs, favoring my left foot.

"You okay?"

"Yeah, just twisted my ankle yesterday. I'll just pop a few Advil when we get settled."

Between the steamy July day and the throb in my ankle, I was in a sour mood. A break in the case would elevate my spirits.

THE INTERROGATION room was dim. The fluorescent lights hummed erratically above our heads like deranged bees. One long bulb was out. The protective casing was yellowed and dingy, casting a muted glow on the table.

Oliver Finch sat on one side with his high-priced lawyer. Agent Larson and I occupied the other. Oliver sat in stony silence, his hands clasped on the table, as Agent Larson and I laid out our cases, sticking to generalizations for the time being, trying to gauge his reaction. He fidgeted with his pinky ring occasionally but for the most part maintained his stoic expression.

When Larson was done speaking, Finch turned his head slightly and glanced at the "No Smoking" sign plastered to the right of the door. He reached into his shirt pocket, removed a sleeve of Nicorette gum, pushed one of the Chiclet-shaped pieces through the silver membrane, and popped it into his mouth. Closing his eyes momentarily, he curled his lips up slightly as the rush of nicotine hit his system.

His Armani-clad lawyer warned us that we were harassing an upstanding gentleman who gave generously to the community, blah, blah, blah. He insisted Oliver was a legitimate, albeit ruthless, businessman who invested in hotels and casinos—and the shifting of money was merely a strategic maneuver to make sure his investments were going to the right places. That his dealings with Shangri-La and J & T Tavern go back to a time when Todd Garmin needed an infusion of investment dollars, and Oliver, being a good friend, was happy to help, and to this day continues to invest in the businesses in a perfectly up-and-up manner. Emphasis on *perfectly up-and-up*. As far as his connection to Madison, the lawyer told us Oliver hadn't seen or spoken to Madison since she departed for college ten years ago.

"If I may—" Oliver interrupted his lawyer.

The lawyer touched Oliver's sleeve and glanced at him sideways. He turned back to Agent Larson. "Unless you have evidence that backs up these accusations, I'm afraid we are done here."

"It seems Mr. Finch has something he wants to say," I said to the lawyer, then turned to Oliver. "Is that right?"

Oliver cleared his throat and held up his hand toward his lawyer. "I just wanted to reiterate that I have not seen Madison in ten years. Her mother, Robin, and I did not get along, and she asked me to steer clear of her daughter. And I did . . . even after their deaths."

"What was the issue between you and Robin? Does it have anything to do with the argument you had with Todd right before his death?"

"I have no idea what you're referring to," Oliver said. His steel-gray eyes narrowed slightly, more inquisitive than menacing, but still unsettling. As if reading my mind, he relaxed his facial muscles into neutral territory.

"We have a witness who heard you arguing with Todd a couple of days before he died."

His stoic expression morphed to that of indignation. A flash of anger that dissipated as quickly as it had come on. "So what? We argued. Friends argue from time to time . . . so do business associates. Doesn't mean I was, as you say, laundering money. And some argument I had with Todd ten years ago certainly doesn't have anything to do with Madison's murder."

The lawyer coughed into his fist. "That's enough."

Agent Larson leaned forward, planted her elbow on the table and placed the back of her hand under her chin. "We're just getting started, gentlemen. Just thought you should know where things stand right now. Whether it's money laundering or murder, we will get to the bottom of this."

MADISON

Saturday, June 15, 2019

*I*t's 2:30 a.m. now and I'm in my office. It happened again. I bolted upright in the middle of the night. I could have sworn I let out a scream, but when I glanced over at Rafael, he was fast asleep. Dry tears were caked on my cheeks. My skin was moist and clammy. In this recurring nightmare everything around me is black, but I can make out a shadowy figure walking haltingly toward me. The face is obscured or the light is too dim to make out any features. Is it a man? A woman? A monster? As it looms closer, I can hear it whispering gibberish and I am jolted out of sleep fearing its intention.

I could use a hit right now, but I want to keep my promise to Rafael—that I am weaning off, smoking less.

Speaking of weed . . . I got a call from Edward last month. Which was surprising. But not as surprising as the reason why he was contacting me. He needed some top-grade marijuana for a client and thought of me! Isn't that sweet! I owed him. Big time. Met him in the city, parted with some good stuff and wished him well. He didn't wish me well. But I get that.

Why these nightmares? Why now? Are they an ominous warning that needs to be heeded? A faceless figure burrowed in the recesses of my brain, hellbent on sending a message? My subconscious whispering, "The truth will set you free! Pay your penance! Show some contrition!"

No matter what happens I know Rafael will stick by me.

I'm pretty sure he will.

I think he will.

Maybe he will.

I hope he will.

15

SUNDAY | JULY 14, 2019

"MOM, YOU might want to make yourself scarce," I said, parting the curtains in the living room.

"Tossing me out? I just got here."

I glanced at my watch. She had been here for at least one hour.

"Dad's here. We got into a bit of a tiff on our way back from New Paltz and he wants to talk to me."

"A tiff about me?"

"Yeah, but it's actually my fault because of this stupid scheme I cooked up to try and get you two to reconcile." I waited a beat, then added, "I'm just afraid you'll . . . you know what."

"Oh my God, just say it, Susan. Drink. The word is *drink*." She reached into her purse and pulled out what appeared to be a dark blue poker chip. She rubbed it between her thumb and pointer, then held it up. "See what I got on June fifteenth? I'm proud of this, Susan. Six months. Not a drink. Sure I crave the damn shit, but I'm doing okay. What happened between your father and me is not going to set me back. Trust me on that. There are a whole host of other things more likely to shove me off the wagon." She wagged the chip at me, then added, "Like you making a big f-ing deal out of it."

The doorbell rang.

Mom stood up. I thought she would slip out the back, but she limped toward the front door. She took a deep breath and opened it.

"Will," she said as she squeezed past him.

"Vera," he replied in a similar monotone.

"She didn't need to leave on my account," Dad said when she was out of earshot. She turned momentarily and waved.

"She was just leaving anyway. What's up?" I led him to the living room and we plopped down on the couch.

"I want to apologize for my grousing in the car the other day and banging heads with you about Irving." He ran his fingers through his hair and sighed. "I'll admit, I have a tiny blind spot when it comes to friends and family."

It was a decent-enough apology and one I was willing to accept. We were knocking heads quite a bit lately, some of it his fault, some of it mine.

"Apology accepted."

A thin smile broke out on his face. "Appreciate that."

I slapped my palms on my thighs, then stood. "I want to show you something."

Dad followed me to my home office—a three-season porch converted into a small room—at the back of the house.

I decided to put the whiteboards I'd bought for the Trudy Solomon case back into use. A dingy white sheet was draped over the board to hide it from prying eyes. As I lifted the sheet, Dad eyed the board. His gaze landed on a picture of Madison.

He sighed. "So young."

Our suspects' photos were lined up in a horizontal row: Rafael Garmin, Annabelle Pratt, Irving Feinberg, Jacob Bowman, Oliver

Finch, Edward Moore, David Cox. I surveyed the board. "They all lied. They all have secrets. They all have motives. But they all have solid alibis . . . well, everyone except Rafael and Oliver. And of course, there is the unknown sub."

"Right. Could be a drug dealer, a drug client, or the person who stands to get in trouble if Madison's conscience-clearing involves someone else, perhaps an old friend." Dad backed away from the whiteboard. "And of course, this could still be a random robbery gone south."

"If Rafael was having an affair, that makes him my number one."

"What makes you think Rafael was having an affair?" Dad asked, his eyes focused on Rafael's photograph. "Edward said he was devoted to her."

"Edward hadn't been around them this past year . . . well except to score some weed. Dr. Samantha Fields told me that Madison was suspicious. I just haven't found anything concrete . . . yet."

"You gotta use your instincts, Susan." Dad punched at his gut. "Chasing flimsy leads and nonexistent evidence will have you running around in circles."

"Methodically following leads and evidence, even if they seem inconsequential, is what good detectives do, Dad. That's what I'm doing here. Digging deeper into the web of secrets and lies surrounding Madison's life. Not to mention, keeping emotions at bay, which you seem not to be able to do."

Dad groaned. "Give me a break. It seems to me that you're the one unable to keep *your* emotions at bay here. You have it in for Rafael for no good reason. You're jumping to the conclusion that he's been unfaithful when nothing has come to light. It feels like you're projecting some kind of personal experience on him."

"Are you kidding me? Didn't you just apologize five minutes ago, admitting that you have, as you put it, a tiny blind spot when it comes to family and friends? I don't have a blind spot. I'm looking at this with eyes wide open."

He stared at the whiteboard. "I just think you're barking up the wrong tree, looking at Madison's family. Excuse me while I take a leak." Dad marched out of the room.

We both needed a few minutes to cool down. I thought about the men who had cheated on me. Would they have killed me to be with their new love? I highly doubted it, but there were plenty of documented cases of this motive: uxoricide, the killing of one's wife. Maybe Dad had a point—a very tiny point—about letting my personal experiences with cheating men cloud my judgment about Rafael. I might not be as instinctual as Dad, but I had a gut, and my gut was not ready to let Rafael off the hook.

"You need to get Oliver Finch back to the interrogation room," Dad said as he hurried back into the room, obviously eager to move the conversation in a different direction. "Out of everyone on this board, he is my number one."

"Larson says she's working another angle on the laundering end. I just need something more than circumstantial on the murder to haul his ass in."

"Find anything on Jacob's computers?"

"Eldridge has got a guy working on it. And it's been given priority status. Unless Jacob was using state-of-the-art encrypted technology, which I highly doubt, the technician should be able to access all his files."

My phone rang. I held it up to Dad. "Freaky," he whispered when he saw Eldridge's name flash on the screen.

"Yeah?" I said to Eldridge as I turned away from Dad.

I plugged one ear as Eldridge spoke.

"Holy shit. How long will it take?"

I nodded as I listened. I turned slightly but didn't need to see Dad's face to feel his exasperation.

"Gotcha. Well, it's a break nonetheless. I just hope it tells us something." I hung up and turned back toward Dad. I tested his patience for a few more seconds.

"What? Are you going to keep me hanging here?"

"You are not to blab a word of this to Irving. I don't want anyone knowing what I'm about to tell you. Got it?"

"I got it, I got it. What is it?"

"Remember Rafael told us that Madison had a journal and kept it with her at all times. Well . . . it was just found."

WHEN I arrived at the station, Eldridge's door was closed. I found Sally in the kitchen pouring coffee into her *Proud Bitch* mug. She peered up, surprised to see me on my day off.

But she knew what that meant.

"Break in the case?" she asked.

"Yeah. Madison's journal was found." I poured myself a cup. "Hopefully it'll shed some light on what was going on with her."

She raised her mug and clinked mine. "Cool."

Eldridge's door opened. "There's my cue," I said as I turned and hurried to his office.

Eldridge motioned for me to sit down. He took his seat, clasped his hands, then placed them squarely on the desk with a gentle thump. "I sent the dive team out this morning—wanted to give them another crack at finding the knife."

The first time Eldridge sent the dive team out, all they found were a couple of Pyrex pie dishes and other random crap.

"No knife. But they found the journal, her wallet, and other small items that were probably in her handbag. All of it found below the far side of the dock."

"And the Louis Vuitton bag?"

"They didn't find it. Those items were probably dumped from the fancy bag into the lake."

"Can the journal be salvaged?"

"That's the sixty-four-thousand-dollar question. There are techniques to dry the pages and read the text. But it will take a few days. Mark can explain better than I can. Something about freeze-drying and infrared luminescence and changing wavelengths. All above my pay grade. I leave the science to the smart guys."

"Are you sure it's even Madison's journal?"

"It was as Rafael described it . . . red leather—although faded—with her initials on the cover." He drummed his fingers on the desk. "So where are we with the other suspects?"

I laid out where the case stood. Pretty much at a standstill. But the journal and Agent Larson's continuing investigation into Oliver Finch provided a sliver of a silver lining.

My phone vibrated in my back pocket, a tingling sensation against my right butt cheek. I let it go to voice mail.

"Keep me apprised, Ford. I got the family, the press, and the sheriff breathing down my neck on this one."

Back at my desk, I checked to see if the caller left a message. The "Bird Lady"—the mnemonic name I assigned to Eleanor Campbell in my phone's contact list—had left a long-winded message about someone who saw something the night of the murder.

I poked my head into Eldridge's office. "Might have a new lead."

He glanced up momentarily from whatever he was reading and flashed a thumbs-up.

"JOHN, THIS is Detective Susan Ford," Eleanor said. "Detective Susan Ford, this is John Snyder."

As John reached out to shake my hand, I held my hands up. "Just getting over a cold."

He retracted his arm. This excuse to avoid handshaking worked so much better than explaining my sweaty palm condition, I planned to use it more frequently in my repertoire of avoidance tactics. We followed John to his kitchen. He placed a tin of butter cookies on the round table and motioned for us to sit. I plucked a cookie from the blue tin and sat down next to Eleanor, across from John.

"I was telling John about possibly seeing Madison and some other person in her car the night of the murder and it got John thinking about something he saw that night as well," Eleanor said. "Well, I'll let John tell it."

John swept his hand over his bald head and scratched at the back of his neck. "Like Eleanor, I had trouble sleeping that night. The humidity. Man, it's something this summer. So I got up to crank up the air conditioner. One of those window models." He leaned over and peered down at the cookies. He lifted a pretzel-shaped one and polished it off in two bites. "As I was saying . . . I was cranking up the air conditioner and I glanced out the window and saw a figure walking along Route 42."

"And what time was this?" I asked.

"Eleven fifty-four." He added, "I looked at my alarm clock before I got out of bed."

"Man? Woman?"

"Hard to tell. But he or she wore what looked like a baseball cap."

"Height? Build?"

"Five nine, ten, or eleven. Definitely not over six feet. But not short either." He examined the cookie tin for a few seconds and removed a round one. "As for build, I'd say slim. Certainly not fat."

"Can you walk me through what you did that night?"

"Sure." He stood quickly and we followed him to his bedroom. "I glanced over at the clock," he said, pointing at a rectangular digital alarm clock on his bedside table. "As I said, it was eleven fifty-four on the dot. I got out of bed on this side." He motioned to the side closer to the window. "I went to adjust the temperature and I peered out the window, like this." In his reenactment of that night, he pretended to fuss with the dials and then looked up and gazed out the window. "That's when I saw a person walking up the road."

I peered out the window, gauging the distance. "Were they on this side of the road, or the far side?"

"The far side. Walking that way," he pointed. "Toward town."

"Was the person strolling? In a hurry?"

"Hmm. Just regular walking."

"Was the person holding anything?"

He closed his eyes momentarily. "A backpack. The person had a backpack on their back. But not like a camping backpack. More like a large school backpack. It had a huge bulge, like it was full."

It was about four miles between where Madison was murdered and the town. John lived halfway between the two. If someone stabbed Madison between 10:30 and 11:00 p.m., that person could easily be at the two-mile mark at 11:54, figuring it takes about twenty minutes to walk one mile, therefore forty to walk two, with perhaps a rest somewhere along the line. The time line matched up with Eleanor's statement of seeing a car turn down Firemans Camp Road at 10:30.

"Anything else you can think of?" I asked.

"The person was smoking." He brought two fingers up to his lips and pantomimed taking a drag from a cigarette.

I called Eldridge and asked him to get a crew out here to canvass the four-mile stretch between Firemans Camp Road and Broadway. Perhaps the knife and the handbag were tossed into the woods from the road. And if there was a cigarette, there was a butt. What do people do with butts after they inhale the last drag? They discard them. And that would be a DNA gold mine.

MADISON

Sunday, June 16, 2019

Mad Bell officially closed its doors today. For the past couple of months, Annabelle and I hardly saw each other. She opted to work in her cramped apartment on most days. We only got together when collaboration over Zoom or Slack or Filestage was less than ideal. That meant one, maybe two times a week. Although we never wandered into conversations about what she was up to with Grandpa, it is without doubt that it was on both our minds. However, there was this one time, about a month ago when she nonchalantly said, "I'd understand if you want to tell your grandmother." I got the feeling that she wanted <u>me</u> to break the news. What a coward! I just glared at her with my best are-you-fucking-kidding-me face. Early on, yes, I considered it. But honestly, none of my business. I've got my own shit to deal with. And in this situation, either way I can't win for losing. Tell Grandma, then Grandpa is mad at me. Don't tell Grandma, then the truth comes out and she finds out that I knew, Grandma is mad at me. I prefer the latter. At least it shows I know how to keep a secret. And trust me, if I have a superpower, that is it.

With Mad Bell in my rearview mirror, a new path lies before me. The reinvention of Madison Garmin Garcia. I've always wanted to write a book. A memoir perhaps. Oh, that would be an interesting way to come clean. No, I prefer fiction. What kind of fiction? I love domestic thrillers. Especially the ones with a deranged family member who has an ax to grind. What would Rafael say? Would he be encouraging and say, "You'd be great at that. Go for it!" Would he laugh and say, "You get the craziest notions sometimes." Would he shrug and say, "It's your life, Madison. Whatever floats your boat." Rafael has always had my back. If I was a betting girl, I would wager that he would spur me on.

Who am I kidding? Write a whole novel? Although, come to think of it, writing is a solitary endeavor and if I end up in prison, it'll keep me busy. See, there's always a silver lining.

16

"YOU EXPECT to find a butt on the side of the road two weeks after it got tossed?" Dad blew on, then sipped his coffee. "*If* it got tossed."

I stared out the window of Defilippi's onto Broadway, the main thoroughfare that ran through the town. It was 7:00 a.m.; traffic was light. A woman pushing a stroller hurried by. I wrapped my sweaty palms around my tall glass of iced coffee. Was Dad being pessimistic or simply realistic?

"Worth a shot. There's also the handbag and knife."

"I'm an old man, Susan, and I could throw a knife pretty far into the woods if I chucked it just right." He cocked his arm back, then flung it forward, demonstrating his imaginary knife throwing skills. "And you want to canvass a nearly four-mile stretch of Route 42?"

"A cigarette butt might be easier to find if the person just flicked it or dropped it. And if this person was smoking while passing by John Snyder's house, we just need to search a few yards past his house. Marty smokes, so—"

"Marty?"

"Ray's partner. I asked him to do a reenactment of smoking and walking along that stretch to figure out when our midnight hiker might have dropped or tossed it."

"Well, while you're playing scavenger hunt, I'll be over at Irving's." He noted my alarm and added, "Don't worry, Susan, I'm not going to divulge anything about the journal or the Route 42 midnight hi—"

"Dad, whether you like it or not, Irving is a suspect. You can't just waltz into his house and have a beer and shoot the shit."

"Jeez, Susan. It's just a friendly visit. See how he's holding up. But fine, point taken." He stood abruptly. "Now, if you'll excuse me, I'm going to order some Hot Dippity Donuts to go."

"WE FOUND three cigarette butts," Marty exclaimed, dropping three small plastic baggies on my desk. "One Marlboro, one Newport, and one of those nasty-smelling clove cigarettes." He laid out the photographs taken at the scene, close-ups of the discarded butts. "And here's a map showing where each one was found along the road." He pointed at the letters. "M for Marlboro, N for Newport, B for Black."

I held up the baggie containing the clove cigarette. "You recognize the brands from the butts?"

"Yeah. Years of smoking made me an expert." He chuckled. "Also, the brand names are close to the filter. And that Black clove cigarette is pretty distinctive."

I turned over the bag and looked for the brand marking. "I thought clove cigarettes were illegal in the US."

"They can't be manufactured or distributed here in the good ol' US of A, but you can buy them online . . . usually from companies in Indonesia."

"Well Marty, you're a fountain of information." I shook the baggies. "I'll get these to the lab."

As I stood, Eldridge called me into his office.

"Do any of our suspects smoke?" he asked as soon as I crossed the threshold.

"When Larson and I interrogated Oliver Finch, he popped a Nicorette into his mouth. Maybe he quit cigarettes, but there are plenty of people who chew them when they can't have the real deal. Also, an old friend of Madison's is a smoker. None of the other suspects, at least that I'm aware of. But a lot of people do it on the QT these days. Especially if others around them shame them about it."

"Yeah, like cancel culture."

"I'm pretty sure that's not what's meant by cancel culture, boss. But yeah, similar, I guess."

He grunted. A cue that this conversation was over.

I slumped into my chair and rubbed the sides of my temples.

Sally planted herself on the edge of my desk. "Is it bad as all that?"

"And then some."

My desk phone rang. "Yeah?" Sally peeled off my desk and headed back to hers. "Okay, cool, I'll follow that up."

Sally twisted around in her chair when I hung up. "New development?"

"That was Joe Randall, the tech guy. He's been digging through Madison's phone and computer and found a text exchange between Madison and one of her clients he thought would interest me. It appears Rafael has not been completely forthcoming about the blissful state of their marriage. This client saw Rafael with another woman and texted Madison about it." I slapped my hand on the desk. "I fucking knew it!"

Sally held up her fist. "Go get him."

ANOTHER TRIP down to the city. But this one was worth the two-hour drive. Couldn't wait to hear how Rafael was going to weasel out of this. I told him there was a new development in the case and I needed to see him sooner rather than later. He said he would leave work early and meet me at his apartment at five o'clock.

He led me into the living room, flicked off the television, and settled on the sofa in front of a half-empty glass of beer. I sat on the love seat to his right.

He leaned forward, his elbows planted on his knees, his hands clasped. "Are you here to report a break in the case?"

"I'm here because we found some messages on Madison's phone that need some explaining." I opened the notes app on my phone. "One of her clients texted: 'Hey Mad, you got time to chat?' Madison replied, 'No. Can you just text me?' The client texted back: 'You know how you suspected Rafael might be stepping out? Well, I saw him at Caledonia this evening. Just thought you oughta know.' Madison then texted: 'You sure it was him?' And she texted back: 'Definitely. They were having a drink at the bar.' I glanced up at Rafael. His eyebrows were furrowed.

"Jesus Christ."

"Gotta know, Rafael. Were you *stepping out*?"

"First of all, no. And second, even if I was, what the fuck does that have to do with anything. Is this the kind of shit you're chasing? Rumors, innuendo, gossip?"

"I'm trying to establish what was going on in Madison's life. Having an affair is motive for murder, in case you haven't been paying attention to, well, life."

"I wasn't having an affair. That woman I met at Caledonia, she's an event planner. I was planning a surprise fifth-wedding-anniversary party. Her name is Claire Montgomery. And I got plenty of email exchanges with her to prove that our so-called relationship was all business." His voice croaked on the word *relationship*. He began to weep. "Madison thought I was having an affair?"

"She suspected as much. She brought it up with her friend Samantha Fields as well."

"Fuck." He sucked in his breath. "She died thinking I was unfaithful. She died not realizing how much I loved her, adored her. I would never . . ." He chugged down the remaining beer.

Watching this upheaval of distress caught me off guard. My eyes started to tear and it took every ounce of willpower and blinking to keep the waterworks at bay. I had to admit, it felt like he was telling the truth. Didn't mean I wasn't going to follow up with this Claire Montgomery or take him up on his offer to read their email exchanges.

I cleared my throat to prevent my voice from cracking. "Give any more thought to why Madison felt she had to clear her conscience?"

He stood. "No. I mean, yes, I have thought about it, but I have no idea."

I tried to read his body language but couldn't tell if he was leveling with me. His emotional outburst left me a bit shaken and between my inflamed sinuses and Dad's insistence that I'm way off base trying to pin this on Rafael, I felt slightly off my game.

As we headed to the front door, Rafael stopped abruptly. "Shit." He massaged his right temple. "I got a call from Jacob's attorney regarding his will. Meant to tell you when you got here, but then you accused me of adultery and murdering my wife and it slipped my mind."

"I'm listening."

"Jacob left all his New Beginnings shares to Madison. Guess he never thought to update his will after she . . ." He sucked in his breath.

"And what about Shangri-La?"

He exhaled. "Seems he left his shares to a company called Mountain Enterprises. Ever hear of it?"

MADISON

Monday, June 17, 2019

I knew it! I fucking knew it! Lenore texted me this afternoon to let me know that she spied Rafael and some middle-aged woman at Caledonia tossing back a few drinks and whooping it up. She thought I "should know." Is this the smoking gun? I didn't want to jump to any conclusions, so I spent the rest of the day talking myself into the possibility that she is a client of Rafael's or a friend of his mother's. But when I asked him about his day, he said he was a slave to his desk and never left the office. I decided not to say anything. Not yet. Perhaps gather more intel? Maybe Grandpa's friend—the retired detective—would be amenable to some private-eye work. And let's face it . . . it's not like I've been the best wife lately. I had my own dalliance. Sure it was just a kiss. But it was still a betrayal. And I wish David would stop badgering me. He thought because he was no longer a client of Mad Bell that I would have a change of heart about being with him. I told him to repair his own marriage or move on. Can I even blame Rafael for seeking refuge in some other woman's bed—I've been moody and frightful to be around lately.

I don't know if my life can get any more complicated. A list of what I need to do:

1. *Cut ties with the properties*
2. *Apologize to Edward*
3. *Get in touch with Crystal*
4. *Confront my past head on, consequences and all*

17

TUESDAY | JULY 16, 2019

I AWOKE in the guest bedroom of Ray's friend from his college days. Ray had contacted him last night to ask if I could crash at his place in Brooklyn. Driving back upstate after my confrontation with Rafael felt daunting. I was drained after accusing him of adultery and murder.

Perhaps I was wrong to jump to conclusions, but what else was I to think? I had three good reasons for speculating he was up to no good. One, Madison confided in Samantha that she suspected Rafael was having an affair.

Two, the thing Madison wanted to get off her chest might have involved Rafael, a secret about him he wasn't keen on having exposed. And three, that text message was damning—a clandestine-seeming meetup at an Upper West Side bar had all the earmarks of an illicit rendezvous.

So, in spite of that heartfelt performance yesterday (or perhaps because of it), I still wasn't taking Rafael's word that it was all an innocent misunderstanding. I planned to meet with Claire Montgomery, party planner to the rich and well-connected (made abundantly clear by the descriptions and testimonials on her company's website).

I grabbed my phone. A text had come in overnight from Agent Larson. *Call me.* I took her up on her offer.

"I got that info you wanted on Oliver Finch," she said. "Finish up your breakfast," she added, muffled, as though she had her hand covering the phone's mouthpiece. "Hold on a sec," she said, clear as day.

While I waited, I heard rustling and at least two indistinct voices on her end.

"Sorry, trying to get my sons to the school bus."

"Should I call back?"

"No. They're out the door. Usually my partner handles morning duties, but she's out of town on business." She sighed. "Too bad you're not in the city. We could meet somewhere around—"

"I'm in Brooklyn. Near Montague Street. I've got some news to share with you as well."

"Great. I'll meet you at Lassen and Hennigs."

I GOT to Lassen and Hennigs before Agent Larson arrived and ordered a yogurt parfait cup and an iced coffee. I snagged a table for two at the back of the restaurant and settled in the chair facing the door.

Although Oliver Finch was tight-lipped during our interrogation, we knew from Dad's "informant" that Oliver Finch and Todd Garmin had some kind of financial connection back in the early 2000s. So Agent Larson had spent the last few days trying to dig up anything related to this so-called loan or investment.

Also nagging me was the fact that Oliver had seen the Garmins two days before their death, and the encounter was not a friendly one. Because Agent Larson had been monitoring Oliver Finch for some time, I had a hunch she could access the kinds of records that would take me longer to obtain. The kind of intel referred to as bread crumbs—credit card usage, cell-phone pings—which would reveal Oliver's whereabouts around the time of the Garmins' death, the week of December 15, 2008.

I spotted the mane of red hair as she whisked by the large panes of glass. She opened the door and glanced around until she saw me waving. She was wearing her standard black pantsuit with white blouse and carrying a brown leather briefcase.

"Fucking heat wave," she said, removing her jacket and hanging it on the back of her chair. "Look," she said, lifting her arms. "I'm already pitted out." She stared at my iced coffee. "I'll be right back."

When she returned to the table, I explained to her why I was in Brooklyn and brought her up to speed on the cigarette-smoking midnight hiker.

"Hmm. When will you get the DNA results?"

"It's on rush, so, hopefully, Thursday or Friday. But it could be early next week. There's a bit of a backlog." I scraped my spoon along the inside of the parfait glass and polished off the last bite of yogurt.

Agent Larson took a long sip of her iced coffee. "Okay, so here's what I got." She reached into her briefcase and removed a few sheets of paper. "I was able to obtain Todd's bank records as it's now tied to our investigation into Oliver Finch and Jacob Bowman. Back in 'ninety-six, Todd and Jacob took out a business loan. The bank paperwork includes the business plan for both Shangri-La and New Beginnings. The deal was that each of them would own a majority share in one of the two properties. As you know, Todd was the majority shareholder in Shangri-La, Jacob the majority shareholder in New Beginnings. They were essentially hedging their bets. If one of the businesses went under, they could at least benefit from the other one's business."

"That makes sense. The area was in a downturn, with the storied hotels closing and the Hasidic groups snapping up the bungalow colonies. There was the promise of gambling, but an investment in a venture like a new hotel at that time would have been a huge gamble." I sipped my iced coffee. "In hindsight, the recovery center was probably the better bet."

"Because of the opioid crisis?"

"Yeah. I heard that New Beginnings has no problem attracting clientele."

Agent Larson shook her head and grimaced. "The Feds dealing with that shit have their hands full. Anyway, back to our business partners . . . and Oliver. In January 2002, six years before his death, Todd applied for a loan for Shangri-La. I guess things weren't going too well. The bank turned him down. So guess who he turned to for help?"

"Our good friend Oliver Finch."

She touched the tip of her nose, signaling I was correct. "In June 2002, Todd opened a new bank account for a business he called Lost Horizons, Inc. Around the same time, Oliver set up a shell company called Sackett Lake Enterprises. A mix of cash and checks between four grand and eight grand started flowing into the Lost Horizons, Inc. bank account from Sackett Lake Enterprises."

"The varying dollar amounts to stave off suspicious activity?"

"Right. Those amounts probably wouldn't trigger a CTR or SAR."

"CTR?"

"Cash Transaction Report. Those generally get triggered with ten-thousand-dollar cash deposits. And to give the whole scheme an air of legitimacy, legit money found its way into that Lost Horizons bank account as well—checks and credit card transactions from guests. About six months after this account was opened, we begin to see checks paid out of the bank to—"

"Let me guess . . . another entity of Oliver Finch's."

"Not exactly." She paused and lifted her eyebrows, definitely for dramatic effect. "A bank account owned by a Charlie Finch."

"Oliver's uncle?"

Agent Larson furrowed her brow. "Yeah. You know of him?"

I explained what my dad found out from interviewing some of Todd's college buddies. And how Charlie Finch set up Oliver's first illegal storefront. "Do you keep tabs on Charlie?"

"He's dead. Died a few years ago. Lung cancer." Agent Larson leaned into the table and lowered her voice. "But you know that other thing you wanted me to look into?"

"Oliver's movements at the time of the Garmins' death?"

She leaned back and smiled. "There's a credit-card transaction at a bed and breakfast in Hurleyville, New York, for the night before the Garmins died."

"Whoa. That's the next town over from where the Garmins lived. So he was in town the morning of their death."

"And then guess what happens to Sackett Lake Enterprises soon after the Garmins died?" She snapped her fingers. "Poof. Dissolved."

I tapped my fingernail against my iced-coffee cup. "Do you mind if I throw out a theory here?"

"Be my guest."

"Todd, desperate for money, turns to his old friend Oliver for the dough. Oliver says yeah sure buddy, but a few strings attached. Tells Todd he needs a front for his money-laundering operation. Todd, perhaps feeling he has no alternative, agrees to the terms. Fast forward six years, to 2008, and Todd wants out or perhaps Todd is skimming. They argue."

"And you think he came back a couple of days later and figured out a way to kill them in a manner that wouldn't garner too much suspicion?"

"I've seen crazier shit. It's not out of the realm of possibility."

"Certainly not going to be easy to prove he had anything to do with their deaths. Staying overnight in a neighboring town is circumstantial, at best."

"It's something to throw at him. Rattle him even more." I leaned forward. "And Rafael just informed me who Jacob named as beneficiaries."

Larson tilted her head slightly forward.

"Jacob never got around to updating his will. Seems his lawyer has been on an extended summer vacation. He bequeathed his 55 percent shares of New Beginnings to Madison . . . giving her total ownership of his one legal business. So that will now end up going to Rafael. But Jacob bequeathed his shares of Shangri-La and J & T Tavern to Mountain Enterprises."

"How lucky for Oliver," Larson said with a sly smile.

"And Rafael." I tapped my finger on the table. "That there could be the motive for murder."

"Jacob's or Madison's?"

"Maybe both." An affair might not be the motive, but coming into the New Beginnings' shares just might be.

BEFORE HEADING back home, I arranged to meet with party planner Claire Montgomery at her midtown office. Interestingly (well, at least to me), her father was the dining-room maître d' at the Cuttman Hotel and her mother was a singer with a trio that made the rounds to various hotels and bungalow colonies in the sixties and seventies. It was almost as if every Jewish person I met in New York had a connection to the Catskills. "My grandparents went to so-and-so bungalow colony" or "My uncle worked at the so-and-so hotel as a [fill in the blank—waiter, bellhop, counselor, lifeguard, dance instructor, bartender, golf caddy]."

Claire was an attractive woman. Her sleek black hair was swept up in a complicated bun. She was slim and tall, and for some odd reason, reminded me of a game-show hostess. Perhaps it was the way she swept her hand across her body when she showed me her kitchen showroom. I pegged her at early forties, so it was not out of the realm of possibility that she could carry on with a twenty-eight-year-old man. Certainly more imaginable than the Irving-Annabelle tryst. Once we were seated in her office, she expressed her horror at what had transpired, although I got the sense she was more horrified over the lost income than the loss of Madison.

I read to her the text message Madison received from her client.

She laughed, then said, "People should really mind their own business. Me having an affair with Rafael? That would be something, all right. Besides the age difference, I'm a very happily married woman." She glanced down at the enormous diamond on her left ring finger and smiled.

"Why meet in an uptown bar? Why not here, in your office?"

"I had an appointment in that area earlier that day, and I live around there. I didn't want to schlep back to my office, so Rafael agreed to meet me at Caledonia. He figured no one would see us." She shrugged and rolled her eyes. "Guess someone saw us."

"Did he ever give you any reason to think their marriage was on the rocks?"

"No. In fact he seemed concerned about her. Said she was 'down in the dumps' and he thought this party would cheer her up. He copped to not being around enough, being a bit of a workaholic. So I could see why she might have been suspicious." Claire's Apple watch pinged. She noted the message, then looked up at me, one perfectly waxed eyebrow arched ever so slightly. "So, do you have any suspects?"

"We're chasing a few leads."

She nodded, waiting for me to elaborate. But that was not going to happen.

MADISON

Sunday, June 23, 2019

O*h boy, joy of joy, spent the weekend with Camilla at Serene Scene.*
Be nice, Madison. I haven't been here in quite a while, and it was
sweet of Camilla to invite me to join her. Rafael was working again this
weekend. Was he? I will not dwell on that.

We borrowed Samantha's car on Friday to get up here. Camilla got
into a little fender bender last week and her car is out of commission for a
couple of weeks. I'll be heading back to the city this evening. But Camilla
says she's going to stay through Monday and will take the Shortline bus
back to the city. I don't mind . . . after a weekend with her I can use the
peace and quiet in the two and half hours back to Brooklyn. Next week-
end I plan to come here alone and do what I need to do. So this might be
my last hoorah here!

Right now the two of us are relaxing around the fire pit. No fire, of
course. It's about a million degrees. And that's in the shade. Global warm-
ing is a bitch. I just don't remember an oppressive heat like this when I
was growing up. Camilla is obsessive about preventing wrinkles. She's got

a cap on to protect her from the sun. Me, I'm a throw caution to the wind kinda girl—no protection, bring on the tan. Bring on the wrinkles! That's what Botox is for.

She just asked me what I'm writing. Man, she's nosy. "C'mon, let me take a peek," she's saying repeatedly to me in her strange British accent. Yeah, right. I don't think so. She's good at getting what she wants. But not this time.

This weekend was a nice diversion for me. I need to figure out what Rafael is up to. I need to figure out what to do with my shares. I need to figure out my career. I need to figure out how to get on in life (and is it even possible to do so with this burden weighing on my conscience?). Man, I got a lot of needs. Which is probably why I need a lot of weed. LOL.

Camilla just glanced over at me and asked me what was so funny. I guess I really laughed out loud.

18

WEDNESDAY | JULY 17, 2019

IT'S BEEN three days since the journal was recovered from the murky bottom of Sackett Lake. Did someone chuck it purposefully, aiming to destroy it? Make it unreadable? Or was it merely of no value to the unsub? Just a piece of evidence someone didn't want in their possession in case caught? The knife was still MIA, as was the Louis Vuitton bag. Did the killer know its value? If it were me, I would've thought twice before tossing a three-thousand-dollar bag in the lake. Eldridge sent the divers back out today for another round.

The technician held the stack of papers like a doctor who just delivered a newborn, cradling it in front of him with two hands. He gently laid each page, encased in polyester film, on the steel counter. He did this without making eye contact.

He coughed into his fist. "These are photographs of the journal pages." He kept his head lowered, his eyes peeled to the papers. "When the journal arrived at the lab, we carefully separated the pages from the binding. We then placed the soggy pages in a freeze-drying chamber to remove the water, which allowed us to peel the pages apart." He cleared his throat, glancing at me momentarily before dropping his head again. "Then the fun part . . . infrared photography. By photographing the water-damaged documents with the aid of light transmitted by the blue-green infrared-blocking filter, the residual ink in the paper fluoresced in the infrared."

I nodded, pretending to understand.

He squinted at me, then added, "Ink has the property of changing the incident visible wavelength into longer invisible wavelengths as the light gets reflected on them."

"So you were able to decipher all the pages?"

"All but one. One page had been torn from the journal. When I separated the sheets, I found the edge of a torn page two pages before the final entry."

"So we're missing the third-to-last thing Madison wrote?"

"Correct." He stepped away from the table and, with a sweeping hand gesture, invited me to start reading.

There were seventeen journal pages laid out before me. One entry missing—torn out by either Madison or the perp. I walked down the line and read each page. It was fascinating to read Madison's perspective of the people and events in her life. Clearly she was wrestling with whether to come clean about something in her past, but none of the entries provided any revelatory clue to what that might be.

Then I read the first two sentences of the last entry, dated June twenty-seventh—two days before she borrowed Samantha Field's car and headed to this area. "Holy shit," I muttered. I glanced over at the technician, who was leaning against the back wall, his eyes riveted on his fingernails. I leaned in closer and read the entry again.

Thursday, June 27

Well, guess who called me out of the blue? Dad's gangsta friend, Oliver Finch. Dad wouldn't allow me to date Rafael, but he had no qualms about doing business with this guy. Said we need to meet—that he has a proposition for me. Am I in a God-father movie? Is he going to make me an offer I can't refuse?

This probably has to do with the properties. Maybe Jacob's behind this? Send in the goon squad to pressure me to sell my shares. Or does Jacob know that I suspect he is laundering money through one or both of the properties? Could my dad have been involved in these financial shenanigans with Oliver? It wouldn't surprise me. A few days before they died, Dad had one hell of a knock-down, drag-out with the guy. Threats were made. On both sides. I remember Mom had an old friend visiting that day. Man, I wonder what she thought?

After Oliver left, Mom was a nervous wreck for the rest of that day, full of I-told-you-so. Apparently she hadn't been happy that this man was part of their lives. And of course, both ignored me when I asked what the fuck was going on. But I have a feeling it had something to do with Dad's business and a loan that Oliver gave him to keep Shangri-La afloat. I may have been stoned half the time, but I wasn't an idiot. Oliver was a shark, and my dad was clearly the guy treading water. Predator . . . and prey.

I think I'm going to meet with Oliver. Why not? It's not like he's going to shoot me, tie cement blocks to my legs, and toss me in the river.

After reading and rereading this June 27 entry, I reread the previous entry, dated June 23, to see if I missed anything. But it was just about a weekend stay at Serene Scene with Camilla. Nothing out of the ordinary.

A SEEMINGLY endless stream of texts from Dad and two voice mails awaited me when I left the lab. One from Dad. One from Rafael.

I texted Dad to let him know that the journal revealed that Oliver Finch *had* gotten in touch with Madison, contradicting what he'd told me and Agent Larson. I added that I would call him shortly. He texted back a thumbs-up emoji. I could feel a lot of impatience in that thumb.

I returned Rafael's call.

"I just got a call from Madison's grandmother." He paused. "She knows. And I know you know."

"So now you know too."

"The question is, how come I wasn't informed of this when *you* found out about Irving and Annabelle?"

"We don't disclose every piece of evidence or witness statement. Why would we? Madison's grandfather's affairs are none of your business."

"If this affair is a motive for my wife's murder, I'd say it is my business." His voice reached an angry pitch.

"As far as we know, Annabelle and Irving were together the night of the murder, which, if true, clears both of them."

"Yeah? Because they told you so? Well, perhaps you should ask Audrey about that. Irving was home with her that night. Which means Annabelle's alibi is bogus. And if you did your job and talked to Audrey, you would've known that days ago."

I let him vent. He was right. Audrey should have been interviewed early on when I was establishing everyone's whereabouts the night of the murder. As much as I accused my father of having blinders on, I wasn't exactly seeing the full panorama myself.

"We found Madison's journal," I finally said.

Silence on the other end of the line.

"Rafael, you there?"

"Yes, sorry. And . . . was it helpful?"

"I can't go into details, but yeah. There's an entry about the suspected money-laundering scheme. I will follow up."

"Great." Again, a beat of silence before he spoke again. "Anything about whatever was bothering her?"

I weighed whether or not he had a right to know what was revealed—or not revealed—in the journal, then told him the truth: "Unfortunately, no."

IRVING AND Annabelle lied, the intent to give each other an alibi. Oliver Finch lied for an obvious reason—he did not want me to know he was in touch with Madison just days before her demise.

I called Dad. Told him about the journal entries and the fact that Annabelle and Irving had lied about their whereabouts the night of the murder—and I was bringing them in for another round of questioning. I ordered him to steer clear of Irving. I got no pushback, only a huge sigh. Then I called Agent Larson and told her I was picking up Oliver.

ANNABELLE FIDGETED with her necklace, a heart dangling from a thin gold chain.

I scanned my notes, then said, "First you tell me you were alone in your apartment, and then, when I told you I found out about you and Irving, the two of you told me you were together that night. Now I come to find that Irving was at his home. Care to explain the discrepancy?"

I was mentally prepared for the fact that this interrogation would be put on hold should she ask for a lawyer, but she just sniffled. "We *were* together that night . . . until about nine o'clock. He owns a cottage in Smallwood that he rents out once in a while, and it was available. He told Audrey he was working late, so he couldn't spend the whole night with me. I had an early client meeting the next morning anyway, so I decided to head home to Brooklyn that night." She plucked a tissue from the box on the table and blew her nose.

"Did you leave right away?"

"Yes." Annabelle uncrossed her legs, then recrossed them the other way. "We left the Smallwood house at the same time, around nine."

"When I drive into the city, it takes me about ninety minutes to get to the George Washington Bridge." I leaned forward. "Would you say that's pretty typical?"

"I guess. Yes."

"So if you left at nine, or even, say, nine fifteen, you would get to the George Washington Bridge at ten forty-five. Only, here's the thing . . . your E-ZPass transponder has you going over the bridge at one fifteen a.m." I showed her the transponder report I had been able to obtain through an expedited subpoena. Not easy to get, but Agent Larson knew how to pull levers. "So, I'll ask again . . . what time did you leave the area? Because from where I'm sitting, it looks like you were still in this area during the time of Madison's mur—"

"I pulled off on Route 6—the overlook, before getting on the Palisades." She slumped in her chair. "I had a few drinks at Smallwood. I was tired and dozing off. I slept there for a few hours."

There were no toll roads between Monticello and the GW Bridge if you took Route 6 instead of the New York Thruway, so I had no way to check out her new version of events.

"You do realize how suspicious this all sounds? Why didn't you just stick with your original alibi that you were home alone? I would have been less likely to poke all these holes in your story."

The funny thing was that I believed her. Perhaps Dad's Spidey senses were taking hold here. He was always harping on me to "trust my instincts." My instinct was telling me that Annabelle was not the murderer. She was just clumsily trying to get herself out of the frame.

"I panicked. I know, stupid. When I heard you found out about me and Irving, I asked Irving to give me an alibi, thinking that would be the end of it. I was nervous because you suspected me, and I just . . . I just . . ." She looked down and wiped away several tears with the tissue she was still clutching. "Sorry," she whispered meekly.

"It certainly is not out of the realm of possibility that you didn't want Madison to tell her grandmother about the affair and—"

"I told you . . . I had no qualms about that." She lowered her head.

"Perhaps." I leaned over the table and waited for her to look at me. When she lifted her head, I said, "I suggest you get yourself a good lawyer, Annabelle. Because if I catch you in a lie again or find even a smidgen of blood in your car, I will arrest you."

"My car?"

"Yeah." I removed the search warrant from my folder and placed it in front of her. "I've got a forensics team analyzing every surface of your car."

She burst into tears.

OLIVER AND his attorney arrived at around five o'clock.

Oliver would not leave the city without his lawyer, hence the delay. I was pretty spent and hoped I wouldn't lose my composure, or worse, fall asleep mid-sentence.

Sally escorted them to the interrogation room, where we let them stew for about fifteen minutes.

At five twenty-five, Eldridge kicked off the proceedings. He hit the record button, made the introductions, noted the time, then leaned back in his chair. He tilted his head in my direction. My cue to start.

I laid the page from the journal on the table in between them. "Go on. Read." They simultaneously bent their heads down, nearly bumping foreheads.

The lawyer finished first, looked up at me, and narrowed his eyes. "I'll need a few minutes, maybe more, with my client."

Eldridge and I stood. "We'll be back in five," he said.

WE GAVE them ten.

I was expecting Oliver to say that although he and Madison intended to meet, they did not. But instead he said, "We met for coffee in Soho on June twenty-eighth. I was interested in buying her shares."

"Why the sudden interest?" I asked.

Oliver shrugged. "Felt the timing was right. Heard the properties were doing well. The opioid crisis. Legalized gambling. A downfall for others. An opportunity for me," he said without the tiniest bit of empathy for those caught up in the tragedies of painkiller and gambling addictions.

"Good timing? I think you met with Madison because she found out about a money-laundering scheme. And she seemed to think you might have been involved. Was she threatening to expose you?"

"*Might* is the operative word here, Detective," the lawyer interjected. He put his reading glasses on and pointed to the paper. "Her exact words are 'Could Oliver be involved in these financial shenanigans?' Not 'I *know* Oliver is involved in these financial shenanigans.' See the difference?"

"Let's read on, shall we?" Eldridge said. "Tell us about this knock-down, drag-out argument you had with Todd."

Oliver cocked his head sideways and moistened his lips with his tongue. "Hmm." He scratched the side of his forehead. "This was in oh-eight? Long time ago." He shook his head. "I'm at a loss here. I mean, if Madison said we were arguing, I'm sure we were. But she was stoned half the time, y'know. So, her recollection of the intensity of our conversation should be taken with a grain of salt. But yeah, Todd and I argued sometimes about the business. I had given him a loan. I figured I had a say in the business. We butted heads occasionally."

"What made you think she would sell her shares to you?"

"I thought if I made a solid-enough offer, she would consider. I knew she wasn't particularly interested in, nor involved with, the day-to-day operations. I figured no harm in reaching out and giving it a shot."

"And? What was her response?"

"She said she would think about it, but she was mulling over other options."

"And did she happen to mention what these other options were?"

"No. I figured I'd let her mull and I'd just come back with a sweeter deal."

Eldridge gently cracked his knuckles. A movement I knew all too well, signaling his impatience.

I decided to change tack. "What's your relationship with Jacob Bowman?" I asked.

"How is this pertinent to Madison Garcia's murder?" the lawyer asked. "My client told you that he met with Ms. Garcia on June twenty-eighth and made her an offer for her shares, which she said she would think about. Mr. Finch has no motive to do Ms. Garcia any harm. And in fact, he would prefer she was still alive, because now her shares end up God knows where."

"This is pertinent because . . . because . . ." The room tilted sideways. A bright light bounced around the room. I blinked rapidly, trying to clear the fog enveloping my brain. I coughed up some phlegm. My eyes fluttered. Then everything went black.

19

THURSDAY | JULY 18, 2019

"HOW ARE you feeling this morning?" Ray asked as he hovered over my side of the bed, a mug in his hand.

"Embarrassed."

"I meant physically." He held out the mug of coffee.

I sat up and took it. "Exhausted, but fine."

His eyebrows shot up. I waited for the *I told you so*. But he just frowned, and said, "You gave us quite the scare."

Two cups of coffee at 6:30 a.m., with nothing to eat all day except antibiotics, had done me in.

That and the stress of two interrogations, neither producing the outcome I had hoped: closure on this case.

"Where's Finch?" I asked.

"Jesus, Susan. That's your concern right now?" Ray walked to the other side of the room. "Eldridge said you are to take it easy today. Finch can wait. He's booked a cottage at Shangri-La. He ain't going nowhere until the interrogation is officially over."

"I never got to ask him what he was doing up here on the day the Garmins died." I sipped the coffee. "Do you know if Eldridge got his DNA?"

"The lawyer nixed that. Told him to get a warrant if he wanted his client's saliva."

"Shit. Shit, shit, shit." I placed the mug on my bedside table and swept the blanket to the side.

"Whoa. Where do you think you're going?"

"Can't a girl pee?"

"Susan, Eldridge is serious. I'm serious. You are not to leave this house today. So go pee, but get your ass back into that bed." He smirked. "As that chick from *Gone with the Wind* said . . . tomorrow is another day."

TOMORROW FELT very far away. After Ray left the room, I called Dad to come over and shoot the shit with me. My brain refused to shut down. Dad would understand. He had an obsessive nature. It's what made him one of the best detectives on the Monticello police force. Now he sat in the chair next to my bed. He wore a pensive expression as I reenacted the interrogation. The expression shifted to that of concerned father as I got to the part about me fainting.

"Well, I'm glad you're all right. You're all right, right?"

"Yeah Dad, I'm all right. It's this damn sinus infection, these antibiotics, the goddamn humidity, combined with the stupidity of not eating anything all day." I pounded my fists on the bedspread. "Oh, and the fact that someone killed Madison Garcia and I am no closer to figuring it out now than I was nineteen days ago." I picked up my phone and it sprang to life upon seeing my face, a wonder, considering the puffiness in my cheeks and my swollen nostrils. "These are the pages from Madison's journal," I said, handing Dad my phone.

He mounted his cheaters on the edge of his nose and scrolled though the images with an occasional "hmm" or grunt. "Interesting," he finally offered up, handing my phone back to me. "Can you send those to me?"

"No. If you want to read them again, just let me know." I placed the phone beside me.

"Fair enough. I get it." He scratched at his chin. "Besides the revelation about Madison and Oliver being in contact, I don't see any smoking gun."

"Yeah, except one page is missing, ripped out."

"Madison could have ripped it out. Perhaps changed her mind about whatever she wrote."

"Perhaps." I reached for a tissue on the bedside table and blew my nose. "Clearly Madison was leading Jacob along. Sounded like she had no intention of selling him her shares but needed him to think so in order to extract information from him. So, he was telling the truth about Madison's intention to sell to him, because he believed that to be true."

"Yet, if Jacob did get wind of what she knew about the money laundering, he might have decided getting rid of her was in his best interest. The same could be said of Oliver. Maybe they were in cahoots." Dad grabbed my phone and held it up to my face. Then he scrolled through the pages again. "Most of her relationships seemed somewhat strained. She was at odds with Annabelle, Camilla, her grandfather, Edward Moore, her in-laws, the client she kissed."

"Even Rafael to some extent—"

The sound of gravel under tires interrupted our conversation. Dad got up and looked out the window. "Vera." He looked back at me. "You plan this?"

"No." Dad looked skeptical, so I quickly added, "I think it's sweet she popped by."

"Huh-uh."

"So I take it you're not going to hang around."

"I'll come back later." He winked. "Bring you some chicken soup."

MOM LEANED her cane on the back of the chair where Dad's ass had been just five minutes earlier. She parked herself on the edge of my bed.

"How's the knee?"

She swatted at the air. "Good enough. It works better than it did before the surgery. So there's that."

Neither of us spoke for a few minutes.

"So, I saw Will was here. Is he still helping with the case?"

Help was the wrong word here, more like consulting, but I let it slide. Semantics. "Yeah. Just exploring the possibilities."

"I heard about Audrey and Irving . . . and Annabelle."

"Word travels fast in these parts. Gonna tell me who you heard this from?"

"A friend of a friend." She grimaced. "You want to know what I think?"

I didn't answer because I knew she would tell me anyway. I blew my nose instead.

"Audrey has never been blind to her husband's infidelities."

"Plural?"

"Yes. And she's had a fling or two in her day too."

"And you know this how?"

"Your father."

"Huh? He knows this?"

"They had an affair."

"What?"

"Long time ago. Right before we split."

"Why are you telling me this now?" My sinuses started to throb as my blood pressure rose.

She puckered her lips, then sighed. "I shouldn't have brought it up."

"Well, you did."

"Can I say something here, and promise me you won't be mad?"

I rubbed the edges of my eyes as my sinuses continued to pulsate. Did I want to hear what she had to say? I knew she was still in the throes of making amends, taking personal inventory, admitting when she was wrong. Maybe this was that. "Sure, tell me."

"You put your dad on a pedestal. But he made mistakes too." She paused, then added, "I know I made mistakes. Big ones." She cleared her throat. "In my newfound clarity, I've come to regret my mistakes, come to terms with them, own them. Especially my actions that have hurt others. I'm not asking for reciprocity. Your dad doesn't need to apologize to me. I'm past that. I'm just asking for understanding."

My mind wandered back to the end of their marriage, when I was thirteen. Mom was deep in the bottle—vodka, to be precise. Dad was deep in a missing-persons case—a case causing him extreme consternation. It shouldn't surprise me that Dad found solace in the arms of another woman. I know it's hard for people to admit when they are wrong or hurtful. I'm not exactly above reproach. No one will mistake me for Mother Teresa.

I have personally experienced two types of regret. The more innocuous of the two: making a wrong personal decision (college major, dessert, piece of furniture) and regretting that choice. In those cases, you are, for the most part, the only person affected (having to stare at a dresser you hate for years, but spent so much money on, so are loathe to replace it). However, regret is usually not a solo act—it tends to involve somebody else, and usually someone with whom you have a relationship. This was the more insidious regret. These regrets are painful to think about—they are usually the events in your life that didn't pan out the way they could have, due to callousness or immaturity. Or selfishness. Upon reflection, I find that this flavor of regret can be traced to acting cavalierly or failing to recognize the relationship as worthwhile, and therefore inflicting damage of some sort or another, no matter whether you were aware of it. This is the regret that eats at you. Sure, you can feel sorry for having been that person. But you also have to deal with the dilemma that there is nothing to be done, except become a better human, or apologize years later. And what good does that really do? The deed has been done—the hurt inflicted. You can examine your past, learn from your mistake. You can't always right it.

What did Madison regret? What did she do that needed to be set right? What prompted her to finally want to make amends? And was there someone she would hurt or incriminate in the process? Hurt so badly it was reason to kill?

"Susan, Susan!" Mom said, waving her hand in front of my face. "Are you listening?"

"Um, yes. You don't need Dad to apologize, you only want him to understand."

She squinted. "Not that. About what I said after that."

My phone rang. Saved by the bell. Well, actually a ringtone.

"Detective Susan Ford."

"It's Rafael." He waited a beat, then continued, "I got a call from a financial advisor—an Alexander Drummond. He said he has been trying to reach Madison for days. She missed an appointment with him, and he was concerned. When he couldn't get ahold of her, he called me."

"He hadn't heard what happened to Madison?"

"No, he said he's been buried in work and never saw the news stories. So, I told him what happened." Rafael inhaled audibly, then quickly exhaled. "I asked him what the appointment was about. He said it was a follow-up meeting to one he had with her in early June but he didn't get into details because he wasn't sure if he could disclose their conversation. I told him that whatever they were meeting about might be pertinent to the case, but he refused to tell me anything about this."

"A financial planner, huh? If he's not a lawyer, then there is no attorney-client privilege."

"Maybe he signed a confidentiality agreement?"

"Do you think this has something to do with the properties?" I asked.

"That crossed my mind."

"Let me see what I can do."

20

FRIDAY | JULY 19, 2019

ALEXANDER DRUMMOND'S office was located in Scarsdale, but I was in no mood to travel eighty miles for a thirty-minute chat. He agreed to speak with me later that afternoon via Zoom. But first up, Oliver Finch (after a solid breakfast of Ray's scrambled eggs and sausage). Chief Eldridge kicked off the interrogation with a round of introductions for the record.

I picked up where I left off. "Here's why your relationship with Jacob Bowman is *pertinent* to this investigation: Madison was onto him and his money-laundering scheme. And since you and Jacob seem to have shared financial interests with money flowing back and forth between your enterprises, it is pertinent with a capital P. And furthermore, your client here stands to gain quite a bit from the death of both Madison and Jacob."

"My understanding is that Mr. Bowman committed suicide. So, unless you have evidence tying my client to Ms. Garcia's murder, we are done here. Unless you can prove that my client is involved in this supposed money-laundering scheme, we are done here. In fact, we should have been done here two days ago after your fainting spell. But here we are."

I ignored the lawyer's objection to this interrogation and turned my attention to Oliver. "You said you argued with Todd a couple of days before he died."

"You said that. I didn't," Oliver sneered. "I recall telling you I had no recollection of that argument. Some friend of Robin's told you that. I'm not disputing that we argued, I'm just saying I have no recollection of it."

"So, what happened after your visit that day? Did you leave, hang around?"

"I would have no reason to hang around," Oliver answered before his lawyer had a chance to intercede.

I opened the folder in front of me and pulled out Oliver Finch's credit-card statement from 2008, placing him in the area on the day of Todd and Robin's death. "Seems you hung around," I said pointing to the bed and breakfast charge.

"Okay, so, I hung around the area. Probably decided to do some sightseeing. Again, this was eleven years ago, so arrest me for a fuzzy memory."

"Here's what I think, Mr. Finch. I think you and Todd argued over that loan you floated to him in 2002. Threats were made. Maybe Todd was planning to expose you. Maybe Todd was stealing from you. No one crosses Oliver Finch, right? So you murdered them in a way that would look like an accident. Madison somehow knew what you did. Maybe she saw you, or maybe her parents told her you threatened them. Perhaps she brought it up when the two of you met. Obviously you can't have her making accusations like that. So you killed her."

Oliver laughed. "Oh man, that's some tale."

The lawyer crossed his arms in front of his chest and leaned forward. "Have you found any *real* evidence that backs up this nonsense? No? Then we're done here."

ELDRIDGE CALLED me into his office after the interrogation. "How do you think that went?"

I knew from his tone, he was not at all pleased, but I ignored the dig. "As well as can be expected, sir, considering we don't have any evidence, and the best we can do is catch him in a lie." This was all I could muster in defense of that cocked-up interrogation. "And speaking of evidence, what's the status of the DNA test on the cigarette butts?"

"Still waiting. Looks like Monday or Tuesday now."

"Shit."

Eldridge knitted his brow and scowled. "I hope you're not hanging your hat on a cigarette butt you found on the side of the road, Ford."

I FIRED up the laptop in one of the interrogation rooms and hit the Zoom link. Alexander Drummond was waiting for me. He glanced at his watch. I glanced at the clock on the wall. I was three minutes late. I was not going to apologize.

I made note of his credentials hanging on the wall behind him, positioned just so that his clients could see he got his undergraduate degree at Yale and received his MBA at Harvard.

A quick background search and I learned he left one of those big New York City corporate accounting firms ten years ago to open a small financial planning and advisory practice with his wife, Elizabeth Drummond, JD.

"Thank you for making time to speak with me," I said.

"Of course. Terrible. Terrible thing that happened. Still can't believe it."

"I'm hoping you can shed some light on why Madison went to see you. It might have bearing on our investigation into her murder."

"I couldn't speak to Rafael without first speaking with my partner, Elizabeth. She handles the legal side of the business. But she said that as long as I didn't sign a confidentiality agreement, I can disclose what the meeting with Madison was about. Now, if Elizabeth had met with Madison, well, client-attorney privilege and all that."

"So I take it you didn't sign a confidentiality agreement?"

"No. Madison was merely seeking advice. She holds shares in two companies." He shuffled through some papers on his desk and held up the one he was looking for. "Here it is. Shangri-La and New Beginnings. She wanted to sell her shares to two different parties and needed advice on how to go about doing that. Then she wanted to take the proceeds from the sale and anonymously gift them to someone. She said a high-school friend who could use the money more than she can."

"Who were the two different parties she wanted to sell to?"

"She didn't give me any names, but she said she was interested in selling her Shangri-La shares to an old associate of her father's and her New Beginnings shares to her father's partner. We were going to get into the details in our second meeting. But she did mention the 'high-school friend.' A woman by the name of Crystal."

"Crystal Booker?"

"She didn't give me a last name. Just Crystal."

THE QUESTION kept coming back to who stood to gain from Madison's death. But the answer seemed to be no one. If Madison *wasn't* killed, she would have sold her Shangri-La shares to Oliver and her New Beginnings shares to Jacob. And that is exactly what they both wanted and expected to happen. So was there someone who did *not* want her to sell her shares? Rafael, perhaps? He did mention how he thought now was not the right time to sell. Not to mention, he was the sole beneficiary of all the New Beginnings shares and Madison's

Shangri-La shares. Camilla, perhaps? She loved staying at Shangri-La and if Madison no longer had an ownership stake, Camilla might have had her privileges revoked. Jacob probably would've taken great pleasure tossing her out on her keister. No more Serene Scene. On the other hand, maybe Madison's murder had nothing to do with the businesses. Something personal? The cast-aside client, David Cox? The betrayed buddy, Edward Moore? The forsaken friend, Sarah Steinberg? The gallivanting grandfather, Irving Feinberg? The philandering partner, Annabelle Pratt? What was I missing?

I CALLED Crystal to ask her when she had last spoken to Madison.

"I told you," she answered. "Hold on, let me put you on speaker." After a pause, she continued, "I haven't spoken to Madison since we graduated high school."

"So, she didn't try to reach out to you? I'm asking because I discovered something that I think she would have wanted to share with you. Maybe there's a message in your email spam folder or Facebook messenger?"

"Hold on a sec," she said. I heard her tapping at a keyboard. "Nothing in my spam folder." The typing continued. "Damn, I can't remember my Facebook password. I'll need to reset it. Give me a sec."

I pictured her going through the motions of resetting her password, a regular habit of mine since I often forgot to make note of them.

"Holy shit. I got a ton of messages and notifications here. Step away from social media for a while, and, bam, it's like you went to another planet, cut off from all the . . . holy shit."

"What? Did you find something from her?"

"Yeah. She sent me a message on June twenty-eighth. What's your email address? I'll cut and paste it into an email."

Hi Crystal—Long time, huh? You're probably wondering why I'm messaging you out of the blue. I saw you the other day in Bloomingdales with your daughter. She is beautiful by the way. That hair. Those eyes. She was having a rough day though. I did a little stalking of you on the Internet—sorry—and I see she is autistic. You haven't posted on Facebook in a while, so I imagine you have your hands full with work and parenting. So, the reason for my message . . .

I'm coming into a bit of money. Not sure how much, but I don't really need it. Nor do I want it. I was thinking of gifting it to a worthy cause. And then I saw you and your daughter in that department store. I was going to say hi, but you had to rush off when she began to make a fuss. My first thought after seeing you and your daughter was donating to an autism research organization. But then I thought, why not actually gift this money to a friend who would better know how to utilize it, whether that means keeping it to help with medical expenses or donating it. No strings attached. Perhaps I feel a bit guilty for ghosting you after That Day.

I also have another favor to ask of you. Yesterday, I met up with a pretty unsavory character. I know something bad about him. He knows something bad about me. A Mexican standoff. Although that sounds racist. Is it? Where does that expression even come from? Maybe it's more like a staring contest. Who will blink first? Or maybe it's more like that car thing where two cars are aimed at each other barreling down the road and the one who veers off, loses. Will I veer? Or will he? Either way, I have no idea what this guy is capable of.

There is a metal file cabinet in my office and taped to the bottom of one of the pullout drawers is a page from my journal that explains everything. If anything happens to me, please contact Detective Susan Ford with the Monticello police department or her father, Will Ford. My grandfather knows how to get in touch with them.

My heart raced as I read this a second time. Madison knew she might be in danger. And she was pointing her finger straight at Oliver Finch. It almost seemed as if she didn't care whether she lived or died, as long as someone worthy benefited from her past misdeed. Was she seeking absolution in this charitable act?

I told Crystal that Madison never had a chance to execute the sale of her shares, so her intentions were never carried out.

"That's okay," she said. "It's the thought that counts."

THE TWO-HOUR drive to Brooklyn was accompanied by two episodes of *My Favorite Murder*. Dad insisted on listening to the podcast, a departure from his typical request to listen to a baseball game or sports news. He had grown fond of the two hosts after I introduced him to the series last year.

"Thanks for inviting me along," he said as he scrolled through my phone to queue up a new episode.

"Well, I thought you would like to tag along." I tapped the steering wheel. "And I can use the company." Which was true, but I also needed a backup driver in case I got lightheaded again. The antibiotics still had me a bit off my game.

I slid into a parking spot about two blocks from Rafael's apartment. He was expecting us. When I called him earlier, I told him I wasn't coming to accuse him of anything this time around, but that I was merely following up on a lead about something I should look for in Madison's office. His response: "Go knock yourself out."

When we arrived, Rafael led us down to Madison's office. "All yours," he said, and left the room.

I slipped on my latex gloves, then knelt next to the three-drawer metal file cabinet. Luckily, there was just this one. I opened the top drawer and felt underneath. Nothing. I pulled out the middle drawer. My fingers slid over an envelope, which I carefully unstuck.

"Ta-da!" The flap was unsealed. On the front were the words: *If you found this, I must be dead.* I plucked the paper from the envelope. It was torn along the left edge. The missing journal page, I presumed. "It's the third to last entry, the one ripped out of her journal, written the week before she was murdered."

I glanced over at Dad. He pursed his lips in anticipation, then he shouted, "For God's sake, Susan, read it!"

Thursday, June 20

I have come to a decision. Next weekend I will unburden myself. I am convinced that outing the truth will allow me to start healing. I will suffer the consequences, surely. But so will Rafael. His reputation is at stake. His livelihood. Our future. All because of me. I thought about asking Rafael what I should do. But I know him all too well. He'll try and talk me out of it.

But this weekend, I will enjoy myself. Heading up to Serene Scene with Camilla tomorrow. Rafael might even drive up on Friday night to join us. That would be so lovely. The calm before the storm.

I looked up at Dad. "There's more, but it was written nine days later. It's scribbled in a different pen at the bottom of the sheet and dated Saturday, June twenty-ninth, the day she borrowed Samantha's car and drove to Sackett Lake."

Saturday, June 29

Sorry, dear journal, for tearing this page out of you. I can't risk Rafael (or anyone for that matter) seeing this before I am ready to confess. I messaged Crystal Booker yesterday. Told her my intentions about gifting the money to her. I also let her know that if anything happens to me, to contact the police and point them toward this note.

I still cannot bring myself to write a confession. Maybe next time. Will there be a next time? If not, ask Oliver Finch. He knows the WHOLE story. I must say, that was a bit of a surprise. He put two and two together. Claims he figured it out after reading the news articles. Told me I should keep it to myself. Not a threat exactly, but clearly not friendly advice. And he's probably not too keen on me holding something over him. He asked me if I ever read Crime and Punishment—*and then lectured me on the folly of confession when no one knows what you've done. He snickered and said, "Clear your conscience some other way." I'm pretty sure this guy sleeps like a baby.*

Meanwhile, I can right a few wrongs. I don't need the shares. I never deserved them in the first place. So I know exactly what I'll do with them now. I've set up a second appointment with Drummond for July 15th.

Tonight I am driving upstate and will contact that detective in Monticello: Susan Ford, Grandpa's friend's daughter. I thought about calling her months ago, back when I asked Grandpa for her number. Probably should have torn this Band-Aid off sooner, but I needed more time to think this through. But I'm ready now. All the pieces are in place. It's time to let everyone know what I did.

I never meant for it to happen.

"Does it say if anyone was joining her on the drive?" Dad asked.

"No."

"Hmm." Dad donned his latex gloves and took the paper from me. "I think Rafael has some more explaining to do. What in the world did

Madison do that would put Rafael's reputation, his livelihood, in jeopardy? Perhaps she stole other clients?"

"Whatever it is, it's connected to Finch."

"And one of them needed to stop her from revealing whatever it was."

Irving's name flashed up on my phone screen. I held my phone up to Dad.

"Take it," Dad said, jutting out his chin.

I tapped the green circle. "How can I help you, Irving?"

"Um, I think I found something that might be of interest to you."

"I'm listening." I looked up at Dad, who was motioning to switch to speaker mode. I shook my head and mouthed, "No."

Irving cleared his throat. "So after we met last week and you showed me that picture, I kept wracking my brain as to who that might be. So I did a little sleuthing. After Todd died, I took possession of his file cabinets. I emptied them but kept the contents in a box in my basement." He blew out a puff of air. "So, I went nosing around down there this morning and found a bunch of photos from his college days, and lo and behold, there were quite a few with that guy."

"Yeah, we are aware they were classmates at BU."

"Oh. Okay. But there's more, which you might not be aware of. I found a notebook and a ledger in which Todd documented a business deal with a company called Sackett Lake Enterprises and a guy named Oliver Finch—he wrote in detail about a loan for Shangri-La in exchange for laundering this guy's money." He sighed. "I wasn't going to say anything about it, afraid I'd sully Todd's reputation, but then I thought it might have some bearing on Madison's murder—maybe even Robin and Todd's deaths. I mean, if Madison found out about this, who knows what these people would do?"

I sucked in my breath and held it for a few seconds. Was this the smoking gun? A treasure trove of neatly stacked documents that tied Oliver Finch to a decades-old money-laundering scheme?

Irving continued: "Also, I found Todd's old mobile phone in the box. A Blackberry. There's no charger, but I'm sure your tech guys can get it going."

I summarized the phone conversation to Dad, who had made himself comfortable on an armchair in the corner of Madison's office.

He stood up and clapped his hands together. "Let's have a little chat with Rafael, and then we sort out the Todd-and-Oliver connection."

Dad started to move toward the door.

"Wait!"

Dad stopped and turned.

"Not yet. I want to talk to Oliver first. Apparently he 'knows the whole story,' whatever that means. And then we'll question Rafael."

"It's your case, Susan," Dad said, then added, "But we're here right now with new information that we can spring on Rafael. Catch him off guard before anyone gets wind of this. Does it really matter who we interview first?"

"I think it does," I said, exasperated that I even needed to explain my strategy to Dad. "I want to make sure I have all the facts. I want the big picture and then drill down from there. The more I know and can spring on Rafael, the harder it will be for him to weasel out of whatever spot he's in. We've got solid incriminating evidence on Finch now . . . and I'm going to leverage it to my fullest advantage."

Dad sighed. "That means schlepping back and forth. Why not get some answers before we leave?"

"You're the one who keeps telling me to trust my instincts." I felt the sharp edges of my fingernails dig into my palms. "Well, my instincts are practically screaming at me to talk to Oliver before talking to Rafael."

21

SATURDAY | JULY 20, 2019

FINCH'S LAWYER slammed his fist on the table. "You better have a damn good reason for dragging us up here on a Saturday morning."

Chief Eldridge leaned forward. "We are investigating the murder of a twenty-eight-year-old woman. How's that for a damn good reason?"

I opened the manila folder in front of me. The top sheet was the journal page we'd found taped to the bottom of Madison's filing-cabinet drawer. I spun it around and placed it between Oliver and his lawyer. Oliver read it first, then leaned back while his lawyer read it.

"What's the 'whole story'?" I asked.

Oliver whispered into his lawyer's ear. The lawyer nodded.

The lawyer spoke first. "Mr. Finch is prepared to tell you what he knows. The whole story, as you put it. In exchange for some assurances against prosecution."

"We are not prepared to mitigate any charges against you if you are involved in Madison Garcia's murder," I said.

"My client did not kill Ms. Garcia. But he does know what she is referring to and he's prepared to give a statement."

"So why the need for immunity?"

"Because what he is about to tell you relates to another criminal matter. One that he had no part of. But one that came to his attention soon after it occurred."

"So you want immunity from an accessory-after-the-fact charge?" The lawyer nodded. "Exactly."

"We are in no position to grant that."

"Then we are in no position to divulge information." The lawyer waited a beat, then added, "But here's why we should make a deal. I'm a really good lawyer, and by that I mean a really, really good lawyer, and you will end up spinning your wheels if you try and charge my client with murder. The accessory-after-the-fact charge is flimsy at best. No one was arrested in that crime. So therefore my client wasn't actually protecting anyone. In fact, until his meeting with Ms. Garcia, his thoughts on the matter were purely conjecture. She confirmed what he surmised. Like I said, I am a very good lawyer, but I still want immunity for my client."

AFTER A couple of hours conferring with the DA, we got the go-ahead to offer immunity on a potential accessory-after-the-fact charge.

"You got your immunity, so let's hear it," Eldridge said. He cracked his knuckles.

Oliver cleared his throat. "Madison accidentally killed her parents. Well, not exactly accidentally. But she didn't mean to kill her parents."

"What?" Eldridge and I turned our heads toward one another. I'm pretty sure I had the same quizzical expression on my face. I turned back to face Oliver. "Madison wasn't even home at the time of her parent's deaths."

"You want the story?"

I gestured for him to continue.

"I was in Hurleyville that day, as you figured out from my credit-card receipt. I was supposed to meet Todd at his house at one o'clock. I had just parked across the street when I got a call from him telling me he was sick—the flu—and needed to postpone our meeting. I was about to pull away when I saw Madison trudge up the driveway and enter the garage. About two minutes later she exited the garage, looked around, and then headed back down the street. By then, the storm had picked up pretty good and I just wanted to head back to the city. So, I didn't think much about it." Oliver took a long sip of water. "Then I read about their death in the *Record*. Carbon monoxide poisoning. Car accidentally left on after Robin came home from the grocery store. The article stated that Madison was at a friend's house all day. Having seen her, I knew that was a lie. If you calculate the time from when Madison entered the garage to the death of her parents, you'll jump to the same conclusion as I did. She snuck into the garage, turned on the motor, and left. A few hours later, they were dead."

Eldridge jabbed the side of my shoe with the toe of his loafer. A subtle nudge, but I got his message loud and clear: *What the hell?*

"And this is what you discussed when you met with her on June twenty-eighth?" I asked.

"Yes. I thought I could use this info for leverage to, um, encourage her to sell her Shangri-La shares to me. The funny thing is, it was almost like she was relieved that someone knew. She said she was planning to come clean anyway. I told her that was a bad idea, and she should make amends some other way. I mean, she didn't intentionally set out to kill them. They weren't supposed to die."

"I don't understand," Eldridge said. "What was she hoping to accomplish?"

"Todd and Robin wouldn't let Madison date Rafael. Madison thought if Rafael saved her parents, they would welcome him into the family with open arms." He put *saved* in air quotes. "Rafael was supposed to be the knight in shining armor, coming to the rescue."

Eldridge and I sat in stony silence. I had so many questions knotted up in my head, I had no idea which one to pluck out first. I had a feeling Eldridge was in the same predicament. "Go on," was all I could think of.

"The scheme was all Madison's idea. At least that's what Madison told me. She would go to the house and start the car, and then come up with some pretense for Rafael to go over there. The idea being that he would show up thirty minutes later and all would be cool." Oliver rolled his eyes. "Only he got a flat tire. The storm hit hard. And she was passed out at her friend's house."

"And she confessed all this to you?"

"Yeah. It was almost cathartic for her. Like I was her priest or something."

I thought back to what Crystal had told me: that Madison said she never made it back to her house. Obviously a lie. But everything else lined up with her account of what happened that afternoon. In light of this revelation, I bet if I read her diary again, I would clearly see the factors that motivated this crazy scheme. Why doing what she did made sense to her at the time, driven by her desire to be with Rafael at any cost (not to mention, her pot-induced hazy state of mind). Her parents paid the price for, well, being parents. Maybe not contenders for "Mother and Father of the Year," but they certainly didn't deserve to die. Looking at it through adult eyes, contemplating becoming a mother herself, I would hazard a guess that she began to see them and their disciplinary actions in a whole new light. Toss on top of that the fact that she was under the impression her marriage—the payoff she got for her crime—was falling apart. No wonder she was wrestling with overwhelming guilt.

One question did manage to make it to the surface. What was Rafael's role in this scheme, and would he kill his wife to keep it a secret?

RAFAEL AND Camilla were ensconced in Serene Scene this weekend. Rafael still didn't know what we'd uncovered under Madison's filing cabinet and I was eager to spring it on him. I merely told him new evidence had come to light and his assistance was needed. In hindsight, my strategy to get Oliver's story before talking to Rafael had paid off in spades. I now had the upper hand. Even Dad conceded that my plan to delay talking to Rafael had been the way to go. Rafael was going to have a lot harder time worming his way out of the questions I had prepared for him.

With my focus on the impending interrogation, I asked Dad if he would head over to Irving's to pick up Todd's old business records and Blackberry. Irving had also found some old photo albums, video cassette tapes, and other stuff from Madison's childhood that he thought Rafael would like to have. So Dad was going to swing by Serene Scene to drop off those items before heading to the station.

My phone pinged. A text message from my mother.

Mom: Car still on the fritz. Can you take me to AA meeting?

Shit.

Me: Can't. Let me ask around and find you a ride.

Desperate, I called Dad and asked if he would pick her up and take her.

"Are you off your rocker?" Dad shouted.

I pulled the phone away from my ear, expecting an onslaught of cursing. But silence followed that initial outburst. I treaded lightly. "I've got my hands full here and I would appreciate this as a favor to me, not Mom."

"Do I have a choice here, Susan? Because it sounds like my arm is being twisted and you're not planning to let go until I give in."

I thought about leveraging what Mom had told me about his affair with Audrey. Remind him that no one was a saint in this family, and on some level, he owed her. But I just couldn't bring myself to play that card. "Please?"

He was none too happy but said he would pick her up on his way to Serene Scene and then drop her off at the Methodist church before heading into the station. With that taken care of, I could now devote all my attention to the impending confrontation.

SALLY ESCORTED Rafael to the interrogation room. The one that Oliver Finch and his lawyer had occupied only an hour earlier. Oliver would be back in the hot seat soon enough. Agent Larson was sending one of her lackeys up here to take possession of whatever it was that Irving had found. I sat across from Rafael and slid the torn journal entry over to his side of the table. I had folded it in half so the only text visible to him was the original journal entry at the top of the page.

Thursday, June 20

I have come to a decision. Next weekend I will unburden myself. I am convinced that outing the truth will allow me to start healing. I will suffer the consequences, surely. But so will Rafael. His reputation is at stake. His livelihood. Our future. All because of me.

He leaned over to read it, then looked up, his thick eyelashes batting rapidly. "Honestly, I have no idea what she is referring to."

Most people who started a sentence with the word *honestly* were not particularly honest. But I decided to play along.

"Is it possible she poached other clients? Perhaps in some illegal way?"

He shook his head. "She's not like that. I mean, yeah, she did it once. Which I explained wasn't illegal." His shoulders slumped.

"Just unethical," I said.

Rafael's hands clenched into fists. "Borderline."

I picked up the folded journal page and placed it on top of the manila folder. "What can you tell us about Oliver Finch?"

He shook his head again. "I have no idea who that is." He sat up straighter. "Really, I don't know. He is a suspect?"

"He's a person of interest."

"Okay. Who is he? Someone Madison knows?" He inhaled slightly. "Knew?"

"He was a business associate of Madison's father. They went to college together and in the early aughts he started laundering money through Shangri-La and J & T Tavern. It seemed to have started up again about three years ago."

Rafael's eyes widened. "So Madison's suspicions about money laundering were true? And you think this is what got her killed?" He unclenched his shaking fists. "You think this guy, Oliver Finch, murdered her?"

"Well, I thought so, yes." I unfolded the torn journal entry. "But then new evidence came to light."

"New evidence?"

"We just spoke to him." I placed the page in front of Rafael and pointed to the lower half of the page this time. "Turns out he knows what you and Madison did."

"What we did? I don't understand."

As Rafael read, tears streamed down his cheeks.

When he looked up, he said, "I didn't murder Madison, if that's where this is going."

"That's where this is going. The way I see it, she was about to ruin you, and you needed to put a stop to it."

Rafael choked on his tears. "I need to call my lawyer."

MY PHONE pinged. I shuffled some papers and peeked under folders, eventually locating it under the pile of crap on my desk.

Dad: Just picked up your mother. On our way to Shangri-La, then I will drop her off at AA, then head to you. What is going on?

Me: Will explain when you get here.

Dad: Ugh!

Rafael's lawyer was on his way up to Monticello from his home on Long Island. We didn't formally charge Rafael, but we told him we were holding him until his lawyer arrived. I asked him if he wanted to contact Camilla, but he said he didn't want to drag her into this. That it was all a big misunderstanding. And knowing her, she would make matters worse by blabbing the situation to Lord knows who.

"Ford, get your ass in here," Eldridge yelled across the bullpen. "Sally, you too!"

Sally and I stood dutifully in front of Eldridge's desk. "Lucky us. I just got a call from the lab. The DNA results from the cigarette butt are in. Guess someone is working overtime on this. Caroline Deaver is going to email them over with her report. I told her to send them directly to you. Should be on its way to you shortly."

"Did Caroline say if there was a match to one of our suspects?"

"Caroline didn't say anything. Her assistant called."

Sally and I hustled back to my desk. She hovered over my shoulder as I wiggled the mouse to my computer and the black screen lit up. "It's in." I opened the report and we both read silently. Sally let out a low whistle. I hit print. Then headed back to Eldridge's office.

"Got a match?" Eldridge asked.

"Not exactly," I said.

"What do you mean 'not exactly.'"

"The DNA on the clove cigarette was a full sibling match to Rafael. And Rafael only has one sib . . . oh shit! My dad. I gotta—"

Eldridge threw up his hands. "But why? Why would Rafael's sister kill Madison?"

"I don't know. Maybe she found out Madison was going to sell her shares and that didn't sit right with her. She loves that place." Crazy theory, yes, but Camilla was slightly off her proverbial rocker. I thought back to the first time I met Camilla at Serene Scene and smelled that spicy-sweet scent, thinking it was her perfume. It was clove.

"Or maybe there's a perfectly innocent reason a cigarette she was smoking was on the side of the road." Eldridge's eyebrows rose slightly as he tilted his head forward. "Like she tossed it out of a car. Being up here as often as she is, she's probably driven up and down that road plenty."

Possibly, but Dad was on his way over to Serene Scene, and I didn't want him conversing with Camilla. Not until I knew what was going on. And I didn't want him leaving Madison's stuff there. There could be something among Madison's personal effects that might shed some light on all this. I dialed Dad's number. My hands were sweating. The phone rang five times.

"Hello?" A woman's voice. My mother's voice.

"Mom?"

"Susan?"

"Yeah. Where's Dad?"

"Your dad left his phone in the car. He just went into Camilla's bungalow with a backpack full of Madison's memorabilia."

"Shit."

"What is it, Susan? Do you need me to get him?"

"No. Just stay in the car. I'm heading there now. I'll be there in ten minutes."

DAD'S CAR was in the Shangri-La parking lot. Mom was nowhere in sight. I parked next to his car. Sally and I jumped out and ran toward Serene Scene.

The front door to the bungalow was ajar. We bounded up the stairs, Sally and I took positions on either side of the door while I gently pushed it open. I peeked in. If I hadn't been in such a frenzied state, I might've laughed at the scene in front of me. Dad was lying on the couch moaning, clutching his ankle. Camilla was knocked out cold on the floor. My mother was holding her cane above Camilla's body. Next to Camilla's outstretched arm, a brown Louis Vuitton bag with a red strap.

Sally called for an ambulance.

I crouched over Camilla, looking up toward Dad. "Dad, you okay?" I felt for Camilla's pulse. She was alive, albeit unconscious.

"Yeah. I tripped going backwards. I think I broke my ankle. But look what I found," Dad said, pointing to the Louis Vuitton bag. "Camilla told me to put Irving's duffel of Madison's stuff behind the room divider with her other bags. When I saw the Louis Vuitton bag, I pulled it out, and asked her where she got it. She charged me, grabbed the bag, and that's when I fell over the cocktail table. That's when Vera came rushing in like the goddamn cavalry."

I rose and walked over to Dad to check him over.

"I thought she was assaulting your father, so I hit her with my cane," Mom chimed in, rather matter-of-factly, given the situation. "I guess I don't know my own strength."

"You guys make a good team." I squatted down next to Dad and whispered in his ear, "Just like Nick and Nora Charles."

Then I called for a second ambulance.

CAMILLA HELD a compact mirror slightly above her head and examined the bruise on her forehead. "I should sue your mother," she said. She snapped it closed and placed it next to her on the white bedsheet.

"I'll pretend I didn't hear that."

"Ah, you have visitors," said a nurse as she walked into the room. "How are we feeling? Headache? Nausea? Fatigue? You suffered a nasty concussion, my dear."

Camilla scowled. "All of the above." She glanced at her bedside table, then back at me. "Where's my phone?"

"Confiscated as evidence. We got a warrant an hour ago."

Her eyes widened. "You can't do that. My whole business is on that phone. I *need* that phone!" She pounded her fists on her thighs. "Has Rafael been here? I need to talk with him."

"He's at the station. With his lawyer."

She picked up her compact mirror, then threw it down again. "Can I use your phone? I'd like to call Rafael."

"You know that is not going to happen. Besides, Rafael's lawyer wisely counseled him to not talk to you." I sat on the chair beside her bed. "You want to tell me what you were doing with Madison's Louis Vuitton bag?"

"She gave it to me. I admired it and she said I could have it."

"So she just gave you a three-thousand-dollar bag?"

Camilla shrugged. "I don't know what you want me to say. She knew I loved it, and I had mentioned that it would be perfect for a photo shoot, so she gave it to me."

"When did she give it to you?"

She drummed her finger on her lip. "Madison stopped by my apartment on her way up here . . . the Saturday that . . ." She placed her palm on her collarbone. "The day she was murdered."

"So Madison gave you her three-thousand-dollar bag on Saturday, June twenty-ninth?"

Camilla stared at her fingernails. "Yeah."

"What time?"

"I don't know. I think around seven o'clock that evening."

"Care to explain how a cigarette butt with your DNA ended up on the side of the road about two miles from the murder scene?"

She lowered her head, then slowly turned toward me. "What road?"

"Route 42."

"You mean a road I drive along all the time? A road which is probably littered with a few of my cigarette butts?" She tittered. "Did you find any other cigarette butts—'cause maybe you should harass those smokers as well."

"Where were you on the night of June twenty-ninth?"

"I'm not answering another one of your inane questions without a lawyer," she said, folding her arms across her chest and pouting like a sullen teenager.

Both our heads turned toward the door when we heard what sounded like a scuffle on the other side. Then a muffled argument. The door swung open and behind Sally stood Luis and Isabela Garcia, their expressions a mix of concern and anger. Hard to tell which was winning out.

I nodded to Sally. "Let them in."

"What in God's green earth is going on?" Luis roared, rushing to Camilla's bedside.

Isabela ran to the far side of the bed and leaned in to examine the bump on her head. Then she turned toward me. "First you arrest Rafael, and now you are harassing our daughter. What is going on?"

"Rafael and Camilla have some explaining to do. Although they have not been formally charged, they wisely requested lawyers. It ain't looking good for either of them."

22

SUNDAY | JULY 21, 2019

SURPRISINGLY, I woke feeling refreshed.

I had to postpone Rafael's interrogation until this morning—Rafael's lawyer got a flat tire on the New York Thruway and didn't show up until after midnight. On some level I was okay with the delay. I got a good night's sleep and felt better prepared for whatever bullshit those siblings would shovel my way.

"Well, you look well rested," Ray said, handing me a cup of coffee. "And chipper."

I parked myself at the kitchen table. "Don't I? It's amazing what a break in the case can do for your mood."

"And a round of antibiotics. So, what's your take?"

"The circumstantial evidence is certainly pointing toward those two."

"Do you think they were in cahoots?"

I shrugged. "Hopefully today's interrogation sheds some light on Rafael's potential motive. Sure, he stood to gain financially, but he's already quite well off. We found no evidence of another woman in his life. And according to his friends, he was devoted to Madison, talked about having kids, even planning a lavish surprise fifth anniversary party."

"And you think Camilla is capable of such a brutal act?"

I scratched at the back of my neck. "I just thought of something. Hold on a sec." I ran upstairs and retrieved my notepad, then hurried back to the kitchen.

I leafed through the pages. "Here it is." I handed the notebook to Ray and pointed to my notes. "Annabelle told me that Camilla took self-defense classes earlier this year. And the place where she took them also offers weapons training."

Ray scanned the page, then handed the notebook back to me. "So you think she learned how to use a knife at this place?"

"A plausible assumption. Would you do me a favor?"

"Depends."

"Would you get in touch with SD and SD—that's the name of the self-defense studio—and ask the owner if Camilla enrolled in the weapons-training classes, and specifically which weapons she learned to use." I tilted my head left, then right, emitting two barely audible cracks.

Ray came up behind me and massaged my shoulders. "I can look into that."

I drooped my head as he worked out the few knots along the right trapezius muscle.

"If Rafael was involved in this come-to-the-rescue scheme that got her parents killed, he'll be facing prison time," Ray said as he worked his fingers down my shoulder blade. "And if he knew Madison was itching to come clean, that is certainly motive. A strong motive, if you ask me."

"And his alibi is less than rock solid. Home alone."

"What about Finch?" Ray asked as he dug his thumbs into my lower neck. "Do you think he factors into the murder?"

"If Madison was going to expose his money-laundering operation, I would imagine he would do anything to stop her. And even though he has a rock solid alibi, he certainly could have sent someone to do his dirty work. Usually these guys are a million miles away from the crime scene."

"I saw a couple of Feds last night at the station picking up the ledgers Irving found." Ray worked his fingers down my spine. "The smoking gun?"

I let my shoulders slump as Ray worked out the kinks. I tilted my head and looked up at him, a satisfied smile plastered on my face. "Hopefully there's enough there to nail Finch."

I ARRIVED at the station at nine o'clock. Rafael showed up with his lawyer at nine thirty.

Camilla was to be released from the hospital at one o'clock, due to arrive here at two o'clock. Sally had resumed guard duty outside Camilla's hospital room, relieving her partner, Ron, at six o'clock this morning. The directive was to keep visitors out, especially Rafael. We didn't need them getting their story straight.

Eldridge and I waited until Rafael and his lawyer, Jonathan Mansfield, settled in. Then we entered the interrogation room. I took the seat across from Rafael.

Charcoal rings under Rafael's eyes told me he did not get a good night's sleep. Nor did he bother to shave this morning. His hands lay flat on the table in front of him, his breathing was somewhat labored. He glared ahead as though he was bracing for a verbal assault. He had that animal-trapped-in-a-cage look and he wasn't going down without a fight.

"Now where were we . . . ah yes, Madison's journal entries." I removed the torn page from the manila folder and placed it in between

Rafael and Jonathan Mansfield. "Oliver Finch told us that Madison, in an attempt to get her parents to welcome you into her family with open arms, planned for you to rescue them. Only between the flat tire and the storm, the plan went awry. You were late getting to her house. They died. And Madison wanted to finally clear her conscience."

"No. I refuse to believe that."

"Which part? The plan? Or the fact that she wanted to confess to clear her conscience?" I could feel pressure start to build in my sinuses. "From where I'm sitting you have motive. This little secret coming out would ruin you. You have a flimsy alibi. You could have easily driven up here Saturday night, let's say to surprise her. The two of you go out to Sackett Lake for a midnight swim. Like old times. Only instead of swimming, you stab her. Then you walk back to wherever you parked your car, and head home." I turned my head into my elbow and sneezed, as daintily as I could.

"This is cra—"

Jonathan Mansfield held up his palm. "Detective, do you have any evidence linking my client to Madison's murder? A weapon? Blood? DNA? A witness? A phone ping off a local tower?"

"Right now, Rafael is facing an accessory-after-the-fact murder charge. And that's only if he had nothing to do with Madison's scheme, and merely withheld information."

The lawyer slammed his hand on the table. "This is all pure conjecture. Rafael is distraught over these allegations. *All* of these allegations. He will not confess to a murder he didn't commit. And he was not party to Madison's scheme a decade ago, if in fact there was such a scheme."

I slowly exhaled, knowing I was short on evidence to build an airtight case against Rafael that would stand the scrutiny of a jury. Motive I had. But that's all I had.

CAMILLA RECLINED lazily in her chair, gazing at her fire-engine-red fingernails. She yawned. "Can we get on with this?" Her British accent in full flower.

"I'm sorry. Are we keeping you from a prior engagement?" Eldridge said, sarcasm dripping off every syllable.

Her lawyer, Deborah Bergstrom, sat ramrod straight. "Let's just proceed with the questioning, shall we?" She shot Camilla a stern look and Camilla sat up straighter.

"You seem to think this is a joke, Camilla," I said. "We've got enough evidence against you to start building a case. And I'm pretty sure the deeper we dig, the more we'll unearth."

"Dig away. I have nothing to hide."

"You've already explained what you were doing with the Louis Vuitton bag," I said sarcastically, knowing full well that her explanation was ludicrous. But I had other angles I wanted to explore and so I let it go . . . for the time being. "So, let's start with your whereabouts on Saturday, June twenty-ninth."

"On the last Saturday of every month, I decompress. I stay off social media. I read and meditate. I never go out. You can ask anyone."

"I've gone through your Instagram grid. I've seen photos posted on the last Saturday of the month for the past year."

"Those are scheduled posts. In fact, the majority of my posts are prescheduled."

"Prescheduled?"

Camilla made a face.

An "okay boomer" face my daughter, Natalie, has thrown my way when I mention how things *used to be.*

"I believe I mentioned this to you before. Every Sunday I prepare all my posts for the week. I use a scheduling app to upload all my content and captions and set the date and time for it to post depending on when my followers are most likely to be checking their socials."

"So, you were home all of Saturday night into Sunday morning?"

"I decompress for the entire day. From the minute I wake up Saturday morning until the minute I go to sleep on Saturday night. On Sunday morning I was planning to meet my brother for breakfast, and then, well—" She slouched back in her chair. "Check my phone's GPS or tracking or whatever you look at if you don't believe me. I never left my apartment."

"You mean your phone never left your apartment. We've seen enough criminal cases these days where the perps are smart enough not to take their phones to the scene of the crime." I opened the manila folder and removed a photograph of the red journal. "Have you seen this before?"

"No."

I pulled out the photograph of the June twenty-third entry. "It says here . . ." I said, pointing to a line of text, "that you asked her if you could read it. So, I'll ask again, have you ever seen this journal?"

She bent over to look more closely at the photograph. "Yeah. I guess that could be her red leather journal. It looks different . . . quite ruined."

"It was. But I bet the person who tossed it into the lake had no idea that there are techniques for resurrecting the ink."

Deborah Bergstrom glanced at the photograph. "I can understand Camilla's confusion. This waterlogged journal probably bears no resemblance to the one she saw Madison writing in."

I turned to Camilla. "Have you ever read Madison's journal? Perhaps snuck a peek?"

"Absolutely not! She always kept that thing with her. Besides, I respected her privacy. I never laid eyes on it." As if I didn't quite get the message, she added emphatically, "Never."

"Well, her portrayal of you is not particularly flattering. Were you aware that she found you . . ." I searched for the right word, "pretentious?"

Camilla let out a demure snort.

"I'll admit. You got me dead to rights there. I'm a bit, as you say, pretentious. You can even say I'm a bit flaky. It's part of my persona as an influencer. My accent . . . it's for fun. I like playing a part. I had no idea it bothered Madison so much that she had to write about me in her journal."

I scooped up both photographs and placed them back in the folder.

"Okay. Moving on. Are you aware of Rafael's role in the alleged accidental killing of Madison's parents?"

"Yes. My father filled me in yesterday. He told me that you're accusing Rafael of killing Madison to cover up some nonsense about the two of them scheming to have Rafael rescue Madison's parents."

Camilla leaned over and whispered in her lawyer's ear. Deborah Bergstrom nodded, then said, "Camilla is not feeling well. Her head is starting to ache. She'd like to adjourn for the day. And just so you know, Camilla decided not to press assault charges against Vera Ford."

I glanced over at Camilla, who raised her eyebrows ever so slightly, giving off a don't-mess-with-me vibe. I decided not to address Ms. Bergstrom's last statement. I was still waiting for confirmation from the self-defense studio that she took weapons-training classes. The tech guys were scouring her phone for any incriminating evidence, and her laptop was en route to the lab. So a break at this point was fine by me.

"Sure, let's break for the day. You're free to go, but not back to the city. So make yourself comfy at Serene Scene. We'll convene first thing in the morning."

WHEN I got home, Ray was waiting for me in the living room. "How did it go?"

He listened as I filled him in on the interrogation, and nodded but didn't say anything. Except an "ah" or a "shit" every now and again.

"I left a message for the owner of that self-defense studio," Ray said. "A Mel Genaro. Still haven't heard back."

I opened my briefcase and pulled out the manila folder. I laid each journal entry across the coffee table, creating two rows. Ray sat down next to me, and we read silently.

I leaned back against the cushions. "Do you mind if I theorize out loud?"

"Sure. Go for it."

I pointed to the journal page dated June 23. "Camilla tried to goad Madison to let her take a peek at the journal, so obviously she was curious. Let's assume she manages to get hold of the journal. Maybe while Madison was in the shower or sleeping. And she reads the passage from June twentieth."

"The one where Madison mentions that whatever she is about to confess will ruin Rafael."

"Yeah. And it's clear from our conversations with others that Camilla is very devoted to Rafael. One could even say weirdly devoted. In the course of this investigation, I've heard countless times that she would do *anything* for him."

Her devotion to her brother was obsessive, bordering on neurotic. Following him to Boston University, then to Brooklyn. Calling him her Romeo. Dr. Samantha Fields recognized it. Even Madison found it bizarre. In her journal she wrote, "*She follows Rafael around like a puppy dog, I know she would do anything for him.*"

"Okay, so there's your possible motive. What about opportunity?"

I closed my eyes and pressed my palms against my eyelids. I searched the darkness for an epiphany. I lowered my hands as my eyes fluttered open. "According to Camilla, Madison stopped by her apartment the evening of Saturday, June twenty-ninth to supposedly give her the Louis Vuitton bag. What if Camilla lured Madison to her apartment with the hope of hitching a ride up here with her. Then, once up here, she convinces Madison to go for a 'midnight swim' for old times' sake. She kills Madison, then dumps the journal and the contents of the bag into the lake. But knowing Camilla, there is no way she is going to toss a three-thousand-dollar Louis Vuitton bag in the muck. So she hangs on to it."

Ray nodded. "One problem with your theory: she didn't have a car to get back to the city. And she met up with Rafael early the next morning."

I tapped the side of my head. "Oh, I think I figured that out too. And, if I'm right, I can even prove it."

23

MONDAY | JULY 22, 2019

"WERE YOU able to get it?" I asked Sally.

Sally twitched her eyebrows skyward and smiled. "Yup. Coffee?"

"Sure."

She reached up into the cabinet and pulled out a mug. "Black, right?"

I nodded. "And?"

"And . . . I downloaded both video files to a thumb drive." She reached into her pocket and held up the thumb drive. "I think you're going to like what you see." She tossed it to me.

I hurried over to my desk and fired up my computer. I inserted the thumb drive and watched the two videos.

Sally came up behind me. "When does Camilla get here?"

"In an hour." I swiveled around and did my best impersonation of jazz hands. "And then it's showtime."

❊

THE BUMP on Camilla's head looked less fierce. The bruising was now a slight protuberance, surrounded by a yellowish-green discoloration of her skin. She sat straight up this time, her expression neutral as she stared straight ahead. A hint of clove drifted off Camilla's sweater when she shifted in her chair. Camilla's lawyer, Deborah Bergstrom, frowned slightly as I typed into my laptop.

I directed everyone's attention to the television screen behind me. I opened the file that I had downloaded earlier from the thumb drive. "Ready?"

All eyes turned up to the flat screen mounted on the wall. I kept my eyes on Camilla.

The video filled the screen. The time code read 12:52AM 063019. A tall, slim figure in a baseball cap and backpack opened the front door to the Shortline bus terminal, head down. The person walked over to the counter and paid cash for a bus ticket, then glanced around and took a seat in the corner of the room, slightly out of the camera's sightline. I fast forwarded the video to 2:55 a.m. The figure stood and stretched, mostly out of view. With head down, the person exited the door to the waiting bus. I stopped the video.

"You can't seriously think that's Camilla," Deborah Bergstrom said.

I ignored the remark and opened the next file. A grainy black-and-white image filled the screen. This footage was courtesy of the bus's mounted camera. We watched the back of the person with the baseball cap walk up the aisle of the bus and stop at a seat about three quarters of the way down. The person shimmied off the backpack and hoisted it into the rack above the seats, then turned slightly before sitting. I stopped the tape. Under a Red Sox baseball cap, Camilla's face stared back at everyone in the room.

"I seriously think that's Camilla," Eldridge said in his best deadpan.

"Madison wrote in her journal that you once took the Shortline bus to get home. I will admit, it took me a while to figure out how you got back to the city in the middle of the night. But lo and behold, turns out there is an early, *early*-morning bus. Who knew?" I waited a beat, then added, "Apparently you did."

Camilla sucked her lips into her mouth and pressed down hard.

Deborah Bergstrom placed her fingertips on Camilla's arm, signaling her to keep quiet.

There was a knock at the door. Ray poked his head in. "Susan, I need to talk to you."

I glanced at Eldridge, who turned to Ray. "Now?"

"Yeah. It's important."

Eldridge clenched his teeth, then called for a ten-minute recess.

I caught a glimmer of relief in Deborah Bergstrom's eyes.

"THIS BETTER be good," Eldridge said to Ray as we stepped out of the interrogation room.

"More fuel for your fire," Ray replied.

"I'm pretty sure we don't need more fuel," Eldridge shot back. "You interrupted us at a crucial juncture."

"If you want to go in with full guns blazing, your pistol better be loaded with all its rounds," Ray countered.

I knew Ray would only barge in if he had a good reason, and there was only one reason I could think of. "You talked to the SD guy?"

"Yeah. Mel Genaro."

"The SD guy?" Eldridge asked.

I filled Eldridge in on this piece of the puzzle—the self-defense class Camilla took.

"She did gun and knife training," Ray explained. "But here's the interesting part . . . the instructor said she called him in late June to ask him specific questions about knives and techniques for using them. He told her about the various places on the torso in which she could inflict the most damage and how to go about doing it. He thought it was a bit strange. But then again, he thought *she* was a bit strange. Mentioned the weird accent."

"Okay, this was worth the interruption," Eldridge said. "Anything else we should know?"

"Yeah. So the instructor recommended a particular knife. Guess which one?"

"A plain reverse tanto," I replied.

"Yup," Ray said.

"The tech guys said we'll have her phone logs later this morning," I said. "And her laptop should be here shortly. Hopefully we'll find a Google search for knives or, better yet, an online purchase."

Eldridge nodded toward the interrogation door. "Let's finish this."

When we opened the door, Camilla was sobbing. Heaving, really. Trying to catch her breath as she wailed. Deborah Bergstrom rubbed her palm in circles on Camilla's back in an attempt to calm her down.

As I watched Camilla convulse, the one thing that really stuck in my craw was that I'd treated her as a collaborator. I took her at her word that she'd spent the entire weekend of June 29 in Brooklyn. I did not recognize her attempts to steer me in wrong directions (*"Have you gotten in touch with Sarah Steinberg? She once stabbed someone. Sarah accused Madison of stealing Rafael. Said she would get back at her one day."*) I did not become suspicious after Annabelle told me about Camilla's self-defense training (*"It was Camilla's idea, actually. A friend of hers got mugged earlier this year, so she enrolled at SD and SD in the spring . . . for those who are interested, he also offers weapons training."*) And as I mentioned to Ray earlier, her devotion to her twin brother. Lots of neon signs pointed toward Camilla, and I didn't even see them flashing.

The water was muddied, of course, with the mob-related money-laundering angle and her friends and family trying to cover up other misdeeds. Now the question was whether she committed murder solo or in cahoots with Rafael.

Eldridge and I reclaimed our seats across from Camilla and Deborah Bergstrom.

Camilla choked on a sob, then looked up at me. Her pupils were dilated. Her hair disheveled. She leaned over the table and stabbed a finger at me. "I did nothing wrong!" she screamed. "I am being framed!"

I ignored Camilla's outburst. "We got in touch with the owner of SD and SD." I let that statement hang in the air for a few beats.

Camilla jerked upright, blinking rapidly. "What? Who?"

"Mel Genaro. Told us you enrolled in his weapons training class. And not just any weapon, Camilla. Seems you had a particularly keen interest in knives. So keen that you contacted him last month to ask about stabbing techniques and which knives would inflict the most damage."

Camilla opened her mouth, but before she could speak, Deborah clamped her hand around Camilla's forearm.

"We are going to formally arrest Camilla," I said, as Eldridge nodded. "We'll be back in ten minutes. And when we return, we'll expect a full confession. Maybe you can explain to Camilla that it's the best way forward."

TEN MINUTES later I poked my head into the interrogation room. Camilla had calmed down. Her head lay on her arms, which were folded on the table. Deborah Bergstrom was knitting a child's sweater. She looked up at me.

"It reduces stress. I always keep a ball and needles in my bag." She bent over and placed the half-knitted sweater, ball of yarn, and knitting needles back in her bag. "Camilla will not confess to a crime she didn't commit."

I addressed Camilla: "We have sufficient evidence to charge you, Camilla, and will be taking you into custody now. I'm just waiting for Eldridge to finish up the paperwork."

Camilla raised her head slightly and tilted it toward me. "You'll be sorry, Detective, for causing me and my brother all this pain and anguish."

Deborah tapped Camilla's shoulder, then silently admonished her with a lethal stare.

"My lawyer wants me to be quiet." Camilla sneered. "So, not another peep out of me."

I directed my attention to Deborah. "If Camilla makes bail—and I have a feeling she will—she is to stay in the area."

A MISSED-CALL notification lit up my phone. I had muted it during the interrogation and forgot to turn the sound back on. It was from Agent Ginger Larson. I wasted no time returning her call.

"Oh man, we got ourselves a gold mine. A treasure trove of malfeasance," Larson exclaimed. "Todd documented everything. And when I say everything, I mean everything. If only Jacob had been as forthcoming, we could have really nailed Finch to the wall."

"Can you connect the dots from the earlier money-laundering scheme with Todd to the one that started up three years ago with Jacob?"

"That's what we're working on now. Jacob's computer and phones gave us nothing. So they must have used burners. But my team knows how to connect dots."

"I bet Oliver couldn't pass up the opportunity to worm his way back into the businesses. With gambling heating up in the area and his knowledge of Shangri-La and J & T Tavern, he probably gave Jacob no choice."

She sighed. "I wish I hadn't leaned on Jacob as hard as I did. I'm feeling a bit guilty that I didn't go easier on him, recognize his role as patsy and perhaps even offer up witness protection."

It wasn't as if I didn't come down hard on him either. We both had a hand in letting Jacob think he was cornered. We were both experienced enough to know that everyone has a breaking point. Did we step over the line? If Dad were here, he would have said, "Woulda, shoulda, coulda gets you nowhere." That seemed a tad flippant in this circumstance.

"We can't second-guess ourselves. We did our jobs and Jacob did have alternatives," I said with just enough conviction.

"Yeah, I know. Easier said than done." She grunted softly. "It's funny that what got Finch caught was a murder he had nothing to do with."

I FOLDED my arms on my desk and laid my head on my top forearm. I closed my eyes and started drifting into sleep. A tap on my shoulder startled me. I wiped an inch of drool from the edge of my lip with my sleeve and sat bolt upright. "Yeah?" I said groggily.

"Sorry," Sally whispered. "Joe rang. He said he found something on Madison's phone that you'll want to see. He's in Eldridge's office now."

I reached into my side drawer and popped an Altoid.

Joe spun around in his chair when I entered Eldridge's office. "Oh, man, Susan, you're gonna love this. I mean, what people have on their phones these days. Madison has a ton of apps on her phone and this one was low priority for a data pull, but then I thought, what the hell, maybe it's worth a look."

"Spill it," Eldridge said. I silently thanked him for his impatience.

"Yeah. Okay. So, Madison has an app on her phone to feed her cat remotely."

"Rafael mentioned an automatic cat feeder when I paid him a visit a few weeks ago. He didn't say anything about it being tied to an app."

"It's possible he didn't know about it," Joe surmised. "But here's the kicker, the feeder also has a built-in camera." Joe held up an iPhone.

"This phone is a clone of Madison's iPhone. All her photos, text messages, browsing history, apps, etcetera, etcetera are downloaded to this phone, so we don't lose the original data." He tapped on an app called CatCam. "So check this out. On June twenty-ninth at around nine forty-five p.m.—which is right after she rang your number—Madison activates the feeder and camera. Now watch what happens."

Eldridge and I leaned in closer to the iPhone and watched a black cat nibbling kibble. After a few seconds, a pair of slippered feet came into view. Then, a hand appeared in the frame, and rubbed the neck of the cat. I recognized the ring. Rafael's wedding band. A few more minutes ticked by, and then Penguin backed away from the feeder and the screen went dark.

Joe tapped at the phone. "The camera is also motion-activated. This way the owner can check to see whenever their cat nibbles or drinks. This feeder has a one-hundred-and-sixty-degree night-vision HD camera and a microphone." Joe's eyebrows twitched in excitement. "Man, I gotta get me one of these. Anyway, Rafael triggers it when he walks into the kitchen for a little midnight snack. You can even hear him humming."

We stared at each other for a few seconds, then burst out laughing.

A fancy cat feeder had just verified Rafael's alibi. He was in his apartment that night, like he'd said he was. There was no way Rafael could have been anywhere near Monticello at the time of Madison's murder.

"Well, that cat camera just cleared Rafael of Madison's murder." Eldridge flexed his jaw. "What about his role in Madison's parents' death? I don't think an app on Madison's phone is gonna help us sort that out."

"I'm still on the fence with that, sir. The one person who knows what really happened that day is dead." I rubbed my lower lip. "I think that case is going to be like the season finale of *The Sopranos* . . . an unsatisfying ending."

I KNOCKED on the door to Dad's apartment. His friend Harry opened it and stepped aside.

"I was just leaving. He's all yours." Harry tipped an imaginary hat as I slipped by him.

"How's the foot?" I said, tapping the plastic boot.

Dad swatted my hand away. "Never mind that. It's fine. How's the case?"

I filled him in on this morning's revelations: the cat camera (met with an outburst of "hot diggity dog"), the bus-station video and the discussion with the weapons-training instructor about the knife. I also let him know that Camilla made bail and was biding her time at Serene Scene.

"Sounds like you got enough to charge her."

I wasn't so sure. "Would love to have blood DNA on the Louis Vuitton or find the actual murder weapon. A confession would be nice."

"Well, with Rafael cleared as a suspect, I have an idea as to how you might get a confession out of Camilla."

My eyebrows sprang upward. "Do tell."

24

FOR THE first time in nearly four weeks, the morning air had a slight chill to it. The humidity had ratcheted down from oppressive to uncomfortable. Even Moxie, who was less than eager to go on long walks this summer, bounded down the stairs aware of the change in the weather.

Ray and I followed her as she led us through a narrow path that ran alongside our house.

"You think it's a sign?" Ray asked. "A turn in the weather, a turn in your case?"

"God works in mysterious ways."

"Have you told Rafael he's no longer a suspect?"

"Eldridge did. Because he hasn't pissed off Rafael like I have, Eldridge thought it best if he was the one to run Dad's idea by Rafael, see if he's game."

Moxie sniffed at a patch of tall grass before ripping off a few blades to chew. She trotted down to a fallen tree trunk and did her business.

We let her meander about for a few more minutes before reversing direction and heading back to the house.

"So is he? Game?"

"Took some convincing, but yeah, he's game."

JOE PARKED the midnight-blue minivan in Lot A of Shangri-La. The tinted windows shielded us from prying eyes.

Rafael twiddled his thumbs.

Joe twisted around in his seat as he pulled a small object out of his bag. "No need to be nervous, man. Piece of cake."

Rafael bit down on his lower lip and rocked slightly back and forth. "Let's just get this over with."

Joe handed Rafael what looked like an ordinary car fob with two keys attached to add authenticity to the device.

Getting Rafael to "wear a wire" was easier than we thought it would be. He steadfastly refused to believe his twin sister had murdered his wife, that there must be some other explanation or proof to counter and repudiate the abundance of circumstantial evidence. He told us the only reason he agreed to do this was, as he put it, "to clear her good name."

"Is this the recording device?" Rafael asked, turning over the fob.

Joe nodded. "And transmitter, so we can hear. The top button, the one with the lock symbol, is the power button. If you press it, you'll know it's powered on because it will vibrate."

"This one?" Rafael asked, pointing to the top button.

"Yeah. The device is voice activated, so once it's powered on there is no need to push any of the other buttons. They are just for show."

"What's the range on this?" Rafael asked.

"For transmitting, about two miles. For picking up conversations, about thirty feet. But voices beyond twenty feet become harder to hear. So try to stay within fifteen feet."

"You don't even have to have it out," I added. "You can wear it in the front pocket of your jeans."

"So, let's test it, shall we?" Joe said.

Rafael looked down at the fob in his palm and shoved it in his pocket. "Okay, I'm turning it on." He paused for a moment. "I just felt the vibration."

"Great!" Joe exclaimed.

"Sure beats strapping a tape recorder to my chest with duct tape," Rafael said.

Joe chuckled. "We're more James Bond than *Carlito's Way* these days."

I ran through some best practices with him. "Start off nice and nonconfrontational. Share in the disbelief of what is happening and that the police have it all wrong."

"They do have it all wrong."

"See, you're already getting the hang of it." I smiled at my lame joke. He didn't. "Then I need you to start asking questions about the evidence, as we discussed earlier. Poke and prod until she slips up."

"She's not going to slip up, Detective, because she's innocent."

I warned him that if he gave Camilla any indication of what he was up to, whether a written note or showing her the fob in a way that tipped her off, he would not be doing her any favors. And it wouldn't bode well for him either.

"If I need to reach you, I will call your cell phone and you're to pretend it's related to work and needs to be answered. Got it?"

"I hear you loud and clear. If she did this, then she must face the consequences," Rafael said as he slid open the van door and stepped into the parking lot. He turned back to us. "But I'm going to prove you wrong."

Joe and I watched Rafael walk across the parking lot until he was completely out of view.

"Testing, testing," Rafael said, then added, "My sister would never do this." We heard him knock on the door. "Technology saved my ass. Now it will save hers."

About ten seconds later we heard Camilla's voice. "Come in." No hint of a British accent.

"How you holding up?" Rafael asked, followed by the sound of a closing door.

"I didn't do this, Rafael. I'm being railroaded. They couldn't find the actual killer, so they're pinning this on me. All because I have her bag and just happened to be in the area that weekend."

"Yeah. I hear what you're saying. It's crazy. But why didn't you tell them you were up here in the first place?"

"I thought it was wise of me not to tell them. I mean . . . I didn't want to distract them from finding the real killer, which as you can see, is exactly what's happening now." She cleared her throat. "I can use a spot of tea. Want some?"

Rafael must have nodded in the affirmative.

"Okay. Tea for two."

We waited for Rafael to follow up on his question about her withholding information about her whereabouts that weekend, but he remained silent.

Perhaps playing the nonconfrontational card, letting her think her answer was perfectly reasonable.

We heard water run into a metal kettle, then the click-click-click-poof of the gas stove igniting, followed by the clinking of mugs being placed on the counter.

"So, what's your plan?" Rafael finally said. "What does your attorney say?"

"She says everything they have is circumstantial. There's no DNA evidence—"

"Well, there's the cigarette butt they found near Sackett Lake."

"Near? If you consider two miles away near."

"Okay. But what were you doing on the Shortline bus at three o'clock in the morning?"

"Whoa Rafael. Are you interrogating me?"

"I'm just trying to understand what you were doing up here. I'm on your side, Camilla. But if you can't explain it to me, how are you going to explain it to the police . . . or a jury, if it comes to that?"

Smart tactic, I thought.

"Well, everyone is accusing me of murder, so you can only imagine how terrifying this is for me."

"I don't have to imagine. I'm under the microscope as well. So, why don't you just tell me what you did on Saturday and then I'll let it go, okay?"

"Fine. When Madison stopped by my apartment to give me her Louis Vuitton bag, she told me she was coming up here, and asked if I would join her. She said she had a headache and would love someone to come along and share the driving. So, even though it was my de-compress day, I decided to be a good doobie and go with her, knowing I could catch the early-morning bus back to the city."

"So she dropped you off here at Shangri-La and drove off, alone?"

"Yes. She said she was meeting someone. Which I will admit was weird, because it was pretty late by then. Maybe it was that Oliver Finch. Who, if you ask me, is probably the guy who killed her. And then there's the fact that she had a drug habit. Her murder could have something to do with that. Or . . . and I hate to bring this up . . . maybe she was having an affair."

"I'll ignore that remark. But I don't want to hear that shit from you again. Got it?" When she didn't respond immediately, he repeated more forcefully, "Got it?"

"I got it," she answered with a hint of take-a-chill-pill defensive-ness.

"So, how did you get from here to the bus station?"

After a few minutes of silence, Camilla said, "Jacob drove me."

Nice, I thought, *use a dead man as your alibi.* Only she didn't know that Jacob was with his lover when she showed up at the bus station.

I immediately called Rafael.

"Hold on. Gotta take this."

After explaining to him how Camilla's story wasn't possible, he said, "Okay. Thanks for letting me know."

"Who was that?" Camilla asked.

"Just work."

Silence again. Perhaps they were sipping their teas.

"So, Jacob dropped you off at the bus station?" Rafael finally said. "Too bad he's dead. He could have confirmed your story."

"Right? Just my luck."

"Maybe someone saw you get in the car with him."

"I doubt it. I met him in the parking lot and we drove off."

Rafael cleared his throat. "My lawyer told me that he had an airtight alibi for the night of Madison's murder."

"Yeah?" Camilla said in a high-pitched voice.

"That he never left the grounds. People saw him around. And get this . . . he has a girlfriend who claims she was with him all night."

"What are you getting at? Are you saying you don't believe me? Do they really believe his lover, someone who wants to protect him? Airtight my ass."

Oh boy, she was good.

"Let's sit outside," Rafael said.

My phone rang. It was Ray.

I had asked Eldridge to pass along any insight gleaned from Camilla's phone or computer to Ray while I was holed up in this van. I optimistically swiped the phone. "Hey."

"Got something for you," he said.

I punched the air with my fist. "I'm listening."

"First, the good news. There were searches for tanto knives on Camilla's computer."

"When were these searches made?"

"On June twenty-fourth and twenty-fifth."

"What about an online purchase?"

"Well, that's the bad news. She might not be savvy enough to know you can never totally erase your search history, but she probably knows that buying your murder weapon online is a lousy idea."

"Without a purchase receipt, it's circumstantial." I sighed. "Her lawyer could easily poke holes. I can hear her now: 'So she looked up knives after learning about them in self-defense class. What's the crime in that?'"

"Well, she took those classes months ago, but something prompted her to go research them just a few days before Madison's death."

"Maybe she didn't buy it online, but she might have searched for brick-and-mortar stores that carry that knife. Can you check to see if she searched outdoor sports stores or similar retailers?"

"Will do."

I slouched forward, cradling my forehead in my hand. "Listen, I gotta go. They're chatting again."

"Here, let me scoot closer," Rafael said. We heard the scraping of a chair along stone, most likely one of those Adirondack chairs from around the fire pit. "So, where were we?"

"I don't know, Rafael. For some reason you are eager to play detective with me. Next thing you'll be asking me is where I hid the knife."

"That's not funny. And you know it. If you're innocent, then you have nothing to worry about. It just so happens that you've lied about a number of things, and that just makes you look suspicious to them."

"Wow! That's ripe coming from you. Seems you've got a few secrets in your life, and I'm sure you've done your fair share of lying. What I want to know is how did she rope you into killing her parents?"

"I had nothing—NOTHING—to do with that!" Rafael screamed.

"Okay, okay. Take it easy."

The only sound we heard for a few moments was birds chirping, then Rafael said, "Is that what you really think? That I was somehow involved in Madison's insane plot to have me rescue her parents?"

Camilla snorted. "It's not implausible to believe that. She wanted her parents to accept you. I mean, she had you wrapped around her little finger. She would ask you to jump and you'd say, 'How high?'"

The chair scraped against the stone. "How dare you! How could you believe I'd go along with such a crazy scheme?"

"Because you'd do anything for her. And you know it. So, what am I supposed to think? She was going to take you down with her. That little bitch."

"You're supposed to think rationally. But no, that's incredibly hard for you. You're good at being irrational. You need to be the life of the party, the center of attention, the girl with the Jamaican accent or the British accent or whatever crazy notion gets into your head so that people pay attention to you, admire you. I mean, for God's sake, look at your career. It's all about me, me, me. Did it ever occur to you that Madison was hurting over this? That her past actions were torturing her? That after all these years she needed to come clean so she could move forward? I had nothing to do with this, but even if I had to suffer the consequences of her past actions, so be it. I would rather she were alive right now!"

"Listen to yourself, Rafael. She was going to ruin you and here you are defending her. When I read what she wrote in that fucking journal, I knew that something had to be done. I did this for you. For—"

"You did what? You did what for me? Camilla, what are you saying?" Rafael paused, then whispered to us, "Camilla just stormed off toward the lake."

Joe turned to me. "That was as close to a confession as I think we're going to get."

"Unfortunately, still shy of a full-throated admission to make it stick. But there was something else she said that proves she was lying to us during the interrogation. And I can't wait to throw it back in her face."

ELDRIDGE MOTIONED me to take a seat on the chair across from him. He put his elbows on his desk, tucked his knuckles under his chin and peered over his reading glasses. "Bottom line it," he said.

"Rafael came through—although I think he was hoping she would prove her innocence, not dig herself into a deeper hole." I slapped my open palms on my thighs. "Turns out Camilla did take a sneak peek at Madison's journal. And it was the trigger. She went ballistic when she read that Madison was going to ruin Rafael's reputation."

"So Camilla thought that whatever Madison was going to confess was going to ruin Rafael, and, as the devoted sister, she put a stop to it."

"And the irony is that he probably had nothing to do with Madison's crazy scheme."

"But if that is the case, in what way would this ruin *his* reputation?"

"Even if there was a hint of collusion on his part, he would lose clients, might even lose his job. It's the kind of bizarre story that gets twisted around to suit the media's need for eyeballs. They'll have a field day with this. On some level, Madison's murder makes it worse for Rafael. At the very least, she could have attempted to clear his name as an accomplice." Oh, the irony. "Good going, Camilla."

Eldridge grunted. "That confession was flimsy at best. And using her brother to extract it, well, not sure that will stand up in court. I want an airtight case, Ford. Let's dot some *i*'s and cross some *t*'s. By which I mean, connect her to the murder weapon."

I WATCHED Ray cross the floor to my desk. He had that glint in his eye.

"I got something for you," he said, parking his rear end on the edge of my desk. "Camilla browsed a few retail sites." He glanced at the small pad tucked in his palm. "Sawkill Creek Outfitter in Port Jervis, Rock and Snow in New Paltz, and Thruway Sporting Goods in Ellenville. I looked at all the sites, and the one in Ellenville carries a pretty huge selection of knives. Probably a good place to start."

"Wanna come with me?" I asked.

"Can't. Gotta chase down a lead on the case I'm working on." Ray turned his head toward the door. "Hey Will," he shouted, as he motioned Dad over to my desk. "Perfect timing. Susan's looking for a wingman for a ride over to Ellenville."

I was about to object, but when I turned and saw Dad hobbling over with a grin on his face, my resolve weakened. "Hey Dad, you up for a drive?" I asked, hoping he would turn me down. But of course he didn't.

I PLACED Dad's crutches in the backseat as he maneuvered himself into the passenger's seat. Turns out, he had come to the station this morning to shoot the shit with Eldridge, but my expedition appealed to him more.

"Thanks for inviting me along," Dad said as he buckled up.

"Little chance of you being knocked over by a deranged woman with a Louis Vuitton bag in a sporting-goods store."

"Speaking of getting knocked out by a deranged woman . . . your mom was something else. I wished you could've seen her wielding that cane like a billy club. She said her instincts kicked in when she saw me in danger."

"Must mean she still has a thing for you."

"I wouldn't go that far, but she did come visit me at the hospital. And yes, we talked through a few issues."

"So, a truce?"

"Actually, more like a reset. We'll see where it goes from here."

"Well, glad to hear it. And no more butting in from me." I crossed my finger over my heart. "Promise."

Dad nodded off as I turned onto Route 52. I figured I'd let him snooze these last ten minutes of the trip. I knew his ankle was throbbing, but he refused painkillers. Said the pain wasn't *that* bad, and he'd seen too many of his buddies fall prey to Oxycontin. ("A couple of Advil and a shot of whiskey is all I need," he'd informed the doctor.)

After pulling into the parking lot of Thruway Sporting Goods, I killed the ignition and let him doze for another five minutes. I leaned over and whispered, "Dad, we're here."

He snorted and opened his eyes. "Great!" he exclaimed. "Let's put the final nail in the coffin."

WE STRODE up to a young woman behind the counter. I flashed my badge. "Detective Susan Ford, Monticello police."

The woman looked at my dad, then down at his booted foot, then back at me.

"This is ex-detective Will Ford."

"Okay. How can I help you?"

"We'd like to know if anyone purchased a knife between June twenty-fourth and June twenty-ninth?"

"I'm sure we sold a number of knives in that time frame."

I pulled out a photograph of Camilla. "Do you recall if this woman bought a knife?"

She puckered her lips as she squinted at the picture. "Um. I don't know. She doesn't look familiar to me. But we have several folks working here. Maybe it's best if you ask the store manager, Gerry," she said, pointing to a reed-thin, red-bearded man in an animated conversation with a customer.

"Thanks," Dad said.

We approached the store manager, introduced ourselves, and gave him the same spiel.

"I was on vacation that week. But follow me." We followed him to the back of the store and into a small office. He took a seat behind a large metal desk and powered on his computer. Dad sat down in the one chair in the office and leaned his crutches against his thigh. "Broken leg?"

"Ankle."

Gerry nodded. "Okay. We sold a handful of knives. Can you be more specific?"

"A reverse plain tanto?"

"That's pretty specific." He moused down the page. "Ah, yes. Travis—he's one of my best salespeople—sold a tanto on June twenty-sixth. The person paid cash, so there's no name associated with the sale."

"Is Travis here?"

"Should be." Gerry picked up a walkie-talkie. "Travis."

"Yes?" Travis replied.

"Can you come in my office, please?"

"Um, sure thing."

About thirty seconds later, Travis knocked on the door, then opened it.

"Hey Travis. These are detectives with the Monticello police."

His eyes widened and a flash of worry crossed his face. An expression we see all too often when the cops show up unannounced.

"Is . . . is everything okay?"

Gerry held up his hands. "Yeah. Yeah. Just an inquiry about a tanto you sold to someone on June twenty-sixth."

"Yeah. I remember that. I thought it was odd that this woman wanted one of those."

"Is this her?" I said, handing Travis the picture of Camilla.

"No. Older lady. Much older. With a slight accent. But the woman in your picture was in the store at the same time. I remember because she was wearing a Red Sox baseball cap and she was quite hot." He looked sheepishly at Gerry. "She was browsing but never bought anything."

I took out my phone and opened my Instagram app. I held up my phone to show him a picture on Camilla's Instagram grid. "Is this the woman who bought the knife?"

"Yup, that's her," Travis replied.

I turned the phone toward Dad.

"Holy shit."

I turned back to Gerry. "I noticed security cameras on the floor. Please tell me you have footage from that day."

I WHACKED the steering wheel with the palm of my right hand.

"Easy there, Susan."

"What the hell? Or as Camilla would say, 'Bloody hell?'"

Dad drummed his fingers on the dashboard, then stopped abruptly. "Can't believe Camilla got her mother to buy her the knife. I'm guessing Camilla wanted to put a little distance between herself and the murder weapon."

"So Isabela has to know that Camilla did this. A couple of days after buying a knife, Madison gets stabbed. You don't have to be a genius to put those two actions together."

"Maybe they planned it together," Dad said. "Camilla might have told her mother what she had read in the diary. Perhaps they came up with this plan to protect Rafael together. There was no love lost between Madison and Isabela."

"Well, there's only one way to find out."

25

WEDNESDAY | JULY 24, 2019

THE LEGS of the metal chairs scraped along the concrete floor as Eldridge and I positioned ourselves to face Camilla and Deborah Bergstrom. Eldridge placed a covered box on the floor next to his chair.

A hint of clove hung in the air. Twenty minutes ago, I had seen Camilla standing in the designated smoking area on the side of the building. She had the audacity to hold up the cigarette and wave at me. I wanted to march right up to her and tell her what we found, but simply ignored her.

Once again, I powered up my laptop and directed everyone's attention to the flat-screen television behind me. I hit the play button. I kept my eye on Camilla as she watched her mother purchase a reverse tanto knife. She pursed her lips repeatedly, occasionally biting into her lower lip. When the video revealed a tall woman in a baseball cap browsing in the back of the store, Camilla lowered her head and stared at her lap. I hit stop.

"What exactly are we looking at?" Deborah asked.

"I take it you've met Camilla's mother, Isabela Garcia?"

Deborah glanced up at the screen and squinted.

"Are you accusing Isabela of stabbing Madison?"

"Isabela would be incapable of stabbing Madison in the way in which she was stabbed. Isabela has severe arthritis in her right shoulder and hand from carrying heavy trays. We are accusing Isabela of buying the knife for Camilla. The knife that killed Madison. And perhaps you missed it, but Camilla was in the store at the time too." I reversed the footage and stopped when Camilla came into view.

Deborah squinted again.

Camilla leaned forward. "So we were shopping for sporting goods. There is no crime in that."

Deborah placed her hand on Camilla's shoulder and pulled her back. She shook her head and raised her finger to her lip.

"Let's move on, shall we?" I said.

Eldridge tilted slightly to his right, lifted the lid off the box, removed a plastic bag, then laid it in the center of the table. "Something we found when we searched your apartment, Camilla," he said, jutting his chin out toward the bag.

I cleared my throat. "This Red Sox baseball cap seems to be popping up a lot in this case. Madison wrote about Camilla wearing it, someone saw a figure walking down Route 42 on the night of the murder wearing a baseball cap, Camilla was videotaped on a Shortline bus wearing a Red Sox cap, and as we just saw, Camilla wore it while her mother *innocently* shopped for a knife at Thruway Sporting Goods."

Camilla pounded her fist on the table. "You can't just take—"

"Oh, yes we can."

"So Camilla wears a Red Sox hat," Deborah interjected. "Not a crime in New York. Maybe not popular, but certainly not a crime. So what's your point with this?"

Eldridge reached back into the box and pulled out a sheet of paper. He placed it next to the plastic bag.

Camilla and Deborah leaned over to look at it. Deborah slid it over to their side of the table. Deborah sucked in a deep breath. "A DNA report?"

I nodded, then turned to Camilla. "Red hat, red blood. Guess you didn't notice it." I pointed to the rim of the cap where forensics had found a smudge. "Madison's blood."

I CALLED Ginger Larson to let her know we closed the Madison Garcia case. She informed me that she arrested Oliver Finch. ("We have enough to convict him on a whole host of charges," she exclaimed. "Thanks to Irving for storing Todd's records and not tossing that Blackberry.")

As I hung up, Sally waved me over.

"Rafael is up front. He wants to speak with you."

I hurried out to the reception area and found Rafael pacing the floor. "You wanted to see me?"

Rafael lowered himself onto one of the plastic chairs along the wall and started to cry. He balled his fists into eyes, perhaps an attempt to quell the outpouring.

"I'm . . . I'm sorry." He gulped at the air and sat up a little straighter, composing himself. "I'm just completely lost here. Why in the world would Camilla do this? Why?"

I sat down next to him. "You'll have to ask her yourself. I can only give you the easy pat answer . . . in her twisted reasoning, she was trying to protect you."

"I won't be talking to her anytime soon. I can't. I won't. What she did was unforgivable."

"I get that." And I did. Forgiving someone who has betrayed you is a monumental endeavor. Sure, my father seems to be on the way to forgiving my mother, but on a scale of one to ten, what my mother did—concealing her role in the disappearance of a local woman—hovers around a four on the betrayal scale. What Camilla did was a clear-cut ten.

※

RAY CLOSED the toilet bowl lid and sat down. "Nice bubbles."

I lifted my hands from the soapy water and examined my pruney fingertips.

"So, case closed?"

"It's pretty solid." I plunged my hands back into the water. "No knife. But we got enough evidence to prove to a jury that she's guilty as fuck."

"What about Isabela?"

"Eh. I don't think the DA will go after her. There's no evidence to prove she was in on it." I shivered slightly as the water entered its lukewarm stage. "I can't imagine she didn't know, but she claims she 'never put two and two together.' Whatever. Will you hand me my towel?"

Ray held open the towel as I stepped out of the bath. He wrapped it around me.

"Did you get a confession out of Camilla?"

"Camilla agreed to cooperate if we left her mother out of it. At that point, we knew we weren't going to pursue charges against Isabela, so we let Camilla think she got her wish."

"So this was all about protecting Rafael?" If he rolled his eyes any higher, they would have gotten stuck in his forehead.

"Yup." Ray followed me to the bedroom. I pulled a pair of underwear, bra, shorts, and a T-shirt out of my dresser and laid them out on the bed. "As we thought, Camilla got hold of the journal and read the passage about Madison ruining Rafael's reputation. She said she was 'beyond furious' at Madison. That Madison didn't deserve Rafael and her brother was better off without her. That Madison was selfish and manipulative and had no right to bring Rafael down. She admitted that she immediately started planning the murder after reading the journal. She couldn't believe her luck when we found a connection to money laundering. She figured that would get us off her trail. And get this, she asked her mother to buy her the knife because she saw a criminal do this on a cop series and get away with it."

Ray snorted.

"Right?" I sat down on the edge of the bed and started to dress. "Camilla knew that Madison was coming up here that Saturday. Rafael had mentioned it to her earlier in the day. She said it was like the opportunity presented itself on a silver platter. So she called Madison and asked her if she could stop by under the false pretense of needing Madison to bring something to Isabela. But when Madison got to Camilla's apartment, Camilla told her she would appreciate a lift up here so she could deliver it herself. Madison was game. Camilla then convinced Madison to go for a midnight swim for 'old times' sake.' Again, Madison was game."

"Which explains the bathing suit on the backseat."

"When I asked her about the location of the knife, she glared at me and said, 'Buried somewhere in the woods. Good luck finding that.'"

26

THURSDAY | JULY 25, 2019

DAD HELD up a metal spatula and waved it at me. His buddies milled around the grill, holding their plates out as he mounted burgers on their buns.

"Glad you can make it to our little shindig," Dad said, pointing the spatula at a nearby table. "Grab a plate and a bun."

"What's the occasion?"

"No occasion. But with the break in the humidity we thought we should fire up the ol' grill."

I walked over to the table, grabbed a plate, then slathered my bun with ketchup. I picked up a bag of potato chips and headed back to Dad, who already had a burger balancing on the spatula.

"Thanks," I said, as he slid the burger on my bun. "Grab your crutches and come take a walk with me. Someone can take over for a bit."

Dad signaled to Harry, who happily took the spatula from him.

"All good?" Dad said, a hint of concern in his voice.

"Oh, yeah. Just wanted to let you know that we're officially closing the book on the Garcia case."

"Did you hear about Irving?"

"No. How's he holding up?"

"He's grateful to you, Susan. He appreciates how dogged you've been. Which, of course, also mucked up his little side fling."

"Side fling? The guy was having an affair with a woman his granddaughter's age."

"Yeah, well, Audrey threw him out on his keister. He says he's going to move to the city. Start anew."

"With Annabelle?"

"Seems so."

"Hmm."

Dad pointed at a bench and we headed toward it. "So I heard from Eldridge that you won't be pressing charges against Isabela."

"We got our murderer. Isabela is just going to have to live with what she has wrought. Her daughter in jail. Her son is not speaking to her. But Luis is sticking by her side."

"And what about Rafael?" Dad asked. He leaned his crutches against the bench and sat down. I joined him. "Was he party to Madison's scheme to make him the hero of the day?"

"I don't think we'll ever really know. Rafael claimed that if he knew he had to get to that house at a certain time and realized he couldn't make it, he would have called 9-1-1." I shrugged. "I'd like to give him the benefit of the doubt. Which, by the way, goes against my nature."

"Well, it doesn't go against my nature. I tend to give people the benefit of the doubt."

I laughed.

"Don't laugh, Susan. It's true. It's better than thinking the worst of people." He stooped over slightly and scratched the skin at the edge of his cast. "If I've learned anything in my life it's that most people try to do the right thing. Do they always succeed? Of course not. But at this stage in my life, I refuse to be a cynical old man, grousing about this, that, and the other thing. If I want to get my ass out of bed every day, I have to believe that the people around me are essentially good-hearted. Because, well, the alternative means being depressed and pissed off all the time. And I've got what? Ten good years left, maybe? I'm not going to waste my precious little time left on this earth being a sour fart."

I stifled a laugh this time.

"Oh, and if you need my help in the future, you know where to find me."

I put my arm around his shoulders. "We do make a pretty good team."

JUNE 29, 2019

CAMILLA LIT the thin black cigarette, then inhaled deeply. She cranked open the living-room window, peered down, and blew a line of smoke out toward the street. Pedestrians scurried along the pavement, sweating in this incessant summer humidity. The heat was enough to make anyone crazy, she thought.

She stubbed the cigarette out on a small dish she kept on the sill. Today was decompression day. But she needed to call her mother. She pulled out one of her burner phones. One of three she had bought for her plan.

"Today's the day," Camilla said when her mother answered. "Rafael just texted me to tell me that Madison is driving up to Shangri-La tonight. By herself."

"Are you sure—"

"Mom, we talked about this. This is the best solution. The only one, really."

"Maybe you can get Rafael to talk to her. Reason with her."

"Ha! Like Madison can be reasoned with." After a stretch of si-lence, Camilla continued, "I told you what she wrote in her journal. You agreed you would support me. I mean, for God's sake, you helped me purchase the knife."

"Are you sure it can't be traced back to me?"

"You paid cash. There is no way anyone can tie the purchase to you. You did your part. The rest is up to me." Camilla sighed, annoyed with her mother's sudden cold feet. She glanced up at the microwave clock. 7:52 p.m. "She'll be here soon. Gotta go."

Camilla deposited the cigarette butts in the trash and sprayed the room with a lavender air freshener. The doorbell rang.

"Hey!" Camilla said, opening the door. "Really appreciate you do-ing this favor for me."

"Sure. So, what is it you want me to take to Isabela?"

"She's having a July Fourth party and I have two of her Pyrex pie plates."

"Oh. Okay."

"Love the bag by the way," Camilla said, eyeing the Louis Vuitton bag. "Would love to use it in a photo shoot."

Madison hugged the bag closer to her hip. "Sorry, Camilla, but I'm not letting this bag out of my sight for a minute. If anything happens to it, I think Rafael will kill me. You should've seen his jaw hit the floor when I told him it cost three thousand dollars."

"Men! They don't understand. Hey! I got a great idea. Why don't I join you? I can really use a respite at Serene Scene after the crazy week I've had."

"Um, I guess so. But I'm meeting Jacob tomorrow about Shan-gri-La business. And then I'm seeing, um, an old friend. I don't plan to come back here until Monday."

"No problem. I don't need to be back in the city until early next week. Let me just throw some stuff in my backpack." Camilla took a few steps toward the bedroom, then turned back to Madison. "Oh, and don't tell anyone I'm coming with you. I want to surprise my mom. If you tell Rafael, he might let it slip."

Madison shrugged. "I doubt he would do that, but sure."

Camilla retrieved the knife from her bedside table. She slipped it into the side pocket of her backpack.

She made sure her phone was powered on and attached it to its cord. She had read somewhere it would trick the police into believing she was home.

Who leaves the house without their phone these days?

"Okay! All set! Just have to go to the bathroom." Camilla wanted to be sure that no one saw them leaving the brownstone together. "Why don't I meet you down by the car?"

MADISON GLANCED over at Camilla and thought: *This is a mistake. Camilla's the last person I should be with. If she gets wind of what I'm planning to do. Well, I don't know what she'd do. Talk me out of it, I guess.*

"I gotta pee," Camilla said as Madison sped down Route 17. "Just pull over. There."

"There's a gas station a few miles ahead. I can stop there."

"You know I won't pee in a public restroom. Just pull off. I'll pee behind the car."

"Fine." Madison parked the car along the shoulder and put the hazards on. Camilla jumped out.

Madison picked up her phone and dialed the number her grandfather had sent her a while back. The daughter of his friend who was a police detective. *Just a quick call to ask if she's around tomorrow or Monday to meet.* But the call went to voice mail. She glanced at the clock on the dashboard: 9:40 p.m.

The passenger's-side door swung open, and Camilla got back in. "All set."

"I just want to check on Penguin and fill his bowl," Madison said. "I should have done it like an hour ago." Madison tapped on the CatCam app, activated the feeder, and watched as Penguin ate. She smiled when she saw Rafael's hand pet the cat. When she bought the feeder, she'd decided not to tell Rafael about the little camera and microphone—she used it occasionally to spy for fun. And, perhaps not for fun, if someone was in that house who ought not to be.

"Music preference?" Madison asked as she scrolled through her Apple Music app.

"How about some Harry Styles. *Sign of the Times?*"

Camilla cranked up the volume and they sang as they rolled down the highway. When the song ended, Camilla picked up Madison's phone.

Madison glanced sideways, then cleared her throat to get Camilla's attention. "So, you know who called me out of the blue a few months ago? Sarah Steinberg. Remember her?"

Camilla stopped scrolling. "No."

"Really? The girl who went to juvie for stabbing Joanna."

Camilla shrugged. "I don't remember her. I mean, I remember Joanna, just not this other girl."

"You were tight with Joanna, right?"

"Yeah, I guess."

"You do remember she got stabbed?"

"Kinda." Camilla leaned her head against the headrest and stared out the sunroof. "So why did this Sarah chick get in touch with you?"

"Part of her twelve-step program. She was making amends. Wanted to apologize. Funny thing, I should have been the one apologizing to her. I threw myself at Rafael when he was dating her."

Madison waited for a response, but Camilla continued to gaze at the stars.

"Do you mind if we don't talk?"

"Sure. Whatever."

✳

CAMILLA FOUND the song she was searching for. "With Every Heartbeat" by Robyn. That had been her and Joanna's song. She leaned her forehead against the window and thought about that night at the party when Joanna told her they were through. ("I prefer boys," Joanna had said, then cruelly added, "I was just experimenting with you.") Everyone at the party was stoned or drunk—including Joanna. Others were ensconced in one of several bedrooms having sex. It was so easy to snatch one of the kitchen knives. Framing Sarah was an unplanned opportunity—the dummy left her locker open. The authorities even found a burn book with rants against half her classmates. And with her less-than-stellar reputation, everyone was inclined to pin it on her.

The turn signal pulled Camilla out of her reverie. "I've got a brilliant idea!" Camilla exclaimed as Madison steered off the exit toward Monticello. She twisted around in her seat and zipped open Madison's duffel.

"Hey, what are you doing?"

Camilla pulled out a bathing suit. "Good. You brought one. Let's go for a midnight swim down at Sackett Lake." *Midnight* in air quotes, as it was only ten fifteen.

"What? Are you insane?"

"It's a perfectly sane idea. In fact, it's a marvelous idea. It's been what? Ten years since we did it. Please, please, please. It'll be fun!"

Madison glanced at her with a tired smile. "Y'know what, Camilla? Yes. Yes! Let's do that."

A fist bump sealed the plan. And Madison's fate. Camilla turned on the overhead map light and rummaged through her backpack. After she found what she was looking for, she clicked off the light. She turned away from Madison and slipped on a pair of clear latex gloves. Then she reached into the side pocket of her backpack and removed the knife. She glanced at Madison and took two deep breaths.

Madison pulled into the parking lot at the edge of Sackett Lake.

Camilla clutched the knife in her right hand. *Just do what you were taught.*

Camilla took another deep breath. *Now or never.* She swung her arm around and hit her first target, Madison's lung. In two quick successive swings she tore into Madison's flesh. Heart, then liver. Her body jerked slightly, but not enough to thwart the targeted assault. Camilla was surprised at the lack of blood spatter. Her gloved hand was bloody, as was the lower part of her right arm and her upper left thigh, but the car was mostly unscathed. She opened the passenger's-side door and got out. Glanced around. Nary a soul.

She carefully removed the bloody gloves and tucked them into her shorts pocket. She then slid the folded knife into her back pocket. She walked to the water's edge and washed away the blood from her arm and thigh, then headed back to the car.

From her backpack, she pulled a fresh pair of latex gloves and put them on. She shut the passenger's-side door, then opened the rear door. She removed the two pie plates from the large plastic bag and laid them on the ground. She undressed, quickly removing her T-shirt, bra, shorts, underwear, and flip-flops, and dropped her clothes into the now empty plastic shopping bag.

Naked, she reached into the backseat again and grabbed the Louis Vuitton bag. She peeked inside. *There it is, that fucking journal.* She carried the pie plates and the Louis Vuitton bag to the end of the dock. She chucked the pie plates as far as she could throw. They were merely a pretense to hitch a ride. She didn't want to risk them being found and associated with her, especially if her fingerprints were on them. She was about to fling the Louis Vuitton bag and its contents into the water, but hesitated. Instead, she held the bag upside down and dumped Madison's journal and whatever else was in there into the lake. Then headed back to the car. She pulled a shirt, bra, underwear, jeans, sneakers, and a baseball cap out of her backpack. She re-dressed and tucked her hair under the baseball cap. She tied a knot to seal the bag of bloody items and stuffed it into her backpack along with the Louis Vuitton bag. She touched the rim of the cap, pulling it down gently. She glanced around again. Then she set off.

About one mile down the road, she veered into the woods. She walked about ten minutes and found a good spot. She removed a trowel from her backpack and dug a two-foot-deep hole. She placed the bag of bloody clothes, the knife, and the trowel in the hole, lit a match and tossed it in. When the items were sufficiently burned, she got back down on her knees and filled the hole in with the dirt and leaves she just removed. She stepped back to admire her work.

Camilla walked back to the main road and continued down Route 42. Somewhere around the halfway point, she shimmied off her backpack and retrieved a cigarette. She savored the clove taste and smell. The aroma reminded her of her semester abroad when she was first introduced to the product. ("An exotic cigarette for an exotic girl," her girlfriend had whispered in her ear at a bar in London.) Tears rolled down her cheeks as she thought of that time. *That lovely time.* But she'd missed her family. She missed Rafael. She wanted to come back to America as a more captivating and intriguing person, someone Rafael would respect and admire and want to show off to his friends. What's the harm in reinventing oneself, she thought. *So Madison thinks I'm pretentious,* she thought. *Madison is dead. She can't hurt Rafael. I did what needed to be done. One day I will tell Rafael the truth. When enough time has passed and he has found true happiness. And he will thank me for saving him from Lord knows what if Madison had her way.*

Lost in thought, Camilla dropped the cigarette butt and stubbed it out with her toe. She continued on the final two miles to the Shortline bus station. She knew there would be cameras, so she lowered the cap on her head. Keep your head down, she reminded herself.

There were only a few people in the bus station. She checked her watch. Twelve forty-five. With that little detour into the woods, it took her about one and a half hours to hike from the parking lot at Sackett Lake to the Shortline bus terminal. She paid cash at the counter and was given a paper ticket. She spied a seat in the corner of the bus station. The bus was due to arrive in two hours. She reached into her backpack and pulled out a paperback, *The Secret History*.

When her scheduled bus was announced over the speakers, she stood, stretched, pulled the baseball cap down over her forehead, and heaved the backpack onto her shoulders. *So close.* She boarded the bus, strode halfway down the aisle, shimmied off her backpack, then inserted it into the overhead rack. She glanced toward the front of the bus as she collapsed into her seat. As the bus pulled away from the station, she sighed. *Done.*

THE END

ACKNOWLEDGMENTS

NONE OF this—not my debut novel, not this novel, not my next novel—would have been possible without my husband, Lew McCreary. When I told him a few years ago I wanted to try my hand at writing a novel, there was no mistaking that look of surprise mingled with a tad of amusement (and perhaps a minor eye roll). Writing novels is Lew's territory. He is brilliant. And if you don't believe me, pick up one of his literary masterpieces, *Mount's Mistake* or *The Minus Man*. After that initial reaction (and he swears he never rolled his eyes), he got behind me 100 percent. I am very lucky to have his support and his wisdom. He is a master at the crafts of writing and storytelling.

Many thanks to the supportive publishing team at CamCat Publishing: Sue Arroyo, Laura Wooffitt, Meredith Lyons, Bill Lehto, Abigail Miles, Maryann Appel, Gabe Schier, Elana Gibson, Kayla Webb, Jessica Homami, Sophie Slusher, Ellen Leach, and Helga Schier, editor extraordinaire. In my wildest imagination, I couldn't have dreamed up a better editor to work with. With every thoughtful suggestion, you have challenged me as a writer, giving me the confidence to bring more vitality and depth to the narrative.

I love how my characters come to life through the wonderful voicing of Rachel Fulginiti. You have captured Susan Ford exactly as I had imagined she would sound.

I'd like to thank my critique readers: Shelly Strickler, Sari Breuer, Sarah Sperling, and Marie Joyce. They hold no punches and I appreciate them for that. I'd also like to thank Margo McCreary, Patti Daboosh, and Harrison Anastasio—my sounding boards when I needed a reality check on sticky plot points and questionable scenes. And a big thank-you to Bob and Toby Stone for answering my endless questions about lawyers and legal issues.

Thank you to librarians and bookstore buyers who have added my books to their shelves, bookstagrammers and BookTokkers who have creatively shared my books with their followers, and to Stephanie Hockersmith (@pieladybooks) for the beautiful piecrust depicting this novel's cover. Instagram is a yummier place with her magnificent "book cover" pies. They are truly works of art.

Family is everything to me. Their support and love sustain me. Larry and Shelly Strickler, also known as Mom and Dad. My sisters, Karyn Anastasio and Sari Breuer. My daughters and stepdaughters, Hayley Dill, Taylor Dill, Molly McCreary, and Hannah McCreary.

ABOUT THE AUTHOR

MARCY McCREARY is the author of *The Disappearance of Trudy Solomon,* a Killer Nashville Silver Falchion 2022 Finalist in the Best Investigator category. After graduating from George Washington University with a BA in American literature and political science, she pursued a career in the marketing field, holding executive positions in marketing communications and sales at various magazine publishing companies and content marketing agencies. She has two daughters and two stepdaughters who live in Brooklyn, NY, Nashville, TN, Madison, WI, and Seattle, WA. She lives in Hull, MA, with her husband, Lew, and black lab, Chloe.

If you liked

Marcy McCreary's *The Murder of Madison Garcia,*

you'll like

Ash Bishop's *The Horoscope Writer.*

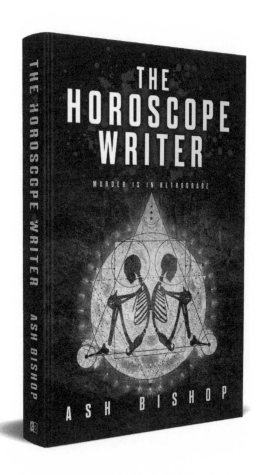

CHAPTER

1

DETECTIVE LESLIE Consorte didn't like being woken up in the middle of the night. In fact, he didn't like it enough to have turned off his cell phone and taken his home phone off the hook. The desk sergeant, a busybody named Roman Stevenson, had felt the situation warranted sending a unit by his house to pound on his door until he had dragged himself out from under warm sheets, grumbling, groaning, and belching out every cussword known to man, and a few based loosely on Latin roots: *crapepsia, shitalgia, cockpluribus.*

Stevenson hadn't been wrong. Leaning on his car door and surveying the damage, Leslie dreamed of the stacks of paperwork headed his way. A fifth-year cop named Lapeyre dressed in uniformed blues approached, picking through the crime scene, not so much to preserve evidence as to preserve his clothes. Lapeyre was a handsome kid, close-cropped black hair, dark skin, driven, focused, taller than Leslie by half a foot.

"It goes on for another three miles."

"This is a grisly thing here."

Leslie squinted his eyes, staring down the dilapidated Clairemont street. Clairemont was proof positive that racism was a baseless concept, or, put more simply, that white people could fuck up a community just as efficiently as any other race. It was a rotten little housing project of about fourteen hundred units: dirt lawns; peeling paint; ugly, unwashed cars and motor homes and non-working boats.

This street, Triana, was particularly bad because it was smeared with blood, muscle and bone. Someone had been dragged behind the bumper of a GMC truck. For about a mile.

"What are we looking at?"

"Dispatch got a call at 12:03. A neighbor reported hearing screaming, squealing tires, and then a grinding sound. Desk jockey logged it as a domestic dispute, though I think that's a bit of an under-classification."

"That's funny, Lapeyre. Any chance we can identify the victim?"

"It's unlikely. There's only about a third of the body left. It shook loose from the car down by the mesa."

Leslie crouched in the street, running his hand over the drying blood.

"Radley found fragments of a jawbone on the next block over. We might be able to get a dental match. I also managed to extricate a patch of hair from the fender of the murder car. I've bagged it for a DNA analysis. A SID team is prepping the car for impound on Derrick Drive. What do you want to do about this?"

"Let's knock on a door or two."

Leslie and Lapeyre walked up the nearest driveway, Leslie's suit looked like he carried it to work in a plastic bag. The top button was loose on the shirt, his tie hung low, the edges of the cuffs were frayed, and the collar was badly wrinkled. Leslie believed it was possible to machine wash and dry his dress shirts. The collar, it seemed to him, was the only part that didn't turn out so great.

Before they reached the door Leslie pulled Lapeyre to a stop.

"I forgot something," he said. He dug around in his pocket, finally drawing out a shiny, metallic object roughly the size of a billfold. He handed it to Lapeyre.

Lapeyre fumbled with it, trying to get it open with shaky hands. "Is this what I think it is?" he said.

"Congratulations, Detective. The captain passed word down to me as I was leaving work. I was going to tell you tomorrow, but I guess this is tomorrow."

Lapeyre didn't say anything else, but his eyes never left the badge. It reminded Leslie of his ex-wife's expression when he'd first popped open the engagement ring box. "It's a good moment, Lapeyre. You only make detective once, if you're lucky. Enjoy it." Leslie waited a moment while Lapeyre polished the badge on the front of his shirt. "Okay, let's solve this case, huh? After you, Inspector."

"Are you going to show me how to grill a witness?"

"I will show you the ways of the master."

The nearest house was a tiny three bedroom, one bathroom with a rotting fence and a weed-strewn yard. Leslie knocked on the door. They waited a few minutes. Lapeyre pulled out his badge to look at it again and Leslie told him to put it away. He knocked again, louder this time. No one answered. They moved to the next house, walking directly across the lawn. It was a small structure, probably close to seven hundred square feet. The roof was dilapidated, and a Trump flag waved above the faded painting of a bald eagle stretched across the garage, wings wide.

They knocked and waited. No one answered.

On the third house, a blond woman in her fifties came to the door. She was wearing pajamas covered by a tattered robe. Her hair was unwashed and had a frizzy-fried texture Leslie always associated with the very poor and the chemically addicted. She smelled of recently smoked cigarettes.

"Yes?" the woman said. She was rubbing her eyes and blinking at them.

Leslie knew Lapeyre was waiting for him to speak but he didn't. After an awkward silence Lapeyre finally said, "Sorry we woke you."

"What do you need?" the woman asked; her voice held a slight edge.

"We were hoping you saw something tonight. There's been a crime. Outside your home, all up and down the street."

"That's terrible. I'm sorry I can't help you."

Leslie didn't like her, but he tried to remain professional. He leaned in and sniffed her.

"What the hell are you doing?" she said.

She smelled like very strong alcohol. Maybe 100 proof. "There was a brutal murder fifteen feet from your house," he said.

"I didn't see anything. I was sleeping."

"The murderer dragged his victim through the street. He tore the victim's body to pieces. His flesh is part of your asphalt now. It's part of your street."

"I don't know anything." The woman said, her shoulders shook in a quick jagged motion, but she got them under control again immediately.

"You watched it from the window."

"No."

"I don't know how much you saw, but it was enough to send you back to the kitchen. A decent person calls the police. Lets us get here in time to help, maybe. But you poured yourself a shot." Leslie sniffed again. "Several shots. Did it work? Did it make you forget the sounds?"

"Get out of my house!" the woman said angrily. "I'll call the cops."

Leslie idly waved his badge. "We're not in your house."

"I'll call my brother then. He'll kick your ass right out of here."

"Go ahead and call him. We'll wait," Leslie told her.

The poor, rugged blonde took a step back and pulled her phone from her pajama pocket. Then she lurched forward and struck Leslie with her phone-clinched fist. Lapeyre moved to interfere, but Leslie called him off with a curt head shake. With her other hand she clawed at him for a moment, like a sick bird, then she fell to her knees, crying.

"We need to know everything you can remember. The coloring, height, and weight of the victim. The same for the killer." His voice softened. "If you tell us everything you saw, it will help you forget. I promise."

The woman remained on the floor. Leslie pulled Lapeyre aside. "Get a statement," he said. "Be as gentle as possible."

"Yeah, right. Thanks," Lapeyre said.

"I'm going to go check out the murder car. Join me when you can." Leslie moved back out of the house without looking at the crumpled form of the woman on the floor, still sobbing. He walked slowly up the street to Derrick Drive.

He had been suffering from acute lower back pain for the last thirteen years. The cause had never been completely diagnosed but Leslie figured it to be a combination of too many nights chasing low-lifes down alleyways, too many hours behind desks perched on cheap chairs, his tendency to buy his own furniture and mattresses at thrift stores, and all the collective stresses of trying to keep a city safe from itself. The mileage of life.

The pinching pain caused him to shuffle his feet when he walked, and he always appeared to be leaning slightly forward.

When he reached Derrick Drive, he followed the portable lights, flares, and flashbulbs to the murder car—which was, in fact, a murder truck. He pulled on a pair of rubber gloves and pointed his belt light at the truck's bumper. A SIDs guy, short for Scientific Investigation Division, was already swabbing at it with a Q-tip. Leslie didn't recognize him, but then as all the other departments felt the pinch of deep budget cuts, the SIDs were growing like weeds.

Leslie ran his light along the left side of the truck. He noted deep, jagged scratch marks in the faux chrome of the bumper, on the right fender, and just above the tailpipe. The SID was working over his shoulder on the taillight. Leslie told him, "It looks like the victim tried to keep up with the car long as he or she could. They must have been affixed to the bumper by something other than their arms. Make sure you run tests for trace elements of rope, tape, whatever the hell kind of epoxy could stick a person to a vehicle long enough to grind their bones to dust."

"Of course."

Leslie looked again at the long, snaking red swath as it disappeared down the street and around the corner. "No motive. Few witnesses. Not much left of the body. This must have made a hell of a racket, though. Make a visual record of the entire trail. Then call the fire department out to turn a hose on it. I don't want people waking up to find this on their street."

"You want to destroy the evidence?"

"No. Gather the evidence but do it quickly and get this massacre cleaned up."

"Are you sure, sir? Whitmire's going to be pissed if we compromise—"

"You SIDs guys are supposed to facilitate our investigation, not run it. Guy gets butchered in the street; it still belongs to homicide; right?"

"Yeah."

Leslie slid his hand into a rubber glove and gingerly felt around the back of the bumper. Something sticky transferred from the bumper to his index finger. He held it up to the light. It looked like candy from a toy store vending machine. He lifted it up for the pale man with the camera and the plastic baggies to see.

"Got an idea of what this is?" Leslie asked him. It wasn't quite the right texture to be brain or flesh.

The SIDs man shone a light on it, moving his face just inches from its quivering surface. Leslie turned his wrist to give him a better look, and it split, letting an inky mess free to run down onto his knuckles.

"Looks like sclera," the man said, taking it from Leslie gingerly and dropping it into one of his bags.

"I made detective because of my tenacity, not my brains."

"I'm pretty sure you found an eyeball, sir."

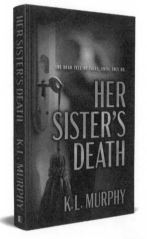
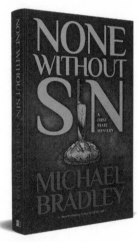
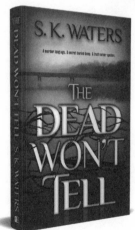

CamCat
Books

VISIT US ONLINE FOR MORE BOOKS TO LIVE IN:

CAMCATBOOKS.COM

CamCatBooks   @CamCatBooks   @CamCat_Books